THE ROVER

JOSEPH CONRAD

Sleep after toyle, port after stormie seas,
Ease after warre, death after life, does greatly please
—EDMUND SPENSER

HEART OF OAK SEA CLASSICS
Dean King, Series Editor

Foreword by
Dean King

Introduction by
John B. Hattendorf

AN OWL BOOK
HENRY HOLT AND COMPANY   NEW YORK

Henry Holt and Company, LLC
Publishers since 1866
115 West 18th Street
New York, New York 10011

Henry Holt ® is a registered
trademark of Henry Holt and Company, LLC.

Published in Canada by Fitzhenry & Whiteside Ltd.,
195 Allstate Parkway, Markham, Ontario L3R 4T8.

Library of Congress Cataloging-in-Publication Data

Conrad, Joseph, 1857–1924.
The rover / by Joseph Conrad; foreword by Dean King ;
introduction by John B. Hattendorf.—1st owl/heart of oak ed.
    p.   cm. — (Heart of oak sea classics series)
ISBN 0-8050-6263-7 (pbk.)
1. Napoleonic Wars, 1800–1815—Fiction.   I. Title.   II. Series.
PR6005.O4R6   1999

823'.912—dc21   99-14966
                                                          CIP

Henry Holt books are available for special promotions and premiums.
For details contact: Director, Special Markets.

First Published in 1923
First Owl/Heart of Oak Edition 1999

Designed by Kate Nichols
Cartography by Jeffrey L. Ward

Printed in the United States of America

1   3   5   7   9   10   8   6   4   2

HEART OF OAK

Come cheer up, my lads, 'tis to glory we steer,
To add something new to this wonderful Year:
To honour we call you, not to press you like slaves,
For who are so free as the sons of the waves?

CHORUS:
Heart of Oak are our ships, Heart of Oak are our men,
We always are ready,
Steady, boys, steady,
We'll fight and we'll conquer again and again.

We ne'er see our foes but we wish them to stay;
They never see us but they wish us away:
If they run, why we follow, and run them on shore,
For if they won't fight us, we cannot do more.

Heart of Oak, etc.

They swear they'll invade us, these terrible foes,
They'll frighten our women, and children, and beaux;
But should their flat-bottoms in darkness get o'er,
Still Britons they'll find to receive them on shore.

Heart of Oak, etc.

We'll still make them run and we'll still make them sweat,
In spite of the Devil, and Brussels Gazette:
Then cheer up, my lads, with one voice let us sing
Our soldiers, our sailors, our statesmen, and King.

Heart of Oak, etc.

—DAVID GARRICK

Source: C. H. Firth, *Naval Songs and Ballads*. Publications of the Navy Records Society, vol. 33 (London, 1908), p. 220.

FOREWORD

THIS CHILLING TALE of the last days of Citizen Peyrol, a French Brother of the Coast (Indian Ocean pirate), who arrives at the Port of Toulon after having been in the eastern seas for forty-five years, is one of Joseph Conrad's most overlooked novels. *The Rover*, a sort of nautical psychological thriller, as you might expect from Conrad, takes place—in theory—shortly after the siege of Toulon (September 7–December 19, 1793), the battle in which Captain Bonaparte drove out British and Royalist forces, making his name and securing a major moral victory for the fledgling Republic.

When Peyrol, with a small fortune jacketed to his body, returns to France after a life of roving the seas, the atmosphere is one of intense paranoia, as the military mercilessly persecutes suspected Bourbon sympathizers. Settling on the Mediterranean coast near Toulon, with a view of the Petite Passe between the Porquerolles and Cape Esterel, Peyrol hides his treasure in a well and takes a room at Escampobar Farm. Here, the seaman emeritus becomes ensnared in a love triangle involving the beautiful but disturbed Arlette, her erstwhile lover, Scevola—a sans-culotte who participated in the bloody murdering of Royalists after the recapture of Toulon, when Arlette's parents were both slain—and a Lieutenant Réal, who shows up at the farm one day with an unstated purpose. Réal presents a threat to both Peyrol, who fears persecution by the army, and Scevola, who fears losing Arlette.

The psychological self-destruction of the civil war that took place in Toulon is embodied in this tragic femme fatale. "There is no more visible reflection of the massacres at Toulon than appears in the half-demented character of Arlette in Joseph Conrad's *The Rover*," wrote the historian Oliver Warner in *A Portrait of Lord Nelson*. "Conrad knew the place, its legends, and living descendants of loyalists and republicans with the nearness of one who began his seafaring in their company. The legends he imbibed were not of a kind out of which fairy-tales arise."

With Nelson blockading the coast and the French army and navy feverish, the atmosphere at Escampobar Farm is indeed heavy, brooding. Conrad slowly builds the tension, as Peyrol, the hard-bitten mariner, restores the abandoned tartane of Arlette's dead father. Meanwhile, Jack Bolt, a lieutenant of the 22-gun sloop HMS *Amelia*, a lookout for Nelson's fleet, sneaks ashore to see what has become of the Royalist sympathizers living at Escampobar, and Lieutenant Réal's callous motive for visiting the farm becomes apparent. He wants Peyrol to embark on a suicidal mission that involves carrying false dispatches in the tartane, pretending to attempt escape at all costs (which means being battered into immobility by the British warships), and ultimately allowing himself to be captured, thus duping Nelson with the false documents and allowing the French fleet in Toulon to escape the blockade.

It is both a dangerous and despicable role to play, allowing dispatches to be taken by the enemy. One might recall that in the first sea action of the war, the gallant French Captain Mullon of the *Cléopâtre*, a canon shot from Pellew's HMS *Nymphe* having pulverized his back and hip, died chewing to pieces what he thought to be the list of French coast signals. But Peyrol has a mind of his own, and his own purposes. Here, Conrad explored what he explored best: the heart and soul of the true sailor, struggling to be an honorable and independent man when all seems to conspire against him.

Many thanks to John B. Hattendorf, the Ernest J. King Professor of Maritime History at the Naval War College in Newport, Rhode Island, for his insightful introduction to this Heart of Oak Sea Classics edition of *The Rover*.

—Dean King

INTRODUCTION

JOSEPH CONRAD (1857–1924) was one of the great writers of the English language and, certainly, the greatest who began his working life as a seaman in a square-rigged sailing ship. His years of experience, as he worked his way up from seaman, to mate, to master, infused him with a level of insight into the nature of sea and sailor that no other writer of his caliber has attained. Above all, his observant, character-building days at sea created a remarkable resource for his fiction writing.

At their best, Conrad's masterpieces of literary art delve deeply into the shaded meanings of human experience. While *The Rover* is not among his most-read works, it is a wonderful addition to the Heart of Oak Sea Classics series, bringing both an inside perspective to the maritime life of France during the naval wars of the French Revolution and Empire and, through the character Peyrol, a great portrayal of the wisdom of a lifelong mariner. *The Rover* also combines great literary art with the swiftness of an adventure novel at sea. As such, it provides an interesting comparison for and complement to Patrick O'Brian's more modern and highly praised Aubrey-Maturin novels, which are set in the same period.

In most of his works, Conrad used his own experiences as sources. Normally, he set his characters in the time frame of his contemporary world, creating romantic adventure by transporting them to the distant ports and countries he had known as a seaman. Born in Poland in

1857, he spent his early years with his parents in northern Russia, where his father was exiled for political reasons. When he was nine, the authorities allowed the family to return to Poland because his father was dying. Orphaned, the boy was raised by his uncle in Krakow and, as a teenager, began to express a wish to go to sea.

When Conrad was approaching seventeen, his uncle reluctantly granted him permission to join the French merchant marine. In the great port of Marseilles, probably armed with a letter of introduction from his uncle, he contacted the shipping firm Déléstang & Fils, and, in the summer of 1874, sailed to St. Pierre, Martinique, in the West Indies, as a passenger on board *Mont Blanc*, a 394-ton three-masted barque. The following year, he sailed as an apprentice in the same ship on a similar voyage to the West Indies, returning in the storm-damaged ship to Le Havre, and, in 1876, after a six-month wait for a berth, he signed on as a steward (but probably took on a range of other activities as well) in the newer barque *Saint-Antoine*. On returning from that voyage, he was ashore for a year in Marseilles, where he found himself so destitute that he attempted suicide. Surviving, he determined to make a fresh start.

In 1878, Conrad attempted to join the U.S. Navy in Villefranche but was rejected. Frustrated in his efforts to find employment, he took passage on a steamer on a circuitous route from Marseilles, via Constantinople, to Lowestoft, England. At the age of twenty and knowing scarcely a word of English, he signed on as a seaman on a coastal steamer in the North Sea. From 1878 to 1894, he rose through the ranks from seaman to officer in the British merchant service, passing examinations for both mates' and masters' certificates and becoming a British citizen. He served on several voyages as a second mate, was chief mate on two ships, and commanded another. These experiences at sea became the grist for a prolific thirty years of writing, from 1894 until his death in August 1924.

Published in November 1923, *The Rover* was the last novel that Conrad completed. (Another set in the same historical period, entitled *Suspense*, remained incomplete at the time of his death.) Despite the fact that *The Rover* came late in his career, a substantial portion of it derives from his earliest sea experiences in the 1870s. The life and countryside of the south coast of France made an indelible impression on Conrad's imagination, an impression that would come to life years later in *The Rover*.

Even more important, the men Conrad lived with in the forecastle of the *Saint-Antoine* and their relationships became the bedrock upon which he built much of his later fiction. The first mate, a forty-two-year-old Corsican named Dominic Cervoni (1834–1890), deeply impressed the nineteen-year-old and became a father figure to him. A tough but charismatic sailor, Cervoni evoked respect for his skill and experience at sea and embodied courage, leadership, and adventure. In his younger days, he had been a kind of maritime Mafioso, engaging in such illegal activities as gunrunning and filibustering. Before that, he had been a member of the "Brotherhood of the Coast," a group of buccaneers operating in the Indian Ocean and the China seas.

As Conrad wrote of Cervoni in his volume of essays and memoirs *The Mirror of the Sea*:

> His thick black moustaches [were] curled every morning with hot tongs by the barber at the corner of the quay. . . . For want of more exalted adversaries, Dominic turned his audacity fertile in impious stratagems against the powers of the earth, as represented by the institution of Customs-houses and every mortal belonging thereto—scribes, officers, and guardacostas. . . . He was the very man for us, this modern and unlawful wanderer with his own legend of loves, dangers, and bloodshed. He told us bits of it in measured, ironic tones. He spoke Catalonian, the Italian of Corsica and the French of Provence with the same easy naturalness.

No wonder the young seaman found such a man fascinating. After Conrad left France in 1878, he never saw Cervoni again, but the consummate sailor lived on in his creative imagination. He became the prototype for Nostromo in the work of that name, as well as for Peyrol.

In *The Rover*, Conrad, now weary and approaching the end of his life and, perhaps, imagining himself in the same mold as Cervoni, contemplated how the Corsican might have ideally ended his life, defiant to the end. One cannot help but think that Conrad, reflecting his characteristic irony and pessimism, might have been writing his own epitaph.

Conrad's early experiences certainly formed a key source for *The Rover*, but they were not the only influences. In 1922, when he wrote the novel, having just witnessed the First World War, he saw similarities and many more contrasts with the last great war, which had engulfed Europe from 1793 to 1815. Among the memories of his youthful days in Poland were nationalistic views about the Napoleonic period. On the one hand, it had been a sad time when Poland lost its autonomy, falling under Russian domination. On the other, the era had inspired heroic beliefs and actions, providing moments of greatness for many ordinary people. In one sense, his return to this period and to his youth in distant lands was a rejection of the present.

At the end of 1919, as Conrad and his family settled into Oswalds, a Georgian-era home in the village of Bishopsbourne, near Canterbury, he planned his future work. His goal was to write a large novel on the Napoleonic period (this would be the unfinished book *Suspense*) and, related to that work, a short story that would appeal to a popular audience. This would eventually evolve into *The Rover*. As 1920 passed, Conrad became bogged down in *Suspense*. To release his frustration, he turned to the short story in early December. After writing 5,000 words, he decided to expand it into a short novel. However, first he decided to take his wife for a holiday on Corsica, where he could recapture the feel of the Mediterranean and refresh his spirit.

They left England on January 23, 1921, and drove across France, stopping en route at Rouen, Chartres, Orléans, Avignon, and Marseilles. After several days in Marseilles, they ferried to Corsica, staying in Ajaccio, where Napoleon was born. While Conrad apparently did not write during these months, he did read at the Ajaccio Library and absorb the local atmosphere. On the waterfront, he talked to seamen and studied the Mediterranean boats. By the end of March, he was ready to leave. After a few days at Bastia on the island's northeast coast, he and his wife ferried to Nice and then traveled on to Toulon, where Conrad carefully observed the scene and countryside that, within a few months, would dominate *The Rover*.

In April, Conrad returned to work, his travels having revived a large range of memories and reflections on his youthful experiences. Nonetheless, he continued to struggle with the writing of *Suspense*, and his wife's relapse into illness distracted him. While gathering together a collection of his shorter pieces, he considered including *The Rover*, and, in December, turned to it again. This time, the writing went better, and it became clear that the work was a novel and not a short story. Conrad finished a first draft in June of 1922 and a revised draft in mid-July. He hoped to serialize it in *The Pictorial Review*, an American magazine, but this never happened. The novel was published by Fisher and Unwin in London, and by Doubleday & Company in the United States, on December 3.

Three days later, an anonymous reviewer for the *Times Literary Supplement* aptly described the book:

> Mr. Conrad's story, as a remark on the wrapper assures us, is in no sense historical; and the letter of that statement is quite true. But it is no less true that the author has laid his course for the past, dipping under the horizon line beyond which, for us, lies history.... What has emerged ... is not the full dress and detail of a historical novel. It is the subtilized past, through the aroma and the intuitive touches, which comes alive....

In *The Rover*, Conrad presents the reader with a series of vivid images of the Mediterranean. Capsulizing them in the book's final paragraph, he wrote: "The blue level of the Mediterranean, the charmer and deceiver of audacious men, kept the secret of its fascination—hugged to its calm breast the victims of all the wars, calamities and tempests of its history, under the marvelous purity of the sunset sky."

Conrad had created another stirring work about the sea, successfully portraying the stress and strain that the Royal Navy caused Toulon while bottling up the French fleet. His dramatic shifts from the perspective of the lonely French sailor to the blockading English warship, and even to Nelson himself, created great drama. As the *Times Literary Supplement* reviewer described it:

> State designs and private emotions interweaving make an honestly thrilling tale of action, with the glint of its time. The sea chase, ending in the destruction of Peyrol and his treasured boat, is a worthy climax; and the glimpse of Nelson which follows is as convincing as far as it goes. It was good that the great novelist of sailing ships should have pictured at last, if only in a flash, the greatest sailor.

Peyrol, a "man of dark deeds, but of large heart," as Conrad described him, is the old salt who desires rest but at the same time cannot resist one last defiant act. Through his descriptions of Peyrol and the novel's thrilling end, Conrad created a historical image of a particular time and place. Yet, unlike much modern historical fiction, it is not based on precise historical detail from flawless research. It is rather an impressionistic tour de force, giving a distinct sense of a past time and place. The historian will find numerous small errors in fact, which, however wrong, do not detract from the novel's literary achievement.

Precisely dating the action of *The Rover* is also a confusing business. While no dates are mentioned, several references imply them. In the future, Lieutenant Réal would sail away "with the Toulon fleet on the great strategical cruise which was to end in the battle of Trafalgar," which dates the action before 1805. Conrad wrote that "the years of political changes ending with the proclamation of Napoleon as consul for life had not touched Peyrol except as to his strong thick head of hair, which was nearly all white." Thus, Conrad is writing about the period leading up to 1804. But another reference mentions the forthcoming Peace of Amiens in 1802. Most prominently, however, the reader finds Admiral Lord Nelson conducting a distant blockade off Toulon, just having received news that the French were preparing an expedition for Egypt. The great battle of the Nile would take place in August 1798.

The names of Conrad's naval officers also deserve some comment. Certainly, the French naval officer whom Conrad calls Citizen Renaud was *Capitaine de Vaisseau* Jean-Marie Renaud, the French Navy's senior officer in the Indian Ocean in 1793, from whom Peyrol had received a warrant to bring home a prize-ship to Toulon. On the British side, there was an officer named Vincent. Richard Budd Vincent was commissioned as a lieutenant in 1790 and promoted to commander in 1802. In February 1805, while convoying merchant ships in the 20-gun sloop *Arrow*, Vincent gallantly fought against two French frigates in the Mediterranean near Gibraltar. Although he was forced to surrender his sinking ship, the *Arrow* and another vessel had successfully defended the convoy. In April 1805, Vincent was made postcaptain.

The geography of the region and waters around Toulon is accurate (see map, pages 2–3), as is Peyrol's beloved 40-ton tartane. This type of vessel, usually called a tartana in English, but *tartane* in French, was single-masted and rigged with one large lateen sail and one or two small jibs set from a bowsprit. Commonly found in the western Mediterranean, it was normally used for trading and fishing. While tartanas varied in size (from roughly 27 feet long and 9 feet in beam to 65 feet long with a 15-foot beam), they characteristically had a high stem and a pointed stern with a high stern post.

While Conrad accurately portrayed the native Mediterranean craft, historians will quibble over the names and descriptions of the British ships. The narrative places Nelson in his most famous command, the 100-gun *Victory*, but, in fact, during 1798, he flew his flag in the 74-gun ship-of-the-line *Vanguard*. There was, indeed, an HMS *Amelia* in the British fleet at this time, but she was not a 22-gun sloop of war as described but rather a 38-gun frigate. Like the fictional *Amelia*, the real HMS *Amelia* was French-built. Designed by the naval architect Sané and constructed in the naval dockyard at Brest, she was commissioned in 1785 as *La Prospérine*. HMS *Dryad* captured her off Cape Clear on 13 June 1796, and she served in the Royal Navy from that time until she was broken up in 1816.

Such small details might distract some readers of *The Rover*, but one should not forget Conrad's intentions. In commenting on an earlier book that had also touched on actual events, he explained that he had not done a great deal of research on the subject, but that "it was a matter of great interest to me to see how near actuality I managed to come in a work of imagination." Enclosing a copy of the same letter with *The Rover*, Conrad noted that it, too, was "a work of pure imagination."

—John B. Hattendorf

THE ROVER

New
Harbor

Old
Harbor

Mishan, the King's
Powder Magazine

Fort
St. Louis

Little Road

Le Goulet

Great Road

Fort de Balaguer

Gulf
of Veche

Cape
Monegau

Mediterranean Sea

©1999 Jeffrey L. Ward

THE
ROADS and HARBOR of
TOULON
with a sketch of
the Adjacent Country

Bay

of

Toulon

Porte de la
Querquerane

Cape Cépet

0 .5 1
Miles

Mouth of the Rhône

Marseilles

Mediterranean Sea

0 10 20 30
Miles

Giens

Toulon

Cape Sicié
Cape d'Escampaberion
Ile de Porquerolles

Petite Pass

Cape
Esterel

Bay d'Hyères

Iles d'Hyères

43°

55 Fathoms
upon This Bank

5°

6°

43°

CHAPTER I

~❧~

AFTER ENTERING AT break of day the inner roadstead of the
Port of Toulon, exchanging several loud hails with one of
the guardboats of the Fleet, which directed him where he
was to take up his berth, Master-Gunner Peyrol let go the anchor of
the sea-worn and battered ship in his charge, between the arsenal and
the town, in full view of the principal quay. The course of his life,
which in the opinion of any ordinary person might have been
regarded as full of marvellous incidents (only he himself had never
marvelled at them), had rendered him undemonstrative to such a
degree that he did not even let out a sigh of relief at the rumble of the
cable. And yet it ended a most anxious six months of knocking about
at sea with valuable merchandise in a damaged hull, most of the time
on short rations, always on the lookout for English cruisers, once or
twice on the verge of shipwreck and more than once on the verge of
capture. But as to that, old Peyrol had made up his mind from the first
to blow up his valuable charge—unemotionally, for such was his character, formed under the sun of the Indian Seas in lawless contests with
his kind for a little loot that vanished as soon as grasped, but mainly
for bare life almost as precarious to hold through its ups and downs,
and which now had lasted for fifty-eight years.

While his crew of half-starved scarecrows, hard as nails and rav-
enous as so many wolves for the delights of the shore, swarmed aloft
to furl the sails nearly as thin and as patched as the grimy shirts on

their backs, Peyrol took a survey of the quay. Groups were forming along its whole stretch to gaze at the new arrival. Peyrol noted particularly a good many men in red caps and said to himself: "Here they are." Amongst the crews of ships that had brought the tricolour into the seas of the East, there were hundreds professing sans-culotte principles; boastful and declamatory beggars he had thought them. But now he was beholding the shore breed. Those who had made the Revolution safe. The real thing. Peyrol, after taking a good long look, went below into his cabin to make himself ready to go ashore.

He shaved his big cheeks with a real English razor, looted years ago from an officer's cabin in an English East Indiaman captured by a ship he was serving in then. He put on a white shirt, a short blue jacket with metal buttons and a high roll-collar, a pair of white trousers which he fastened with a red bandana handkerchief by way of a belt. With a black, shiny low-crowned hat on his head he made a very creditable prize-master. He beckoned from the poop to a boatman and got himself rowed to the quay.

By that time the crowd had grown to a large size. Peyrol's eyes ranged over it with no great apparent interest, though it was a fact that he had never in all his man's life seen so many idle white people massed together to stare at a sailor. He had been a rover of the outer seas; he had grown into a stranger to his native country. During the few minutes it took the boatman to row him to the step, he felt like a navigator about to land on a newly discovered shore.

On putting his foot on it he was mobbed. The arrival of a prize made by a squadron of the Republic in distant seas was not an everyday occurrence in Toulon. The wildest rumours had been already set flying. Peyrol elbowed himself through the crowd somehow, but it continued to move after him. A voice cried out, "Where do you come from, *citoyen*?"—"From the other side of the world," Peyrol boomed out.

He did not get rid of his followers till the door of the Port Office. There he reported himself to the proper officials as master of a prize taken off the Cape by Citoyen Renaud, Commander-in-Chief of the Republican Squadron in the Indian Seas. He had been ordered to make for Dunkerque but, said he, having been chased by the *sacrés Anglais* three times in a fortnight between Cape Verde and Cape Spartel, he had made up his mind to run into the Mediterranean where, he had understood from a Danish brig he had met at sea, there were no English men-of-war just then. And here he was; and there were his ship's papers and his own papers and everything in order. He mentioned also that he was tired of rolling about the seas, and that he longed for a period of repose on shore. But till all the legal business was settled he remained in Toulon roaming about the streets at a deliberate gait, enjoying general consideration as Citizen Peyrol, and looking everybody coldly in the eye.

His reticence about his past was of that kind which starts a lot of mysterious stories about a man. No doubt the maritime authorities of Toulon had a less cloudy idea of Peyrol's past, though it need not necessarily have been more exact. In the various offices connected with the sea where his duties took him, the wretched scribes, and even some of the chiefs, looked very hard at him as he went in and out, dressed very neatly, and always with his cudgel, which he used to leave outside the door of private offices when called in for an interview with one or another of the "gold-laced lot." Having, however, cut off his queue and got in touch with some prominent patriots of the Jacobin type, Peyrol cared little for people's stares and whispers. The person that came nearest to trying his composure was a certain naval captain with a patch over one eye and a very threadbare uniform coat who was doing some administrative work at the Port Office. That officer, looking up from some papers, remarked brusquely, "As a matter of fact you have been the best part of your life skimming the seas, if the truth were known. You must have been a deserter from the Navy at one time, whatever you may call yourself now."

There was not a quiver on the large cheeks of the gunner Peyrol.

"If there was anything of the sort it was in the time of kings and aristocrats," he said steadily. "And now I have brought in a prize, and a service letter from Citizen Renaud, commanding in the Indian Seas. I can also give you the names of good Republicans in this town who know my sentiments. Nobody can say I was ever anti-revolutionary in my life. I knocked about the Eastern seas for forty-five years—that's true. But let me observe that it was the seamen who stayed at home that let the English into the Port of Toulon." He paused a moment and then added: "When one thinks of that, *citoyen* Commandant, any little slips I and fellows of my kind may have made five thousand leagues from here and twenty years ago cannot have much importance in these times of equality and fraternity."

"As to fraternity," remarked the post-captain in the shabby coat, "the only one you are familiar with is the Brotherhood of the Coast, I should say."

"Everybody in the Indian Ocean except milksops and youngsters had to be," said the untroubled Citizen Peyrol. "And we practised republican principles long before a republic was thought of; for the Brothers of the Coast were all equal and elected their own chiefs."

"They were an abominable lot of lawless ruffians," remarked the officer venomously, leaning back in his chair. "You will not dare to deny that."

Citizen Peyrol refused to take up a defensive attitude. He merely mentioned in a neutral tone that he had delivered his trust to the Port Office all right, and as to his character he had a certificate of civism from his section. He was a patriot and entitled to his discharge. After being dismissed by a nod he took up his cudgel outside the door and walked out of the building with the calmness of rectitude. His large face of the Roman type betrayed nothing to the wretched quill-drivers, who whispered on his passage. As he went along the streets he looked as usual everybody in the eye; but that very same evening he vanished from Toulon. It wasn't that he was afraid of anything. His mind was as calm as the natural set of his florid face. Nobody could know what his forty years or more of sea-life had been, unless he told them himself. And of that he didn't mean to tell more than what he had told the inquisitive captain with the patch over one eye. But he didn't want any bother for certain other reasons; and more than anything else he didn't want to be sent perhaps to serve in the fleet now fitting out in Toulon. So at dusk he passed through the gate on the road to Fréjus in a high two-wheeled cart belonging to a well-known farmer whose habitation lay that way. His personal belongings were brought down and piled up on the tailboard of the cart by some raga-muffin patriots whom he engaged in the street for that purpose. The only indiscretion he committed was to pay them for their trouble with a large handful of assignats. From such a prosperous seaman, how-ever, this generosity was not so very compromising. He himself got into the cart over the wheel, with such slow and ponderous move-ments, that the friendly farmer felt called upon to remark: "Ah, we are not so young as we used to be—you and I."—"I have also an awk-ward wound," said Citizen Peyrol, sitting down heavily.

And so from farmer's cart to farmer's cart, getting lifts all along, jogging in a cloud of dust between stone walls and through little villages well known to him from his boyhood's days, in a landscape of stony hills, pale rocks, and dusty green of olive trees, Citizen Peyrol went on unmolested till he got down clumsily in the yard of an inn on the outskirts of the town of Hyères. The sun was setting to his right. Near a clump of dark pines with blood-red trunks in the sunset, Peyrol perceived a rutty track branching off in the direction of the sea.

At that spot Citizen Peyrol had made up his mind to leave the high road. Every feature of the country with the darkly wooded rises, the barren flat expanse of stones and sombre bushes to his left, appealed to him with a sort of strange familiarity, because they had remained unchanged since the days of his boyhood. The very cartwheel tracks scored deep into the stony ground had kept their physiognomy; and far away, like a blue thread, there was the sea of the Hyères roadstead with a lumpy indigo swelling still beyond—which was the island of Porquerolles. He had an idea that he had been born on Porquerolles, but he really did not know. The notion of a father was absent from his mentality. What he remembered of his parents was a tall, lean, brown woman in rags, who was his mother. But then they were working together at a farm which was on the mainland. He had fragmentary memories of her shaking down olives, picking stones out of a field, or handling a manure fork like a man, tireless and fierce, with wisps of greyish hair flying about her bony face; and of himself running bare-footed in connection with a flock of turkeys, with hardly any clothes on his back. At night, by the farmer's favour, they were permitted to sleep in a sort of ruinous byre built of stones and with only half a roof on it, lying side by side on some old straw on the ground. And it was on a bundle of straw that his mother had tossed ill for two days and had died in the night. In the darkness, her silence, her cold face had given him an awful scare. He supposed they had buried her but he didn't know, because he had rushed out terror-struck, and never stopped till he got as far as a little place by the sea called Almanarre, where he hid himself on board a tartane that was lying there with no one on board. He went into the hold because he was afraid of some dogs on shore. He found down there a heap of empty sacks which made a luxurious couch, and being exhausted went to sleep like a stone. Some time during the night the crew came on board and the tartane sailed for Marseilles. That was another awful scare—being hauled out by the scruff of the neck on the deck and being asked who the devil he was and what he was doing there. Only from that one he could not run away. There was water all around him and the whole world, including the coast not very far away, wobbled in a most alarming manner. Three bearded men stood about him and he tried to explain to them that he had been working at Peyrol's. Peyrol was the farmer's name. The boy didn't know that he had one of his own. Moreover, he didn't know very well how to talk to people, and they must have misunderstood him. Thus the name of Peyrol stuck to him for life.

There the memories of his native country stopped, overlaid by other memories, with a multitude of impressions of endless oceans, of the Mozambique Channel, of Arabs and negroes, of Madagascar, of the coast of India, of islands and channels and reefs; of fights at sea, rows on shore, desperate slaughter and desperate thirst, of all sorts of ships one after another: merchant ships and frigates and privateers; of reckless men and enormous sprees. In the course of years he had learned to speak intelligibly and think connectedly and even to read and write after a fashion. The name of the farmer Peyrol, attached to his person on account of his inability to give a clear account of himself, acquired a sort of reputation, both openly, in the ports of the East and, secretly, amongst the Brothers of the Coast, that strange fraternity with something masonic and not a little piratical in its constitution. Round the Cape of Storms, which is also the Cape of Good Hope, the words Republic, Nation, Tyranny, Liberty, Equality, and Fraternity, and the cult of the Supreme Being came floating on board ships from home, new cries and new ideas which did not upset the slowly developed intelligence of the gunner Peyrol. They seemed the invention of landsmen, of whom the seaman Peyrol knew very little—nothing, so to speak. Now, after nearly fifty years of lawful and lawless sea-life, Citizen Peyrol, at the yard gate of the roadside inn, looked at the late scene of his childhood. He looked at it without any animosity, but a little puzzled as to his bearings amongst the features of the land. "Yes, it must be somewhere in that direction," he thought vaguely. Decidedly he would go no further along the high road. . . . A few yards away the woman of the inn stood looking at him, impressed by the good clothes, the great shaven cheeks, the well-to-do air of that seaman; and suddenly Peyrol noticed her. With her anxious brown face, her grey locks, and her rustic appearance she might have been his mother, as he remembered her, only she wasn't in rags.

"Hé! La mère," hailed Peyrol. "Have you got a man to lend a hand with my chest into the house?"

He looked so prosperous and so authoritative that she piped without hesitation in a thin voice, "*Mais oui, citoyen*. He will be here in a moment."

In the dusk the clump of pines across the road looked very black against the quiet clear sky; and Citizen Peyrol gazed at the scene of his young misery with the greatest possible placidity. Here he was after nearly fifty years, and to look at things it seemed like yesterday. He felt for all this neither love nor resentment. He felt a little funny as it were, and the funniest thing was the thought which crossed his mind that he could indulge his fancy (if he had a mind to it) to buy up all this land to the furthermost field, away over there where the track lost itself sinking into the flats bordering the sea where the small rise at the end of the Giens Peninsula had assumed the appearance of a black cloud.

"Tell me, my friend," he said in his magisterial way to the farm-hand with a tousled head of hair who was awaiting his good pleasure, "doesn't this track lead to Almanarre?"

"Yes," said the labourer, and Peyrol nodded. The man continued, mouthing his words slowly as if unused to speech. "To Almanarre and further too, beyond the great pond right out to the end of the land, to Cape Esterel."

Peyrol was lending his big flat hairy ear. "If I had stayed in this country," he thought, "I would be talking like this fellow." And aloud he asked:

"Are there any houses there, at the end of the land?"

"Why, a hamlet, a hole, just a few houses round a church and a farm where at one time they would give you a glass of wine."

CHAPTER II

∽

C ITIZEN PEYROL STAYED at the inn-yard gate till the night
had swallowed up all those features of the land to which his
eyes had clung as long as the last gleams of daylight. And
even after the last gleams had gone he had remained for some time
staring into the darkness in which all he could distinguish was the
white road at his feet and the black heads of pines where the cart track
dipped towards the coast. He did not go indoors till some carters who
had been refreshing themselves had departed with their big two-
wheeled carts piled up high with empty wine-casks, in the direction
of Fréjus. The fact that they did not remain for the night pleased
Peyrol. He ate his bit of supper alone, in silence, and with a gravity
which intimidated the old woman who had aroused in him the
memory of his mother. Having finished his pipe and obtained a bit of
candle in a tin candlestick, Citizen Peyrol went heavily upstairs to
rejoin his luggage. The crazy staircase shook and groaned under his
feet as though he had been carrying a burden. The first thing he did
was to close the shutters most carefully as though he had been afraid
of a breath of night air. Next he bolted the door of the room. Then sitting on the floor, with the candlestick standing before him between his
widely straddled legs, he began to undress, flinging off his coat and
dragging his shirt hastily over his head. The secret of his heavy movements was disclosed then in the fact that he had been wearing next his
bare skin—like a pious penitent his hair-shirt—a sort of waistcoat

made of two thicknesses of old sail-cloth and stitched all over in the manner of a quilt with tarred twine. Three horn buttons closed it in front. He undid them, and after he had slipped off the two shoulder-straps which prevented this strange garment from sagging down on his hips he started rolling it up. Notwithstanding all his care there were during this operation several faint chinks of some metal which could not have been lead.

His bare torso thrown backwards and sustained by his rigid big arms heavily tattooed on the white skin above the elbows, Peyrol drew a long breath into his broad chest with a pepper-and-salt pelt down the breastbone. And not only was the breast of Citizen Peyrol relieved to the fullest of its athletic capacity, but a change had also come over his large physiognomy on which the expression of severe stolidity had been simply the result of physical discomfort. It isn't a trifle to have to carry girt about your ribs and hung from your shoulders a mass of mixed foreign coins equal to sixty or seventy thousand francs in hard cash; while as to the paper money of the Republic, Peyrol had had already enough experience of it to estimate the equivalent in cartloads. A thousand of them. Perhaps two thousand. Enough in any case to justify his flight of fancy, while looking at the countryside in the light of the sunset, that what he had on him would buy all that soil from which he had sprung: houses, woods, vines, olives, vegetable gardens, rocks and salt lagoons—in fact, the whole landscape, including the animals in it. But Peyrol did not care for the land at all. He did not want to own any part of the solid earth for which he had no love. All he wanted from it was a quiet nook, an obscure corner out of men's sight where he could dig a hole unobserved.

That would have to be done pretty soon, he thought. One could not live for an indefinite number of days with a treasure strapped round one's chest. Meantime, an utter stranger in his native country the landing on which was perhaps the biggest adventure in his adventurous life, he threw his jacket over the rolled-up waistcoat and laid his head down on it after extinguishing the candle. The night was warm. The floor of the room happened to be of planks, not of tiles. He was no stranger to that sort of couch. With his cudgel laid ready at his hand Peyrol slept soundly till the noises and the voices about the house and on the road woke him up shortly after sunrise. He threw open the shutter, welcoming the morning light and the morning breeze in the full enjoyment of idleness which, to a seaman of his kind, is inseparable from the fact of being on shore. There was nothing to trouble his thoughts; and though his physiognomy was far from being vacant, it did not wear the aspect of profound meditation.

It had been by the merest accident that he had discovered during the passage, in a secret recess within one of the lockers of his prize, two bags of mixed coins: gold mohurs, Dutch ducats, Spanish pieces, English guineas. After making that discovery he had suffered from no doubts whatever. Loot big or little was a natural fact of his free-booter's life. And now when by the force of things he had become a master-gunner of the Navy he was not going to give up his find to confounded landsmen, mere sharks, hungry quill-drivers, who would put it in their own pockets. As to imparting the intelligence to his crew (all bad characters), he was much too wise to do anything of the kind. They would not have been above cutting his throat. An old fighting seadog, a Brother of the Coast, had more right to such plunder than anybody on earth. So at odd times, while at sea, he had busied himself within the privacy of his cabin in constructing the ingenious canvas waistcoat in which he could take his treasure ashore secretly. It was bulky, but his garments were of an ample cut, and no wretched customs-guard would dare to lay hands on a successful prize-master going to the Port Admiral's offices to make his report. The scheme had worked perfectly. He found, however, that this secret garment, which was worth precisely its weight in gold, tried his endurance more than he had expected. It wearied his body and even depressed his spirits somewhat. It made him less active and also less communicative. It reminded him all the time that he must not get into trouble of any sort—keep clear of rows, of intimacies, of promiscuous jollities. This was one of the reasons why he had been anxious to get away from the town. Once, however, his head was laid on his treasure he could sleep the sleep of the just.

Nevertheless in the morning he shrank from putting it on again. With a mixture of sailor's carelessness and of old-standing belief in his own luck he simply stuffed the precious waistcoat up the flue of the empty fireplace. Then he dressed and had his breakfast. An hour later, mounted on a hired mule, he started down the track as calmly as though setting out to explore the mysteries of a desert island.

His aim was the end of the peninsula which, advancing like a colossal jetty into the sea, divides the picturesque roadstead of Hyères from the headlands and curves of the coast forming the approaches of the Port of Toulon. The path along which the sure-footed mule took him (for Peyrol, once he had put its head the right way, made no attempt at steering) descended rapidly to a plain of arid aspect, with the white gleams of the Salins in the distance, bounded by bluish hills of no great elevation. Soon all traces of human habitations disappeared from before his roaming eyes. This part of his native country was more foreign to him than the shores of the Mozambique Channel, the coral strands of India, the forests of Madagascar. Before long he found himself on the neck of the Giens Peninsula, impregnated with salt and containing a blue lagoon, particularly blue, darker and even more still than the expanses of the sea to the right and left of it from which it was separated by narrow strips of land not a hundred yards wide in places. The track ran indistinct, presenting no wheel-ruts, and with patches of efflorescent salt as white as snow between the tufts of wiry grass and the particularly dead-looking bushes. The whole neck of land was so low that it seemed to have no more thickness than a sheet of paper laid on the sea. Citizen Peyrol saw on the level of his eye, as if from a mere raft, sails of various craft, some white and some brown, while before him his native island of Porquerolles rose dull and solid beyond a wide strip of water. The mule, which knew rather better than Citizen Peyrol where it was going to, took him presently amongst the gentle rises at the end of the peninsula. The slopes were covered with scanty grass; crooked boundary walls of dry stones ran across the fields, and above them, here and there, peeped a low roof of red tiles shaded by the heads of delicate acacias. At a turn of the ravine appeared a village with its few houses, mostly with their blind walls to the path, and, at first, no living soul in sight. Three tall platanes, very ragged as to their bark and very poor as to foliage, stood in a group in an open space; and Citizen Peyrol was cheered by the sight of a dog sleeping in the shade. The mule swerved with great determination towards a massive stone trough under the village fountain. Peyrol, looking round from the saddle while the mule drank, could see no signs of an inn. Then, examining the ground nearer to him, he perceived a ragged man sitting on a stone. He had a broad leathern belt and his legs were bare to the knee. He was contemplating the stranger on the mule with stony surprise. His dark nut-brown face contrasted strongly with his grey shock of hair. At a sign from Peyrol he showed no reluctance and approached him readily without changing the stony character of his stare.

The thought that if he had remained at home he would have

probably looked like that man crossed unbidden the mind of Peyrol. With that gravity from which he seldom departed he inquired if there were any inhabitants besides himself in the village. Then, to Peyrol's surprise, that destitute idler smiled pleasantly and said that the people were out looking after their bits of land.

There was enough of the peasant-born in Peyrol, still, to remark that he had seen no man, woman, or child, or four-footed beast for hours, and that he would hardly have thought that there was any land worth looking after anywhere around. But the other insisted. Well, they were working on it all the same, at least those that had any.

At the sound of the voices the dog got up with a strange air of being all backbone, and, approaching in dismal fidelity, stood with his nose close to his master's calves.

"And you," said Peyrol, "you have no land then?"

The man took his time to answer. "I have a boat."

Peyrol became interested when the man explained that his boat was on the salt pond, the large, deserted, and opaque sheet of water lying dead between the two great bays of the living sea. Peyrol wondered aloud why any one should want a boat on it.

"There is fish there," said the man.

"And is the boat all your worldly goods?" asked Peyrol.

The flies buzzed, the mule hung its head, moving its ears and flapping its thin tail languidly.

"I have a sort of hut down by the lagoon and a net or two," the man confessed, as it were. Peyrol, looking down, completed the list by saying: "And this dog."

The man again took his time to say:

"He is company."

Peyrol sat as serious as a judge. "You haven't much to make a living of," he delivered himself at last. "However! . . . Is there no inn, café, or some place where one could put up for a day? I have heard up inland that there was some such place."

"I will show it to you," said the man, who then went back to where he had been sitting and picked up a large empty basket before he led the way. His dog followed with his head and tail low, and then came Peyrol dangling his heels against the sides of the intelligent mule, which seemed to know beforehand all that was going to happen. At the corner where the houses ended there stood an old wooden cross stuck into a square block of stone. The lonely boatman of the Lagoon of Pesquiers pointed in the direction of a branching path where the rises terminating the peninsula sank into a shallow pass. There were leaning pines on the skyline, and in the pass itself dull silvery green patches of olive orchards below a long yellow wall backed by dark cypresses, and the red roofs of buildings which seemed to belong to a farm.

"Will they lodge me there?" asked Peyrol.

"I don't know. They will have plenty of room, that's certain. There are no travellers here. But as for a place of refreshment, it used to be that. You have only got to walk in. If he isn't there, the mistress is sure to be there to serve you. She belongs to the place. She was born on it. We know all about her."

"What sort of woman is she?" asked Citizen Peyrol, who was very favourably impressed by the aspect of the place.

"Well, you are going there. You shall soon see. She is young."

"And the husband?" asked Peyrol, who, looking down into the other's steady upward stare, detected a flicker in the brown, slightly faded eyes. "Why are you staring at me like this? I haven't got a black skin, have I?"

The other smiled, showing in the thick pepper-and-salt growth on his face as sound a set of teeth as Citizen Peyrol himself. There was in his bearing something embarrassed, but not unfriendly, and he uttered a phrase from which Peyrol discovered that the man before him, the lonely, hirsute, sunburnt and barelegged human being at his stirrup, nourished patriotic suspicions as to his character. And this seemed to him outrageous. He wanted to know in a severe voice whether he looked like a confounded landsman of any kind. He swore also without, however, losing any of the dignity of expression inherent in his type of features and in the very modelling of his flesh.

"For an aristocrat you don't look like one, but neither do you look like a farmer or a pedlar or a patriot. You don't look like anything that has been seen here for years and years and years. You look like one, I dare hardly say what. You might be a priest."

Astonishment kept Peyrol perfectly quiet on his mule. "Do I dream?" he asked himself mentally. "You aren't mad?" he asked aloud. "Do you know what you are talking about? Aren't you ashamed of yourself?"

"All the same," persisted the other innocently, "it is much less than ten years ago since I saw one of them of the sort they call bishops, who had a face exactly like yours."

Instinctively Peyrol passed his hand over his face. What could there be in it? Peyrol could not remember ever having seen a bishop in his life. The fellow stuck to his point, for he puckered his brow and murmured:

"Others too. . . . I remember perfectly. . . . It isn't so many years ago. Some of them skulk amongst the villages yet, for all the chasing they got from the patriots."

The sun blazed on the boulders and stones and bushes in the perfect stillness of the air. The mule, disregarding with Republican austerity the neighbourhood of a stable within less than a hundred and twenty yards, dropped its head, and even its ears, and dozed as if in the middle of a desert. The dog, apparently changed into stone at his master's heels, seemed to be dozing too with his nose near the ground. Peyrol had fallen into a deep meditation, and the boatman of the lagoon awaited the solution of his doubts without eagerness and with something like a grin within his thick beard. Peyrol's face cleared. He had solved the problem, but there was a shade of vexation in his tone.

"Well, it can't be helped," he said. "I learned to shave from the English. I suppose that's what's the matter."

At the name of the English the boatman pricked up his ears.

"One can't tell where they are all gone to," he murmured. "Only three years ago they swarmed about this coast in their big ships. You saw nothing but them, and they were fighting all round Toulon on land. Then in a week or two, *crac!*—nobody! Cleared out devil knows where. But perhaps you would know."

"Oh, yes," said Peyrol, "I know all about the English, don't you worry your head."

"I am not troubling my head. It is for you to think about what's best to say when you speak with him up there. I mean the master of the farm."

"He can't be a better patriot than I am, for all my shaven face," said Peyrol. "That would only seem strange to a savage like you."

With an unexpected sigh the man sat down at the foot of the cross, and, immediately, his dog went off a little way and curled himself up amongst the tufts of grass.

"We are all savages here," said the forlorn fisherman from the lagoon. "But the master up there is a real patriot from the town. If you were ever to go to Toulon and ask people about him they would tell you. He first became busy purveying the guillotine when they were purifying the town from all aristocrats. That was even before the English came in. After the English got driven out there was more of that work than the guillotine could do. They had to kill traitors in the streets, in cellars, in their beds. The corpses of men and women were lying in heaps along the quays. There were a good many of his sort that got the name of drinkers of blood. Well, he was one of the best of them. I am only just telling you."

Peyrol nodded. "That will do me all right," he said. And before he could pick up the reins and hit it with his heels the mule, as though it had just waited for his words, started off along the path.

In less than five minutes Peyrol was dismounting in front of a low, long addition to a tall farmhouse with very few windows, and flanked by walls of stones enclosing not only the yard but apparently a field or two also. A gateway stood open to the left, but Peyrol dismounted at the door, through which he entered a bare room, with rough white-washed walls and a few wooden chairs and tables, which might have been a rustic café. He tapped with his knuckles on the table. A young woman with a fichu round her neck and a striped white and red skirt, with black hair and a red mouth, appeared in an inner doorway.

"*Bonjour, citoyenne,*" said Peyrol. She was so startled by the unusual aspect of this stranger that she answered him only by a murmured "*bonjour,*" but in a moment she came forward and waited expectantly. The perfect oval of her face, the colour of her smooth cheeks, and the whiteness of her throat forced from the Citizen Peyrol a slight hiss through his clenched teeth.

"I am thirsty, of course," he said, "but what I really want is to know whether I can stay here."

The sound of a mule's hoofs outside caused Peyrol to start, but the woman arrested him.

"She is only going to the shed. She knows the way. As to what you said, the master will be here directly. Nobody ever comes here. And how long would you want to stay?"

The old rover of the seas looked at her searchingly.

"To tell you the truth, *citoyenne,* it may be in a manner of speaking for ever."

She smiled in a bright flash of teeth, without gaiety or any change in her restless eyes that roamed about the empty room as though Peyrol had come in attended by a mob of Shades.

"It's like me," she said. "I lived as a child here."

"You are but little more than that now," said Peyrol, examining her with a feeling that was no longer surprise or curiosity, but seemed to be lodged in his very breast.

"Are you a patriot?" she asked, still surveying the invisible company in the room.

Peyrol, who had thought that he had "done with all that damned nonsense," felt angry and also at a loss for an answer.

"I am a Frenchman," he said bluntly.

"Arlette!" called out an aged woman's voice through the open inner door.

"What do you want?" she answered readily.

"There's a saddled mule come into the yard."

"All right. The man is here." Her eyes, which had steadied, began to wander again all round and about the motionless Peyrol. She moved a step nearer to him and asked in a low confidential tone: "Have you ever carried a woman's head on a pike?"

Peyrol, who had seen fights, massacres on land and sea, towns taken by assault by savage warriors, who had killed men in attack and defence, found himself at first bereft of speech by this simple question, and next moved to speak bitterly.

"No. I have heard men boast of having done so. They were mostly braggarts with craven hearts. But what is all this to you?"

She was not listening to him, the edge of her white even teeth pressing her lower lip, her eyes never at rest. Peyrol remembered suddenly the sans-culotte—the blood-drinker. Her husband. Was it possible? . . . Well, perhaps it was possible. He could not tell. He felt his utter incompetence. As to catching her glance, you might just as well have tried to catch a wild sea-bird with your hands. And altogether she was like a sea-bird—not to be grasped. But Peyrol knew how to be patient, with that patience that is so often a form of courage. He was known for it. It had served him well in dangerous situations. Once it had positively saved his life. Nothing but patience. He could well wait now. He waited. And suddenly as if tamed by his patience this strange creature dropped her eyelids, advanced quite close to him and began to finger the lapel of his coat—something that a child might have done. Peyrol all but gasped with surprise, but he remained perfectly still. He was disposed to hold his breath. He was touched by a soft indefinite emotion, and as her eyelids remained lowered till her black lashes seemed to lie like a shadow on her pale cheek, there was no need for him to force a smile. After the first moment he was not even surprised. It was merely the sudden movement, not the nature of the act itself, that had startled him.

"Yes. You may stay. I think we shall be friends. I'll tell you about the Revolution."

At these words Peyrol, the man of violent deeds, felt something like a chill breath at the back of his head.

"What's the good of that?" he said.

"It must be," she said and backed away from him swiftly, and without raising her eyes turned round and was gone in a moment, so lightly that one would have thought her feet had not touched the ground. Peyrol, staring at the open kitchen door, saw after a moment an elderly woman's head, with brown thin cheeks and tied up in a coloured handkerchief, peeping at him fearfully.

"A bottle of wine, please," he shouted at it.

CHAPTER III

THE AFFECTATION COMMON to seamen of never being surprised at anything that sea or land can produce had become in Peyrol a second nature. Having learned from childhood to suppress every sign of wonder before all extraordinary sights and events, all strange people, all strange customs, and the most alarming phenomena of nature (as manifested, for instance, in the violence of volcanoes or the fury of human beings), he had really become indifferent—or only perhaps utterly inexpressive. He had seen so much that was bizarre or atrocious, and had heard so many astounding tales, that his usual mental reaction before a new experience was generally formulated in the words, "*J'en ai vu bien d'autres.*" The last thing which had touched him with the panic of the supernatural had been the death under a heap of rags of that gaunt, fierce woman, his mother; and the last thing that had nearly overwhelmed him at the age of twelve with another kind of terror was the riot of sound and the multitude of mankind on the quays in Marseilles, something perfectly inconceivable from which he had instantly taken refuge behind a stack of wheat sacks after having been chased ashore from the tartane. He had remained there quaking till a man in a cocked hat and with a sabre at his side (the boy had never seen either such a hat or such a sabre in his life) had seized him by the arm close to the armpit and had hauled him out from there; a man who might have been an ogre (only Peyrol had never heard of an ogre) but at any rate in his own way was alarming and wonderful beyond anything he could have imagined—if the faculty of imagination had been developed in him then. No doubt all this was enough to make one die of fright, but that possibility never occurred to him. Neither did he go mad; but being only a child, he had simply adapted himself, by means of passive acquiescence, to the new and inexplicable conditions of life in something like twenty-four hours. After that initiation the rest of his existence, from flying fishes to whales and on to black men and coral reefs, to decks running with blood, and thirst in open boats, was comparatively plain sailing. By the time he had heard of a Revolution in France and of certain Immortal Principles causing the death of many people, from the mouths of seamen and travellers and year-old gazettes coming out of Europe, he was ready to appreciate contemporary history in his own particular way. Mutiny and throwing officers overboard. He had seen that twice and he was on a different side each time. As to this upset, he took no side. It was too far—too big—also not distinct enough. But he acquired the revolutionary jargon quickly enough and used it on occasion, with secret contempt. What he had gone through, from a spell of crazy love for a yellow girl to the experience of treachery from a bosom friend and shipmate (and both those things Peyrol confessed to himself he could never hope to understand), with all the graduations of varied experience of men and passions between, had put a drop of universal scorn, a wonderful sedative, into the strange mixture which might have been called the soul of the returned Peyrol.

Therefore he not only showed no surprise but did not feel any when he beheld the master, in the right of his wife, of the Escampobar Farm. The homeless Peyrol, sitting in the bare *salle* with a bottle of wine before him, was in the act of raising the glass to his lips when the man entered, ex-orator in the sections, leader of red-capped mobs, hunter of the ci-devants and priests, purveyor of the guillotine, in short a blood-drinker. And Citizen Peyrol, who had never been nearer than six thousand miles as the crow flies to the realities of the Revolution, put down his glass and in his deep unemotional voice said: "*Salut.*"

The other returned a much fainter "*Salut,*" staring at the stranger of whom he had heard already. His almond-shaped, soft eyes were noticeably shiny and so was to a certain extent the skin on his high but rounded cheekbones, coloured red like a mask of which all the rest was but a mass of clipped chestnut hair growing so thick and close around the lips as to hide altogether the design of the mouth which, for all Citizen Peyrol knew, might have been of a quite ferocious character. A careworn forehead and a perpendicular nose suggested a certain austerity proper to an ardent patriot. He held in his hand a long bright knife which he laid down on one of the tables at once. He didn't seem more than thirty years old, a well-made man of medium height, with a lack of resolution in his bearing. Something like disillusion was suggested by the set of his shoulders. The effect was subtle, but Peyrol became aware of it while he explained his case and finished the tale by declaring that he was a seaman of the Republic and that he had always done his duty before the enemy.

The blood-drinker had listened profoundly. The high arches of his eyebrows gave him an astonished look. He came close up to the table and spoke in a trembling voice.

"You may have! But you may all the same be corrupt. The seamen of the Republic were eaten up with corruption paid for with the gold of the tyrants. Who would have guessed it? They all talked like patriots. And yet the English entered the harbour and landed in the town without opposition. The armies of the Republic drove them out, but treachery stalks in the land, it comes up out of the ground, it sits at our hearthstones, lurks in the bosom of the representatives of the people, of our fathers, of our brothers. There was a time when civic virtue flourished, but now it has got to hide its head. And I will tell you why: there has not been enough killing. It seems as if there could never be enough of it. It's discouraging. Look what we have come to."

His voice died in his throat as though he had suddenly lost confidence in himself.

"Bring another glass, *citoyen*," said Peyrol, after a short pause, "and let's drink together. We will drink to the confusion of traitors. I detest treachery as much as any man, but . . ."

He waited till the other had returned, then poured out the wine, and after they had touched glasses and half emptied them, he put down his own and continued:

"But you see I have nothing to do with your politics. I was at the other side of the world, therefore you can't suspect me of being a traitor. You showed no mercy, you other sans-culottes, to the enemies of the Republic at home, and I killed her enemies abroad, far away. You were cutting off heads without much compunction. . . ."

The other most unexpectedly shut his eyes for a moment, then opened them very wide. "Yes, yes," he assented very low. "Pity may be a crime."

"Yes. And I knocked the enemies of the Republic on the head whenever I had them before me without inquiring about the number. It seems to me that you and I ought to get on together."

The master of Escampobar farmhouse murmured, however, that in times like these nothing could be taken as proof positive. It behoved every patriot to nurse suspicion in his breast. No sign of impatience escaped Peyrol. He was rewarded for his self-restraint and the unshaken good-humour with which he had conducted the discussion by carrying his point. Citizen Scevola Bron (for that appeared to be the name of the master of the farm), an object of fear and dislike to the other inhabitants of the Giens Peninsula, might have been influenced by a wish to have some one with whom he could exchange a few words from time to time. No villagers ever came up to the farm, or were likely to, unless perhaps in a body and animated with hostile intentions. They resented his presence in their part of the world sullenly.

"Where do you come from?" was the last question he asked.

"I left Toulon two days ago."

Citizen Scevola struck the table with his fist, but this manifestation of energy was very momentary.

"And that was the town of which by a decree not a stone upon another was to be left," he complained, much depressed.

"Most of it is still standing," Peyrol assured him calmly. "I don't know whether it deserved the fate you say was decreed for it. I was there for the last month or so and I know it contains some good patriots. I know because I made friends with them all." Thereupon Peyrol mentioned a few names which the retired sans-culotte greeted with a bitter smile and an ominous silence, as though the bearers of them had been only good for the scaffold and the guillotine.

"Come along and I will show you the place where you will sleep," he said with a sigh, and Peyrol was only too ready. They entered the kitchen together. Through the open back door a large square of sunshine fell on the floor of stone flags. Outside one could see quite a mob of expectant chickens, while a yellow hen postured on the very doorstep, darting her head right and left with affectation. An old woman holding a bowl full of broken food put it down suddenly on a table and stared. The vastness and cleanliness of the place impressed Peyrol favourably.

"You will eat with us here," said his guide, and passed without stopping into a narrow passage giving access to a steep flight of stairs. Above the first landing a narrow spiral staircase led to the upper part of the farmhouse; and when the sans-culotte flung open the solid plank door at which it ended he disclosed to Peyrol a large low room containing a four-poster bedstead piled up high with folded blankets and spare pillows. There were also two wooden chairs and a large oval table.

"We could arrange this place for you," said the master, "but I don't know what the mistress will have to say," he added.

Peyrol, struck by the peculiar expression of his face, turned his head and saw the girl standing in the doorway. It was as though she had floated up after them, for not the slightest sound of rustle or foot-fall had warned Peyrol of her presence. The pure complexion of her white cheeks was set off brilliantly by her coral lips and the bands of raven-black hair only partly covered by a muslin cap trimmed with lace. She made no sign, uttered no sound, behaved exactly as if there had been nobody in the room; and Peyrol suddenly averted his eyes from that mute and unconscious face with its roaming eyes.

In some way or other, however, the sans-culotte seemed to have ascertained her mind, for he said in a final tone:

"That's all right then," and there was a short silence, during which the woman shot her dark glances all round the room again and again, while on her lips there was a half-smile, not so much absent-minded as totally unmotived, which Peyrol observed with a side glance, but could not make anything of. She did not seem to know him at all.

"You have a view of salt water on three sides of you," remarked Peyrol's future host.

The farmhouse was a tall building, and this large attic with its three windows commanded on one side the view of Hyères roadstead on the first plan, with further blue undulations of the coast as far as Fréjus; and on the other the vast semicircle of barren high hills, broken by the entrance to Toulon harbour guarded by forts and batteries, and ending in Cape Cépet, a squat mountain, with sombre folds and a base of brown rocks, with a white spot gleaming on the very summit of it, a ci-devant shrine dedicated to Our Lady, and a ci-devant place of pilgrimage. The noonday glare seemed absorbed by the gemlike surface of the sea perfectly flawless in the invincible depth of its colour.

"It's like being in a lighthouse," said Peyrol. "Not a bad place for a seaman to live in." The sight of the sails dotted about cheered his heart. The people of landsmen with their houses and animals and activities did not count. What made for him the life of any strange shore were the craft that belonged to it: canoes, catamarans, balla-hous, praus, lorchas, mere dug-outs, or even rafts of tied logs with a bit of mat for a sail from which naked brown men fished along stretches of white sand crushed under the tropical skyline, sinister in its glare and with a thunder-cloud crouching on the horizon. But here he beheld a perfect serenity, nothing sombre on the shore, nothing ominous in the sunshine. The sky rested lightly on the distant and vaporous outline of the hills; and the immobility of all things seemed poised in the air like a gay mirage. On this tideless sea several tartanes lay becalmed in the Petite Passe between Porquerolles and Cape Esterel, yet theirs was not the stillness of death but of light slumber, the immobility of a smiling enchantment, of a Mediterranean fair day, breathless sometimes but never without life. Whatever enchantment Peyrol had known in his wanderings it had never been so remote from all thoughts of strife and death, so full of smiling security, making all his past appear to him like a chain of lurid days and sultry nights. He thought he would never want to get away from it, as though he had obscurely felt that his old rover's soul had been always rooted there. Yes, this was the place for him; not because expediency dictated, but simply because his instinct of rest had found its home at last.

He turned away from the window and found himself face to face with the sans-culotte, who had apparently come up to him from behind, perhaps with the intention of tapping him on the shoulder, but who now turned away his head. The young woman had disappeared.

"Tell me, *patron*," said Peyrol, "is there anywhere near this house a little dent in the shore with a bit of beach in it perhaps where I could keep a boat?"

"What do you want a boat for?"

"To go fishing when I have a fancy to," answered Peyrol curtly.

Citizen Bron, suddenly subdued, told him that what he wanted was to be found a couple of hundred yards down the hill from the house. The coast, of course, was full of indentations, but this was a perfect little pool. And the Toulon blood-drinker's almond-shaped eyes became strangely sombre as they gazed at the attentive Peyrol. A perfect little pool, he repeated, opening from a cove that the

English knew well. He paused. Peyrol observed without much animosity but in a tone of conviction that it was very difficult to keep off the English whenever there was a bit of salt water anywhere; but what could have brought English seamen to a spot like this he couldn't imagine.

"It was when their fleet first came here," said the patriot in a gloomy voice, "and hung round the coast before the anti-revolutionary traitors let them into Toulon, sold the sacred soil of their country for a handful of gold. Yes, in the days before the crime was consummated English officers used to land in that cove at night and walk up to this very house."

"What audacity!" commented Peyrol, who was really surprised. "But that's just like what they are." Still, it was hard to believe. But wasn't it only a tale?

The patriot flung one arm up in a strained gesture. "I swore to its truth before the tribunal," he said. "It was a dark story," he cried shrilly, and paused. "It cost her father his life," he said in a low voice . . . "her mother too—but the country was in danger," he added still lower.

Peyrol walked away to the western window and looked towards Toulon. In the middle of the great sheet of water within Cape Cicié a tall two-decker lay becalmed and the little dark dots on the water were her boats trying to tow her head round the right way. Peyrol watched them for a moment, and then walked back to the middle of the room.

"Did you actually drag him from this house to the guillotine?" he asked in his unemotional voice.

The patriot shook his head thoughtfully with downcast eyes. "No, he came over to Toulon just before the evacuation, this friend of the English . . . sailed over in a tartane he owned that is still lying here at the Madrague. He had his wife with him. They came over to take home their daughter who was living then with some skulking old nuns. The victorious Republicans were closing in and the slaves of tyranny had to fly."

"Came to fetch their daughter," mused Peyrol. "Strange, that guilty people should . . ."

The patriot looked up fiercely. "It was justice," he said loudly. "They were anti-revolutionists, and if they had never spoken to an Englishman in their life the atrocious crime was on their heads."

"H'm, stayed too long for their daughter," muttered Peyrol. "And so it was you who brought her home."

"I did," said the patron. For a moment his eyes evaded Peyrol's investigating glance, but in a moment he looked straight into his face. "No lessons of base superstition could corrupt her soul," he declared with exaltation. "I brought home a patriot."

Peyrol, very calm, gave him a hardly perceptible nod. "Well," he said, "all this won't prevent me sleeping very well in this room. I always thought I would like to live in a lighthouse when I got tired of roving about the seas. This is as near a lighthouse lantern as can be. You will see me with all my little affairs to-morrow," he added, moving towards the stairs. "*Salut, citoyen.*"

There was in Peyrol a fund of self-command amounting to placidity. There were men living in the East who had no doubt whatever that Peyrol was a calmly terrible man. And they would quote illustrative instances which from their own point of view were simply admirable. But all Peyrol had ever done was to behave rationally, as it seemed to him, in all sorts of dangerous circumstances without ever being led astray by the nature, or the cruelty, or the danger of any given situation. He adapted himself to the character of the event and to the very spirit of it, with a profound responsive feeling of a particularly unsentimental kind. Sentiment in itself was an artificiality of which he had never heard and if he had seen it in action would have appeared to him too puzzling to make anything of. That sort of genuineness in acceptance made him a satisfactory inmate of the Escampobar Farm. He duly turned up with all his cargo, as he called it, and was met at the door of the farmhouse itself by the young woman with the pale face and wandering eyes. Nothing could hold her attention for long amongst her familiar surroundings. Right and left and far away beyond you, she seemed to be looking for something while you were talking to her, so that you doubted whether she could follow what you said. But as a matter of fact she had all her wits about her. In the midst of this strange search for something that was not there she had enough detachment to smile at Peyrol. Then, withdrawing into the kitchen, she watched, as much as her restless eyes could watch anything, Peyrol's cargo and Peyrol himself passing up the stairs.

The most valuable part of Peyrol's cargo being strapped to his person, the first thing he did after being left alone in that attic room which was like the lantern of a lighthouse was to relieve himself of the burden and lay it on the foot of the bed. Then he sat down and leaning his elbow far on the table he contemplated it with a feeling of complete relief. That plunder had never burdened his conscience. It had merely on occasion oppressed his body; and if it had at all affected his spirits it was not by its secrecy but by its mere weight, which was inconvenient, irritating, and towards the end of a day altogether insupportable. It made a free-limbed, deep-breathing sailor-man feel like a mere overloaded animal, thus extending whatever there was of compassion in Peyrol's nature towards the four-footed beasts that carry men's burdens on the earth. The necessities of a lawless life had taught Peyrol to be ruthless, but he had never been cruel.

Sprawling in the chair, stripped to the waist, robust and grey-haired, his head with a Roman profile propped up on a mighty and tattooed forearm, he remained at ease, with his eyes fixed on his treasure with an air of meditation. Yet Peyrol was not meditating (as a superficial observer might have thought) on the best place of concealment. It was not that he had not had a great experience of that sort of property which had always melted so quickly through his fingers. What made him meditative was its character, not of a share of a hard-won booty in toil, in risk, in danger, in privation, but of a piece of luck personally his own. He knew what plunder was and how soon it went; but this lot had come to stay. He had it with him, away from the haunts of his lifetime, as if in another world altogether. It couldn't be drunk away, gambled away, squandered away in any sort of familiar circumstances, or even given away. In that room, raised a good many feet above his revolutionized native land where he was more of a stranger than anywhere else in the world, in this roomy garret full of light and as it were surrounded by the sea, in a great sense of peace and security, Peyrol didn't see why he should bother his head about it so very much. It came to him that he had never really cared for any plunder that fell into his hands. No, never for any. And to take particular care of this for which no one would seek vengeance or attempt recovery would have been absurd. Peyrol got up and opened his big sandalwood chest secured with an enormous padlock, part, too, of some old plunder gathered in a Chinese town in the Gulf of Tonkin, in company of certain Brothers of the Coast, who having boarded at night a Portuguese schooner and sent her crew adrift in a boat, had taken a cruise on their own account, years and years and years ago. He was young then, very young, and the chest fell to his share because nobody else would have anything to do with the cumbersome thing, and also for the reason that the metal of the curiously wrought thick hoops that strengthened it was not gold but mere brass. He, in his innocence, had been rather pleased with the article. He had carried it about with him into all sorts of places, and also he had left it behind him—once for a whole year in a dark and noisome cavern on a certain part of the Madagascar coast. He had left it with various native chiefs, with Arabs, with a gambling-hell keeper in Pondicherry, with his various friends in short, and even with his enemies. Once he had lost it altogether.

That was on the occasion when he had received a wound which laid him open and gushing like a slashed wine-skin. A sudden quarrel broke out in a company of Brothers over some matter of policy complicated by personal jealousies, as to which he was as innocent as a babe unborn. He never knew who gave him the slash. Another Brother, a chum of his, an English boy, had rushed in and hauled him out of the fray, and then he had remembered nothing for days. Even now when he looked at the scar he could not understand why he had not died. That occurrence, with the wound and the painful convalescence, was the first thing that sobered his character somewhat. Many years afterwards, when in consequence of his altered views of mere lawlessness he was serving as quartermaster on board the *Hirondelle*, a comparatively respectable privateer, he caught sight of that chest again in Port Louis, of all places in the world, in a dark little den of a shop kept by a lone Hindoo. The hour was late, the side street was empty, and so Peyrol went in there to claim his property, all fair, a dollar in one hand and a pistol in the other, and was entreated abjectly to take it away. He carried off the empty chest on his shoulder, and that same night the privateer went to sea; then only he found time to ascertain that he had made no mistake, because, soon after he had got it first, he had, in grim wantonness, scratched inside the lid, with the point of his knife, the rude outline of a skull and cross-bones into which he had rubbed afterwards a little Chinese vermilion. And there it was, the whole design, as fresh as ever.

In the garret full of light of the Escampobar farmhouse, the grey-haired Peyrol opened the chest, took all the contents out of it, laying them neatly on the floor, and spread his treasure—pockets downwards—over the bottom, which it filled exactly. Busy on his knees he replaced the chest. A jumper or two, a fine cloth jacket, a rem-

nant piece of Madapolam muslin, costly stuff for which he had no use
in the world—a quantity of fine white shirts. Nobody would dare to
rummage in his chest, he thought, with the assurance of a man who
had been feared in his time. Then he rose, and looking round the room
and stretching his powerful arms, he ceased to think of the treasure, of
the future and even of to-morrow, in the sudden conviction that he
could make himself very comfortable there.

CHAPTER IV

IN A TINY bit of a looking-glass hung on the frame of the east window, Peyrol, handling the unwearable English blade, was shaving himself—for the day was Sunday. The years of political changes ending with the proclamation of Napoleon as Consul for life had not touched Peyrol except as to his strong thick head of hair, which was nearly all white now. After putting the razor away carefully, Peyrol introduced his stockinged feet into a pair of sabots of the very best quality and clattered downstairs. His brown cloth breeches were untied at the knee and the sleeves of his shirt rolled up to his shoulders. That sea-rover turned rustic was now perfectly at home in that farm which, like a lighthouse, commanded the view of two road-steads and of the open sea. He passed through the kitchen. It was exactly as he had seen it first, sunlight on the floor, red copper utensils shining on the walls, the table in the middle scrubbed snowy white; and it was only the old woman, Aunt Catherine, who seemed to have acquired a sharper profile. The very hen, manœuvring her neck pretentiously on the doorstep, might have been standing there for the last eight years. Peyrol shooed her away, and going into the yard washed himself lavishly at the pump. When he returned from the yard he looked so fresh and hale that old Catherine complimented him in a thin voice on his *"bonne mine."* Manners were changing, and she addressed him no longer as *citoyen* but as Monsieur Peyrol. He answered readily that if her heart was free he was ready to lead her to the altar that very day. This was such an old joke that Catherine took no notice of it whatever, but followed him with her eyes as he crossed the kitchen into the *salle*, which was cool, with its tables and benches washed clean, and no living soul in it. Peyrol passed through to the front of the house, leaving the outer door open. At the clatter of his clogs a young man sitting outside on a bench turned his head and greeted him by a careless nod. His face was rather long, sunburnt and smooth, with a slightly curved nose and a very well-shaped chin. He wore a dark blue naval jacket open on a white shirt and a black neckerchief tied in a slip-knot with long ends. White breeches and stockings and black shoes with steel buckles completed his costume. A brass-hilted sword in a black scabbard worn on a cross-belt was lying on the ground at his feet. Peyrol, silver-headed and ruddy, sat down on the bench at some little distance. The level piece of rocky ground in front of the house was not very extensive, falling away to the sea in a declivity framed between the rises of two barren hills. The old rover and the young seaman with their arms folded across their chests gazed into space, exchanging no words, like close intimates or like distant strangers. Neither did they stir when the master of the Escampobar Farm appeared out of the yard gate with a manure fork on his shoulder and started to cross the piece of level ground. His grimy hands, his rolled-up shirt sleeves, the fork over the shoulder, the whole of his working-day aspect had somehow an air of being a manifestation; but the patriot dragged his dirty clogs low-spiritedly in the fresh light of the young morning, in a way no real worker on the land would ever do at the end of a day of toil. Yet there were no signs of debility about his person. His oval face with rounded cheekbones remained unwrinkled except at the corners of his almond-shaped, shiny, visionary's eyes, which had not changed since the day when old Peyrol's gaze had met them for the first time. A few white hairs on his tousled head and in the thin beard alone had marked the passage of years, and you would have had to look for them closely. Amongst the unchangeable rocks at the extreme end of the Peninsula, time seemed to have stood still and idle while the group of people poised at that southernmost point of France had gone about their ceaseless toil, winning bread and wine from a stony-hearted earth.

The master of the farm, staring straight before him, passed before the two men towards the door of the *salle*, which Peyrol had left open. He leaned his fork against the wall before going in. The sound of a distant bell, the bell of the village where years ago the returned rover had watered his mule and had listened to the talk of the man with the dog, came up faint and abrupt in the great stillness of the upper space. The violent slamming of the *salle* door broke the silence between the two gazers on the sea.

"Does that fellow never rest?" asked the young man in a low indifferent voice which covered the delicate tinkling of the bell, and without moving his head.

"Not on Sunday anyhow," answered the rover in the same detached manner. "What can you expect? The church bell is like poison to him. That fellow, I verily believe, has been born a sansculotte. Every *'décadi'* he puts on his best clothes, sticks a red cap on his head and wanders between the buildings like a lost soul in the light of day. A Jacobin, if ever there was one."

"Yes. There is hardly a hamlet in France where there isn't a sansculotte or two. But some of them have managed to change their skins if nothing else."

"This one won't change his skin, and as to his inside he never had anything in him that could be moved. Aren't there some people that remember him in Toulon? It isn't such a long time ago. And yet . . ." Peyrol turned slightly towards the young man . . . "And yet to look at him . . ."

The officer nodded, and for a moment his face wore a troubled expression which did not escape the notice of Peyrol who went on speaking easily:

"Some time ago, when the priests began to come back to the parishes, he, that fellow"—Peyrol jerked his head in the direction of the *salle* door—"would you believe it?—started for the village with a sabre hanging to his side and his red cap on his head. He made for the church door. What he wanted to do there I don't know. It surely could not have been to say the proper kind of prayers. Well, the people were very much elated about their reopened church, and as he went along some woman spied him out of a window and started the alarm. 'Eh, there! look! The Jacobin, the sans-culotte, the blood-drinker! Look at him.' Out rushed some of them, and a man or two that were working in their home patches vaulted over the low walls. Pretty soon there was a crowd, mostly women, each with the first thing she could snatch up—stick, kitchen knife, anything. A few men with spades and cudgels joined them by the water-trough. He didn't quite like that.

What could he do? He turned and bolted up the hill, like a hare. It takes some pluck to face a mob of angry women. He ran along the cart track without looking behind him, and they after him, yelling: "*A mort! A mort le buveur de sang!*' He had been a horror and an abomination to the people for years, what with one story and another, and now they thought it was their chance. The priest over in the presbytery hears the noise, comes to the door. One look was enough for him. He is a fellow of about forty but a wiry, long-legged beggar, and agile— what? He just tucked up his skirts and dashed out, taking short cuts over the walls and leaping from boulder to boulder like a blessed goat. I was up in my room when the noise reached me there. I went to the window and saw the chase in full cry after him. I was beginning to think the fool would fetch all those furies along with him up here and that they would carry the house by boarding and do for the lot of us, when the priest cut in just in the nick of time. He could have tripped Scevola as easy as anything, but he lets him pass and stands in front of his parishioners with his arms extended. That did it. He saved the patron all right. What he could say to quieten them I don't know, but these were early days and they were very fond of their new priest. He could have turned them round his little finger. I had my head and shoulders out of the window—it was interesting enough. They would have massacred all the accursed lot, as they used to call us down there—and when I drew in, behold there was the *patronne* standing behind me looking on too. You have been here often enough to know how she roams about the grounds and about the house, without a sound. A leaf doesn't pose itself lighter on the ground than her feet do. Well, I suppose she didn't know that I was upstairs, and came into the room just in her way of always looking for something that isn't there, and noticing me with my head stuck out, naturally came up to see what I was looking at. Her face wasn't any paler than usual, but she was clawing the dress over her chest with her ten fingers—like this. I was confounded. Before I could find my tongue she just turned round and went out with no more sound than a shadow."

When Peyrol ceased, the ringing of the church bell went on faintly and then stopped as abruptly as it had begun.

"Talking about her shadow," said the young officer indolently, "I know her shadow."

Old Peyrol made a really pronounced movement. "What do you mean?" he asked. "Where?"

"I have got only one window in the room where they put me to sleep last night and I stood at it looking out. That's what I am here for—to look out, am I not? I woke up suddenly, and being awake I went to the window and looked out."

"One doesn't see shadows in the air," growled old Peyrol.

"No, but you see them on the ground, pretty black too when the moon is full. It fell across this open space here from the corner of the house."

"The *patronne*," exclaimed Peyrol in a low voice, "impossible!"

"Does the old woman that lives in the kitchen roam, do the village women roam as far as this?" asked the officer composedly. "You ought to know the habits of the people. It was a woman's shadow. The moon being to the west, it glided slanting from that corner of the house and glided back again. I know her shadow when I see it."

"Did you hear anything?" asked Peyrol after a moment of visible hesitation.

"The window being open I heard somebody snoring. It couldn't have been you, you are too high. Moreover, from the snoring," he added grimly, "it must have been somebody with a good conscience. Not like you, old skimmer of the seas, because, you know, that's what you are, for all your gunner's warrant." He glanced out of the corner of his eyes at old Peyrol. "What makes you look so worried?"

"She roams, that cannot be denied," murmured Peyrol, with an uneasiness which he did not attempt to conceal.

"Evidently. I know a shadow when I see it, and when I saw it, it did not frighten me, not a quarter as much as the mere tale of it seems to have frightened you. However, that sans-culotte friend of yours must be a hard sleeper. Those purveyors of the guillotine all have a first-class fireproof Republican conscience. I have seen them at work up north when I was a boy running barefoot in the gutters. . . ."

"The fellow always sleeps in that room," said Peyrol earnestly.

"But that's neither here nor there," went on the officer, "except that it may be convenient for roaming shadows to hear his conscience taking its ease."

Peyrol, excited, lowered his voice forcibly. "Lieutenant," he said, "if I had not seen from the first what was in your heart I would have contrived to get rid of you a long time ago in some way or other."

The lieutenant glanced sideways again and Peyrol let his raised fist fall heavily on his thigh. "I am old Peyrol and this place, as lonely as a ship at sea, is like a ship to me and all in it are like shipmates. Never mind the *patron*. What I want to know is whether you heard anything? Any sound at all? Murmur, footstep?" A bitterly mocking smile touched the lips of the young man.

"Not a fairy footstep. Could you hear the fall of a leaf—and with that terrorist cur trumpeting right above my head? . . ." Without unfolding his arms he turned towards Peyrol, who was looking at him anxiously. . . . "You want to know, do you? Well, I will tell you what I heard and you can make the best of it. I heard the sound of a stumble. It wasn't a fairy either that stubbed its toe. It was something in a heavy shoe. Then a stone went rolling down the ravine in front of us interminably, then a silence as of death. I didn't see anything moving. The way the moon was then, the ravine was in black shadow. And I didn't try to see."

Peyrol, with his elbow on his knee, leaned his head in the palm of his hand. The officer repeated through his clenched teeth: "Make the best of it."

Peyrol shook his head slightly. After having spoken, the young officer leaned back against the wall, but the next moment the report of a piece of ordnance reached them as it were from below, travelling around the rising ground to the left in the form of a dull thud followed by a sighing sound that seemed to seek an issue amongst the stony ridges and rocks near by.

"That's the English corvette which has been dodging in and out of Hyères Roads for the last week," said the young officer, picking up his sword hastily. He stood up and buckled the belt on, while Peyrol rose more deliberately from the bench, and said:

"She can't be where we saw her at anchor last night. That gun was near. She must have crossed over. There has been enough wind for that at various times during the night. But what could she be firing at down there in the Petite Passe? We had better go and see."

He strode off, followed by Peyrol. There was not a human being in sight about the farm and not a sound of life except for the lowing of a cow coming faintly from behind a wall. Peyrol kept close behind the quickly moving officer who followed the footpath marked faintly on the stony slope of the hill.

"That gun was not shotted," he observed suddenly in a deep steady voice.

The officer glanced over his shoulder.

"You may be right. You haven't been a gunner for nothing. Not shotted, eh? Then a signal gun. But who to? We have been observing that corvette now for days and we know she has no companion."

He moved on, Peyrol following him on the awkward path without losing his wind and arguing in a steady voice: "She has no companion but she may have seen a friend at daylight this morning."

"Bah!" retorted the officer without checking his pace. "You talk now like a child or else you take me for one. How far could she have seen? What view could she have had at daylight if she was making her way to the Petite Passe where she is now? Why, the islands would have masked for her two-thirds of the sea and just in the direction too where the English inshore squadron is hovering below the horizon. Funny blockade that! You can't see a single English sail for days and days together, and then when you least expect them they come down all in a crowd as if ready to eat us alive. No, no! There was no wind to bring her up a companion. But tell me, gunner, you who boast of knowing the bark of every English piece, what sort of gun was it?"

Peyrol growled in answer:

"Why, a twelve. The heaviest she carries. She is only a corvette."

"Well, then, it was fired as a recall for one of her boats somewhere out of sight along the shore. With a coast like this, all points and bights, there would be nothing very extraordinary in that, would there?"

"No," said Peyrol, stepping out steadily. "What is extraordinary is that she should have had a boat away at all."

"You are right there." The officer stopped suddenly. "Yes, it is really remarkable, that she should have sent a boat away. And there is no other way to explain that gun."

Peyrol's face expressed no emotion of any sort.

"There is something there worth investigating," continued the officer with animation.

"If it is a matter of a boat," Peyrol said without the slightest excitement, "there can be nothing very deep in it. What could there be? As likely as not they sent her inshore early in the morning with lines to try to catch some fish for the captain's breakfast. Why do you open your eyes like this? Don't you know the English? They have enough cheek for anything."

After uttering those words with a deliberation made venerable by his white hair, Peyrol made the gesture of wiping his brow, which was barely moist.

"Let us push on," said the lieutenant abruptly.

"Why hurry like this?" argued Peyrol without moving. "Those heavy clogs of mine are not adapted for scrambling on loose stones."

"Aren't they?" burst out the officer. "Well, then, if you are tired you can sit down and fan yourself with your hat. Good-bye." And he strode away before Peyrol could utter a word.

The path following the contour of the hill took a turn towards its sea-face and very soon the lieutenant passed out of sight with startling suddenness. Then his head reappeared for a moment, only his head, and that too vanished suddenly. Peyrol remained perplexed. After gazing in the direction in which the officer had disappeared, he looked down at the farm buildings, now below him but not at a very great distance. He could see distinctly the pigeons walking on the roof ridges. Somebody was drawing water from the well in the middle of the yard. The patron, no doubt; but that man, who at one time had the power to send so many luckless persons to their death, did not count for old Peyrol. He had even ceased to be an offence to his sight and a disturber of his feelings. By himself he was nothing. He had never been anything but a creature of the universal blood-lust of the time. The very doubts about him had died out by now in old Peyrol's breast. The fellow was so insignificant that had Peyrol in a moment of particular attention discovered that he cast no shadow, he would not have been surprised. Below there he was reduced to the shape of a dwarf lugging a bucket away from the well. But where was she? Peyrol asked himself, shading his eyes with his hand. He knew that the *patronne* could not be very far away, because he had a sight of her during the morning; but that was before he had learned she had taken to roaming at night. His growing uneasiness came suddenly to an end when, turning his eyes away from the farm buildings, where obviously she was not, he saw her appear, with nothing but the sky full of light at her back, coming down round the very turn of the path which had taken the lieutenant out of sight.

Peyrol moved briskly towards her. He wasn't a man to lose time in idle wonder, and his sabots did not seem to weigh heavy on his feet. The *fermière*, whom the villagers down there spoke of as Arlette as though she had been a little girl, but in a strange tone of shocked awe, walked with her head drooping and her feet (as Peyrol used to say) touching the ground as lightly as falling leaves. The clatter of the clogs made her raise her black, clear eyes that had been smitten on the very verge of womanhood by such sights of bloodshed and terror, as to leave in her a fear of looking steadily in any direction for long, lest she should see coming through the empty air some mutilated vision of the dead. Peyrol called it trying not to see something that was not there; and this evasive yet frank mobility was so much a part of her being that the steadiness with which she met his inquisitive glance surprised old Peyrol for a moment. He asked without beating about the bush:

"Did he speak to you?"

She answered with something airy and provoking in her voice, which also struck Peyrol as a novelty: "He never stopped. He passed by as though he had not seen me"—and then they both looked away from each other.

"Now, what is it you took into your head to watch for at night?"

She did not expect that question. She hung her head and took a pleat of her skirt between her fingers, embarrassed like a child.

"Why should I not?" she murmured in a low shy note, as if she had two voices within her.

"What did Catherine say?"

"She was asleep, or perhaps, only lying on her back with her eyes shut."

"Does she do that?" asked Peyrol with incredulity.

"Yes." Arlette gave Peyrol a queer, meaningless smile with which her eyes had nothing to do. "Yes, she often does. I have noticed that before. She lies there trembling under her blankets till I come back."

"What drove you out last night?" Peyrol tried to catch her eyes, but they eluded him in the usual way. And now her face looked as though it couldn't smile.

"My heart," she said. For a moment Peyrol lost his tongue and even all power of motion. The *fermière* having lowered her eyelids, all her life seemed to have gone into her coral lips, vivid and without a quiver in the perfection of their design, and Peyrol, giving up the conversation with an upward fling of his arm, hurried up the path without looking behind him. But once round the turn of the path, he approached the lookout at an easier gait. It was a piece of smooth ground below the summit of the hill. It had quite a pronounced slope, so that a short and robust pine growing true out of the soil yet leaned well over the edge of the sheer drop of some fifty feet or so. The first thing that Peyrol's eyes took in was the water of the Petite Passe with the enormous shadow of the Porquerolles Island darkening more than half of its width at this still early hour. He could not see the whole of it, but on the part his glance embraced there was no ship of any kind. The lieutenant, leaning with his chest along the inclined pine, addressed him irritably.

"Squat! Do you think there are no glasses on board the Englishman?"

Peyrol obeyed without a word and for the space of a minute or so presented the bizarre sight of a rather bulky peasant with venerable white locks crawling on his hands and knees on a hillside for no visible reason. When he got to the foot of the pine he raised himself on his knees. The lieutenant, flattened against the inclined trunk and with a pocket-glass glued to his eye, growled angrily:

"You can see her now, can't you?"

Peyrol in his kneeling position could see the ship now. She was less than a quarter of a mile from him up the coast, almost within hailing effort of his powerful voice. His unaided eyes could follow the movements of the men on board like dark dots about her decks. She had drifted so far within Cape Esterel that the low projecting mass of it seemed to be in actual contact with her stern. Her unexpected nearness made Peyrol draw a sharp breath through his teeth. The lieutenant murmured, still keeping the glass to his eye:

"I can see the very epaulettes of the officers on the quarter-deck."

CHAPTER V

A S PEYROL AND the lieutenant had surmised from the
report of the gun, the English ship which the evening before
was lying in Hyères Roads had got under way after dark.
The light airs had taken her as far as the Petite Passe in the early part of
the night, and then had abandoned her to the breathless moonlight in
which, bereft of all motion, she looked more like a white monument of
stone dwarfed by the darkling masses of land on either hand than a
fabric famed for its swiftness in attack or in flight.

Her captain was a man of about forty, with clean-shaven, full
cheeks and mobile thin lips which he had a trick of compressing
mysteriously before he spoke and sometimes also at the end of his
speeches. He was alert in his movements and nocturnal in his habits.

Directly he found that the calm had taken complete possession of
the night and was going to last for hours, Captain Vincent assumed
his favourite attitude of leaning over the rail. It was then some time
after midnight and in the pervading stillness the moon, riding on a
speckless sky, seemed to pour her enchantment on an uninhabited
planet. Captain Vincent did not mind the moon very much. Of course
it made his ship visible from both shores of the Petite Passe. But after
nearly a year of constant service in command of the extreme lookout
ship of Admiral Nelson's blockading fleet he knew the emplacement
of almost every gun of the shore defences. Where the breeze had left
him he was safe from the biggest gun of the few that were mounted on

Porquerolles. On the Giens side of the pass he knew for certain there was not even a popgun mounted anywhere. His long familiarity with that part of the coast had imbued him with the belief that he knew the habits of its population thoroughly. The gleams of light in their houses went out very early and Captain Vincent felt convinced that they were all in their beds, including the gunners of the batteries who belonged to the local militia. Their interest in the movements of Her Majesty's twenty-two-gun sloop *Amelia* had grown stale by custom. She never interfered with their private affairs, and allowed the small coasting craft to go to and fro unmolested. They would have wondered if she had been more than two days away. Captain Vincent used to say grimly that the Hyères roadstead had become like a second home to him.

For an hour or so Captain Vincent mused a bit on his real home, on matters of service and other unrelated things, then getting into motion in a very wide-awake manner, he superintended himself the dispatch of that boat the existence of which had been acutely surmised by Lieutenant Réal and was a matter of no doubt whatever to old Peyrol. As to her mission, it had nothing to do with catching fish for the captain's breakfast. It was the captain's own gig, a very fast-pulling boat. She was already alongside with her crew in her when the officer, who was going in charge, was beckoned to by the captain. He had a cutlass at his side and a brace of pistols in his belt, and there was a businesslike air about him that showed he had been on such service before.

"This calm will last a good many hours," said the captain. "In this tideless sea you are certain to find the ship very much where she is now, but closer inshore. The attraction of the land—you know."

"Yes, sir. The land does attract."

"Yes. Well, she may be allowed to put her side against any of these rocks. There would be no more danger than alongside a quay with a sea like this. Just look at the water in the pass, Mr. Bolt. Like the floor of a ballroom. Pull close along shore when you return. I'll expect you back at dawn."

Captain Vincent paused suddenly. A doubt crossed his mind as to the wisdom of this nocturnal expedition. The hammer-head of the peninsula with its sea-face invisible from both sides of the coast was an ideal spot for a secret landing. Its lonely character appealed to his imagination, which in the first instance had been stimulated by a chance remark of Mr. Bolt himself.

The fact was that the week before, when the *Amelia* was cruising off the peninsula, Bolt, looking at the coast, mentioned that he knew that part of it well; he had actually been ashore there a good many years ago, while serving with Lord Howe's fleet. He described the nature of the path, the aspect of a little village on the reverse slope, and had much to say about a certain farmhouse where he had been more than once, and had even stayed for twenty-four hours at a time on more than one occasion.

This had aroused Captain Vincent's curiosity. He sent for Bolt and had a long conversation with him. He listened with great interest to Bolt's story—how one day a man was seen from the deck of the ship in which Bolt was serving then, waving a white sheet or table-cloth amongst the rocks at the water's edge. It might have been a trap; but, as the man seemed alone and the shore was within range of the ship's guns, a boat was sent to take him off.

"And that, sir," Bolt pursued impressively, "was, I verily believe, the very first communication that Lord Howe had from the royalists in Toulon." Afterwards Bolt described to Captain Vincent the meetings of the Toulon royalists with the officers of the fleet. From the back of the farm he, Bolt himself, had often watched for hours the entrance of the Toulon harbour on the lookout for the boat bringing over the royalist emissaries. Then he would make an agreed signal to the advanced squadron and some English officers would land on their side and meet the Frenchmen at the farmhouse. It was as simple as that. The people of the farmhouse, husband and wife, were well-to-do, good class altogether, and staunch royalists. He had got to know them well.

Captain Vincent wondered whether the same people were still living there. Bolt could see no reason why they shouldn't be. It wasn't more than ten years ago, and they were by no means an old couple. As far as he could make out, the farm was their own property. He, Bolt, knew only very few French words at that time. It was much later, after he had been made a prisoner and kept inland in France till the Peace of Amiens, that he had picked up a smattering of the lingo. His captivity had done away with his feeble chance of promotion, he could not help remarking. Bolt was a master's mate still.

Captain Vincent, in common with a good many officers of all ranks in Lord Nelson's fleet, had his misgivings about the system of distant blockade from which the admiral apparently would not depart. Yet one could not blame Lord Nelson. Everybody in the fleet understood that what was in his mind was the destruction of the enemy; and if the enemy was closely blockaded he would never come out to be destroyed. On the other hand it was clear that as things were conducted the French had too many chances left them to slip out unobserved and vanish from all human knowledge for months. Those possibilities were a constant worry to Captain Vincent, who had thrown himself with the ardour of passion into the special duty with which he was entrusted. Oh, for a pair of eyes fastened night and day on the entrance of the harbour of Toulon! Oh, for the power to look at the very state of French ships and into the very secrets of French minds!

But he said nothing of this to Bolt. He only observed that the character of the French Government was changed and that the minds of the royalist people in the farmhouse might have changed too, since they had got back the exercise of their religion. Bolt's answer was that he had had a lot to do with royalists, in his time, on board Lord Howe's fleet, both before and after Toulon was evacuated. All sorts, men and women, barbers and noblemen, sailors and tradesmen; almost every kind of royalist one could think of; and his opinion was that a royalist never changed. As to the place itself, he only wished the captain had seen it. It was the sort of spot that nothing could change. He made bold to say that it would be just the same a hundred years hence.

The earnestness of his officer caused Captain Vincent to look hard at him. He was a man of about his own age, but while Vincent was a comparatively young captain, Bolt was an old master's mate. Each understood the other perfectly. Captain Vincent fidgeted for a while and then observed abstractedly that he was not a man to put a noose round a dog's neck, let alone a good seaman's.

This cryptic pronouncement caused no wonder to appear in Bolt's attentive gaze. He only became a little thoughtful before he said in the same abstracted tone that an officer in uniform was not likely to be hanged for a spy. The service was risky, of course. It was necessary, for its success, that, assuming the same people were there, it should be undertaken by a man well known to the inhabitants. Then he added that he was certain of being recognized. And while he enlarged on the extremely good terms he had been on with the owners of the farm, especially the farmer's wife, a comely motherly woman, who had been very kind to him, and had all her wits about her, Captain Vincent, looking at the master's mate's bushy whiskers, thought that these in themselves were enough to insure recognition. This impression was so strong that he asked point-blank: "You haven't altered the growth of the hair on your face, Mr. Bolt, since then?"

There was just a touch of indignation in Bolt's negative reply; for he was proud of his whiskers. He declared he was ready to take the most desperate changes for the service of his king and his country.

Captain Vincent added: "For the sake of Lord Nelson, too." One understood well what His Lordship wished to bring about by that blockade at sixty leagues off. He was talking to a sailor, and there was no need to say any more. Did Bolt think that he could persuade those people to conceal him in their house on that lonely shore end of the peninsula for some considerable time? Bolt thought it was the easiest thing in the world. He would simply go up there and renew the old acquaintance, but he did not mean to do that in a reckless manner. It would have to be done at night, when of course there would be no one about. He would land just where he used to before, wrapped up in a Mediterranean sailor's cloak—he had one of his own—over his uniform, and simply go straight to the door, at which he would knock. Ten to one the farmer himself would come down to open it. He knew enough French by now, he hoped, to persuade those people to conceal him in some room having a view in the right direction; and there he would stick day after day on the watch, taking a little exercise in the middle of the night, ready to live on mere bread and water if necessary, so as not to arouse suspicion amongst the farmhands. And who knows if, with the farmer's help, he could not get some news of what was going on actually within the port. Then from time to time he could go down in the dead of night, signal to the ship and make his report. Bolt expressed the hope that the *Amelia* would remain as much as possible in sight of the coast. It would cheer him up to see her about. Captain Vincent naturally assented. He pointed out to Bolt, however, that his post would become most important exactly when the ship had been chased away or driven by the weather off her station, as could very easily happen—"You would be then the eyes of Lord Nelson's fleet, Mr. Bolt—think of that. The actual eyes of Lord Nelson's fleet!"

After dispatching his officer, Captain Vincent spent the night on deck. The break of day came at last, much paler than the moonlight which it replaced. And still no boat. And again Captain Vincent asked himself if he had not acted indiscreetly. Impenetrable, and looking as fresh as if he had just come up on deck, he argued the point with himself till the rising sun clearing the ridge on Porquerolles Island flashed its level rays upon his ship with her dew-darkened sails and dripping rigging. He roused himself then to tell his first lieutenant to get the boats out to tow the ship away from the shore. The report of the gun he ordered to be fired expressed simply his irritation. The *Amelia*, pointing towards the middle of the Passe, was moving at a snail's pace behind her string of boats. Minutes passed. And then suddenly Captain Vincent perceived his boat pulling back in shore according to orders. When nearly abreast of the ship, she darted away, making for her side. Mr. Bolt clambered on board, alone, ordering the gig to go ahead and help with the towing. Captain Vincent, standing apart on the quarter-deck, received him with a grimly questioning look.

Mr. Bolt's first words were to the effect that he believed the confounded spot to be bewitched. Then he glanced at the group of officers on the other side of the quarter-deck. Captain Vincent led the way to his cabin. There he turned and looked at his officer, who, with an air of distraction, mumbled: "There are night-walkers there."

"Come, Bolt, what the devil have you seen? Did you get near the house at all?"

"I got within twenty yards of the door, sir," said Bolt. And encouraged by the captain's much less ferocious "Well?" began his tale. He did not pull up to the path which he knew, but to a little bit of beach on which he told his men to haul up the boat and wait for him. The beach was concealed by a thick growth of bushes on the landward side and by some rocks from the sea. Then he went to what he called the ravine, still avoiding the path, so that as a matter of fact he made his way up on his hands and knees mostly, very carefully and slowly amongst the loose stones, till by holding on to a bush he brought his eyes on a level with the piece of flat ground in front of the farmhouse.

The familiar aspect of the buildings, totally unchanged from the time when he had played his part in what appeared as a most successful operation at the beginning of the war, inspired Bolt with great confidence in the success of his present enterprise, vague as it was, but the great charm of which lay, no doubt, in mental associations with his younger years. Nothing seemed easier than to stride across the forty yards of open ground and rouse the farmer whom he remembered so well, the well-to-do man, a grave sagacious royalist in his humble way; certainly, in Bolt's view, no traitor to his country, and preserving so well his dignity in ambiguous circumstances. To Bolt's simple vision neither that man nor his wife could have changed.

In this view of Arlette's parents Bolt was influenced by the consciousness of there having been no change in himself. He was the same Jack Bolt, and everything around him was the same as if he had left the spot only yesterday. Already he saw himself in the kitchen which he knew so well, seated by the light of a single candle before a glass of wine and talking his best French to that worthy farmer of sound principles. The whole thing was as well as done. He imagined himself a secret inmate of that building, closely confined indeed, but sustained by the possible great results of his watchfulness, in many ways more comfortable than on board the *Amelia* and with the glorious consciousness that he was, in Captain Vincent's phrase, the actual physical eyes of the fleet.

He didn't, of course, talk of his private feelings to Captain Vincent. All those thoughts and emotions were compressed in the space of not much more than a minute or two while, holding on with one hand to his bush and having got a good foothold for one of his feet, he indulged in that pleasant anticipatory sense of success. In the old days the farmer's wife used to be a light sleeper. The farmhands who, he remembered, lived in the village or were distributed in stables and outhouses, did not give him any concern. He wouldn't need to knock heavily. He pictured to himself the farmer's wife sitting up in bed, listening, then rousing her husband, who, as likely as not, would take the gun standing against the dresser downstairs and come to the door.

And then everything would be all right . . . But perhaps . . . Yes! It was just as likely the farmer would simply open the window and hold a parley. That really was most likely. Naturally. In his place Bolt felt he would do that very thing. Yes, that was what a man in a lonely house, in the middle of the night, would do most naturally. And he imagined himself whispering mysteriously his answers up the wall to the obvious questions—*Ami*—*Bolt*—*Ouvrez-moi*—*vive le roi*—or things of that sort. And in sequence to those vivid images it occurred to Bolt that the best thing he could do would be to throw small stones against the window shutter, the sort of sound most likely to rouse a light sleeper. He wasn't quite sure which window on the floor above the ground floor was that of those people's bedroom, but there were anyhow only three of them. In a moment he would have sprung up from his foothold on to the level if, raising his eyes for another look at the front of the house, he had not perceived that one of the windows was already open. How he could have failed to notice that before he couldn't explain.

He confessed to Captain Vincent in the course of his narrative that "this open window, sir, checked me dead. In fact, sir, it shook my confidence, for you know, sir, that no native of these parts would dream of sleeping with his window open. It struck me that there was something wrong there; and I remained where I was."

That fascination of repose, of secretive friendliness, which houses present at night, was gone. By the power of an open window, a black square in the moon-lighted wall, the farmhouse took on the aspect of a man-trap. Bolt assured Captain Vincent that the window would not have stopped him; he would have gone on all the same, though with an uncertain mind. But while he was thinking it out, there glided without a sound before his irresolute eyes from somewhere a white vision—a woman. He could see her black hair flowing down her back. A woman whom anybody would have been excused for taking for a ghost. "I won't say that she froze my blood, sir, but she made me cold all over for a moment. Lots of people have seen ghosts, at least they say so, and I have an open mind about that. She was a weird thing to look at in the moonlight. She did not act like a sleep-walker either. If she had not come out of a grave, then she had jumped out of bed. But when she stole back and hid herself round the corner of the house I knew she was not a ghost. She could not have seen me. There she stood in the black shadow watching for something—or waiting for somebody," added Bolt in a grim tone. "She looked crazy," he conceded charitably.

One thing was clear to him: there had been changes in that farmhouse since his time. Bolt resented them, as if that time had been only last week. The woman concealed round the corner remained in his full view, watchful, as if only waiting for him to show himself in the open, to run off screeching and rouse all the countryside. Bolt came quickly to the conclusion that he must withdraw from the slope. On lowering himself from his first position he had the misfortune to dislodge a stone. This circumstance precipitated his retreat. In a very few minutes he found himself by the shore. He paused to listen. Above him, up the ravine and all round amongst the rocks, everything was perfectly still. He walked along in the direction of his boat. There was nothing for it but to get away quietly and perhaps . . .

"Yes, Mr. Bolt, I fear we shall have to give up our plan," interrupted Captain Vincent at that point. Bolt's assent came reluctantly, and then he braced himself to confess that this was not the worst. Before the astonished face of Captain Vincent he hastened to blurt it out. He was very sorry, he could in no way account for it, but—he had lost a man.

Captain Vincent seemed unable to believe his ears. "What do you say? Lost a man out of my boat's crew!" He was profoundly shocked. Bolt was correspondingly distressed. He narrated that, shortly after he had left them, the seamen had heard, or imagined they had heard, some faint and peculiar noises somewhere within the cove. The coxswain sent one of the men, the oldest of the boat's crew, along the shore to ascertain whether their boat hauled on the beach could be seen from the other side of the cove. The man—it was Symons— departed crawling on his hands and knees to make the circuit and, well—he had not returned. This was really the reason why the boat was so late in getting back to the ship. Of course Bolt did not like to give up the man. It was inconceivable that Symons should have deserted. He had left his cutlass behind and was completely unarmed, but had he been suddenly pounced upon he surely would have been able to let out a yell that could have been heard all over the cove. But till daybreak a profound stillness, in which it seemed a whisper could have been heard for miles, had reigned over the coast. It was as if Symons had been spirited away by some supernatural means, without a scuffle, without a cry. For it was inconceivable that he should have ventured inland and got captured there. It was equally inconceivable that there should have been on that particular night men ready to pounce upon Symons and knock him on the head so neatly as not to let him give a groan even.

Captain Vincent said: "All this is very fantastical, Mr. Bolt," and compressed his lips firmly for a moment before he continued: "But not much more than your woman. I suppose you did see something real. . . ."

"I tell you, sir, she stood there in full moonlight for ten minutes within a stone's throw of me," protested Bolt with a sort of desperation. "She seemed to have jumped out of bed only to look at the house. If she had a petticoat over her night-shift, that was all. Her back was to me. When she moved away I could not make out her face properly. Then she went to stand in the shadow of the house."

"On the watch," suggested Captain Vincent.

"Looked like it, sir," confessed Bolt.

"So there must have been somebody about," concluded Captain Vincent with assurance.

Bolt murmured a reluctant, "Must have been." He had expected to get into enormous trouble over this affair and was much relieved by the captain's quiet attitude. "I hope, sir, you approve of my conduct in not attempting to look for Symons at once?"

"Yes. You acted prudently by not advancing inland," said the captain.

"I was afraid of spoiling our chances to carry out your plan, sir, by disclosing our presence on shore. And that could not have been avoided. Moreover, we were only five in all and not properly armed."

"The plan has gone down before your night-walker, Mr. Bolt," Captain Vincent declared dryly. "But we must try to find out what has become of our man if it can be done without risking too much."

"By landing a large party this very next night we could surround the house," Bolt suggested. "If we find friends there, well and good. If enemies, then we could carry off some of them on board for exchange perhaps. I am almost sorry I did not go back and kidnap that wench— whoever she was," he added recklessly. "Ah! If it had only been a man!"

"No doubt there was a man not very far off," said Captain Vincent equably. "That will do, Mr. Bolt. You had better go and get some rest now."

Bolt was glad to obey, for he was tired and hungry after his dismal failure. What vexed him most was its absurdity. Captain Vincent, though he too had passed a sleepless night, felt too restless to remain below. He followed his officer on deck.

CHAPTER VI

B Y THAT TIME the *Amelia* had been towed half a mile or so away from Cape Esterel. This change had brought her nearer to the two watchers on the hillside, who would have been plainly visible to the people on her deck, but for the head of the pine which concealed their movements. Lieutenant Réal, bestriding the rugged trunk as high as he could get, had the whole of the English ship's deck open to the range of his pocket-glass which he used between the branches. He said to Peyrol suddenly:

"Her captain has just come on deck."

Peyrol, sitting at the foot of the tree, made no answer for a long while. A warm drowsiness lay over the land and seemed to press down his eyelids. But inwardly the old rover was intensely awake. Under the mask of his immobility, with half-shut eyes and idly clasped hands, he heard the lieutenant, perched up there near the head of the tree, mutter counting something: "One, two, three," and then a loud *"Parbleu!"* after which the lieutenant in his trunk-bestriding attitude began to jerk himself backwards. Peyrol got up out of his way, but could not restrain himself from asking: "What's the matter now?"

"I will tell you what's the matter," said the other excitedly. As soon as he got his footing he walked up to old Peyrol and when quite close to him folded his arms across his chest.

"The first thing I did was to count the boats in the water. There was not a single one left on board. And now I just counted them again and found one more there. That ship had a boat out last night. How I missed seeing her pull out from under the land I don't know. I was watching the decks, I suppose, and she seems to have gone straight up to the tow-rope. But I was right. That Englishman had a boat out."

He seized Peyrol by both shoulders suddenly. "I believe you knew it all the time. You knew it, I tell you." Peyrol, shaken violently by the shoulders, raised his eyes to look at the angry face within a few inches of his own. In his worn gaze there was no fear or shame, but a troubled perplexity and obvious concern. He remained passive, merely remonstrating softly:

"*Doucement. Doucement.*"

The lieutenant suddenly desisted with a final jerk which failed to stagger old Peyrol, who, directly he had been released, assumed an explanatory tone.

"For the ground is slippery here. If I had lost my footing I would not have been able to prevent myself from grabbing at you, and we would have gone down that cliff together; which would have told those Englishmen more than twenty boats could have found out in as many nights."

Secretly Lieutenant Réal was daunted by Peyrol's mildness. It could not be shaken. Even physically he had an impression of the utter futility of his effort, as though he had tried to shake a rock. He threw himself on the ground carelessly saying:

"As for instance?"

Peyrol lowered himself with a deliberation appropriate to his grey hairs. "You don't suppose that out of a hundred and twenty or so pairs of eyes on board that ship there wouldn't be a dozen at least scanning the shore. Two men falling down a cliff would have been a startling sight. The English would have been interested enough to send a boat ashore to go through our pockets, and whether dead or only half dead we wouldn't have been in a state to prevent them. It wouldn't matter so much as to me, and I don't know what papers you may have in your pockets, but there are your shoulder-straps, your uniform coat."

"I carry no papers in my pocket, and . . ." A sudden thought seemed to strike the lieutenant, a thought so intense and far-fetched as to give his mental effort a momentary aspect of vacancy. He shook it off and went on in a changed tone: "The shoulder-straps would not have been much of a revelation by themselves."

"No. Not much. But enough to let her captain know that he had been watched. For what else could the dead body of a naval officer with a spyglass in his pocket mean? Hundreds of eyes may glance carelessly at that ship every day from all parts of the coast, though I fancy those landsmen hardly take the trouble to look at her now. But that's a very different thing from being kept under observation. However, I don't suppose all this matters much."

The lieutenant was recovering from the spell of that sudden thought. "Papers in my pocket," he muttered to himself. "That would be a perfect way." His parted lips came together in a slightly sarcastic smile with which he met Peyrol's puzzled, sidelong glance provoked by the inexplicable character of these words.

"I bet," said the lieutenant, "that ever since I came here first you have been more or less worrying your old head about my motives and intentions."

Peyrol said simply: "You came here on service at first and afterwards you came again because even in the Toulon fleet an officer may get a few days' leave. As to your intentions, I won't say anything about them. Especially as regards myself. About ten minutes ago anybody looking on would have thought they were not friendly to me."

The lieutenant sat up suddenly. By that time the English sloop, getting away from under the land, had become visible even from the spot on which they sat.

"Look!" exclaimed Réal. "She seems to be forging ahead in this calm."

Peyrol, startled, raised his eyes and saw the *Amelia* clear of the edge of the cliff and heading across the Passe. All her boats were already alongside, and yet, as a minute or two of steady gazing was enough to convince Peyrol, she was not stationary.

"She moves! There is no denying that. She moves. Watch the white speck of that house on Porquerolles. There! The end of her jib-boom touches it now. In a moment her head sails will mask it to us."

"I would never have believed it," muttered the lieutenant, after a pause of intent gazing. "And look, Peyrol, look, there is not a wrinkle on the water."

Peyrol, who had been shading his eyes from the sun, let his hand fall. "Yes," he said, "she would answer to a child's breath quicker than a feather, and the English very soon found it out when they got her. She was caught in Genoa only a few months after I came home and got my moorings here."

"I didn't know," murmured the young man.

"Aha, Lieutenant," said Peyrol, pressing his finger to his breast, "it hurts here, doesn't it? There is nobody but good Frenchmen here. Do you think it is a pleasure to me to watch that flag out there at her peak? Look, you can see the whole of her now. Look at her ensign hanging down as if there were not a breath of wind under the heavens. . . ." He stamped his foot suddenly. "And yet she moves! Those in Toulon that may be thinking of catching her dead or alive would have to think hard and make long plans and get good men to carry them out."

"There was some talk of it at the Toulon Admiralty," said Réal.

The rover shook his head. "They need not have sent you on the duty," he said. "I have been watching her now for a month, her and the man who has got her now. I know all his tricks and all his habits and all his dodges by this time. The man is a seaman, that must be said for him, but I can tell beforehand what he will do in any given case."

Lieutenant Réal lay down on his back again, his clasped hands under his head. He thought that this old man was not boasting. He knew a lot about the English ship, and if an attempt to capture her was to be made, his ideas would be worth having. Nevertheless, in his relations with old Peyrol Lieutenant Réal suffered from contradictory feelings. Réal was the son of a ci-devant couple—small provincial gentry—who had both lost their heads on the scaffold, within the same week. As to their boy, he was apprenticed by order of the Delegate of the Revolutionary Committee of his town to a poor but pure-minded joiner, who could not provide him with shoes to run his errands in, but treated this aristocrat not unkindly. Nevertheless, at the end of the year the orphan ran away and volunteered as a boy on board one of the ships of the Republic about to sail on a distant expedition. At sea he found another standard of values. In the course of some eight years, suppressing his faculties of love and hatred, he arrived at the rank of an officer by sheer merit, and had accustomed himself to look at men sceptically, without much scorn or much respect. His principles were purely professional and he had never formed a friendship in his life—more unfortunate in that respect than old Peyrol, who at least had known the bonds of the lawless Brotherhood of the Coast. He was, of course, very self-contained. Peyrol, whom he had found unexpectedly settled on the peninsula, was the first human being to break through that schooled reserve which the precariousness of all things had forced on the orphan of the Revolution. Peyrol's striking personality had aroused Réal's interest, a mistrustful liking mixed with some contempt of a purely doctrinaire kind. It was clear that the fellow had been next thing to a pirate at one time or another—a sort of past which could not commend itself to a naval officer.

Still, Peyrol had broken through: and, presently, the peculiarities of all those people at the farm, each individual one of them, had entered through the breach.

Lieutenant Réal, on his back, closing his eyes to the glare of the sky, meditated on old Peyrol, while Peyrol himself, with his white head bare in the sunshine, seemed to be sitting by the side of a corpse. What in that man impressed Lieutenant Réal was the faculty of shrewd insight. The facts of Réal's connection with the farmhouse on the peninsula were much as Peyrol had stated. First on specific duty about establishing a signal station, then, when that project had been given up, voluntary visits. Not belonging to any ship of the fleet but doing shore duty at the Arsenal, Lieutenant Réal had spent several periods of short leave at the farm, where indeed nobody could tell whether he had come on duty or on leave. He personally could not— or perhaps would not—tell even to himself why it was that he came there. He had been growing sick of his work. He had no place in the world to go to, and no one either. Was it Peyrol he was coming to see? A mute, strangely suspicious, defiant understanding had established itself imperceptibly between him and that lawless old man who might have been suspected to have come there only to die, if the whole robust personality of Peyrol with its quiet vitality had not been antagonistic to the notion of death. That rover behaved as though he had all the time in the world at his command.

Peyrol spoke suddenly, with his eyes fixed in front of him as if he were addressing the Island of Porquerolles, eight miles away.

"Yes—I know all her moves, though I must say that this trick of dodging close to our peninsula is something new."

"H'm! Fish for the captain's breakfast," mumbled Réal without opening his eyes. "Where is she now?"

"In the middle of the Passe, busy hoisting in her boats. And still moving! That ship will keep her way as long as the flame of a candle on her deck will not stand upright."

"That ship is a marvel."

"She has been built by French shipwrights," said old Peyrol bitterly.

This was the last sound for a long time. Then the lieutenant said in an indifferent tone: "You are very positive about that. How do you know?"

"I have been looking at her for a month, whatever name she might have had or whatever name the English call her by now. Did you ever see such a bow on an English-built ship?"

The lieutenant remained silent, as though he had lost all interest and there had been no such thing as an English man-of-war within a mile. But all the time he was thinking hard. He had been told confidentially of a certain piece of service to be performed on instructions received from Paris. Not an operation of war, but service of the greatest importance. The risk of it was not so much deadly as particularly odious. A brave man might well have shrunk from it; and there are risks (not death) from which a resolute man might shrink without shame.

"Have you ever tasted of prison, Peyrol?" he asked suddenly, in an affectedly sleep voice.

It roused Peyrol nearly into a shout. "Heavens! No! Prison! What do you mean by prison? . . . I have been a captive to savages," he added, calming down, "but that's a very old story. I was young and foolish then. Later, when a grown man, I was a slave to the famous Ali-Kassim. I spent a fortnight with chains on my legs and arms in the yard of a mud fort on the shores of the Persian Gulf. There was nearly a score of us Brothers of the Coast in the same predicament . . . in consequence of a shipwreck."

"Yes. . . ." The lieutenant was very languid indeed. . . . "And I daresay you all took service with that bloodthirsty old pirate."

"There was not a single one of his thousands of blackamoors that could lay a gun properly. But Ali-Kassim made war like a prince. We sailed, a regular fleet, across the gulf, took a town on the coast of Arabia somewhere, and looted it. Then I and the others managed to get hold of an armed dhow, and we fought our way right through the blackamoors' fleet. Several of us died of thirst later. All the same, it was a great affair. But don't you talk to me of prisons. A proper man if given a chance to fight can always get himself killed. You understand me?"

"Yes, I understand you," drawled the lieutenant. "I think I know you pretty well. I suppose an English prison . . ."

"That is a horrible subject of conversation," interrupted Peyrol in a loud, emotional tone. "Naturally, any death is better than a prison. Any death! What is it you have in your mind, Lieutenant?"

"Oh, it isn't that I want you to die," drawled Réal in an uninterested manner.

Peyrol, his entwined fingers clasping his legs, gazed fixedly at the English sloop floating idly in the Passe while he gave up all his mind to the consideration of these words that had floated out, idly too, into the peace and silence of the morning. Then he asked in a low tone:

"Do you want to frighten me?"

The lieutenant laughed harshly. Neither by word, gesture nor glance did Peyrol acknowledge the enigmatic and unpleasant sound. But when it ceased the silence grew so oppressive between the two men that they got up by a common impulse. The lieutenant sprang to his feet lightly. The uprising of Peyrol took more time and had more dignity. They stood side by side unable to detach their longing eyes from the enemy ship below their feet.

"I wonder why he put himself into this curious position," said the officer.

"I wonder," growled Peyrol curtly. "If there had been only a couple of eighteen-pounders placed on the rocky ledge to the left of us, we could have unrigged her in about ten minutes."

"Good old gunner," commented Réal ironically. "And what afterwards? Swim off, you and I, with our cutlasses in our teeth and take her by boarding, what?"

This sally provoked in Peyrol an austere smile. "No! No!" he protested soberly. "But why not let Toulon know? Bring out a frigate or two and catch him alive. Many a time have I planned his capture just to ease my heart. Often I have stared at night out of my window upstairs across the bay to where I knew he was lying at anchor, and thinking of a little surprise I could arrange for him if I were not only old Peyrol, the gunner."

"Yes. And keeping out of the way at that, with a bad note against his name in the books of the Admiralty in Toulon."

"You can't say I have tried to hide myself from you who are a naval officer," struck in Peyrol quickly. "I fear no man. I did not run. I simply went away from Toulon. Nobody had given me an order to stay there. And you can't say I ran very far either."

"That was the cleverest move of all. You knew what you were doing."

"Here you go again, hinting at something crooked like that fellow with big epaulettes at the Port Office that seemed to be longing to put me under arrest just because I brought a prize from the Indian Ocean, eight thousand miles, dodging clear of every Englishman that came in my way, which was more perhaps than he could have done. I have my gunner's warrant signed by Citizen Renaud, a *chef d'escadre*. It wasn't given me for twirling my thumbs or hiding in the cable tier when the enemy was about. There were on board our ships some patriots that weren't above doing that sort of thing, I can tell you. But Republic or no Republic, that kind wasn't likely to get a gunner's warrant."

"That's all right," said Réal, with his eyes fixed on the English ship, the head of which was swung to the northward now. . . . "Look, she seems to have lost her way at last," he remarked parenthetically to Peyrol, who also glanced that way and nodded. . . . "That's all right. But it's on record that you managed in a very short time to get very thick with a lot of patriots ashore. Section leaders. Terrorists. . . ."

"Why, yes. I wanted to hear what they had to say. They talked like a drunken crew of scallywags that had stolen a ship. But at any rate it wasn't such as they that had sold the Port to the English. They were a lot of bloodthirsty landlubbers. I did get out of town as soon as I could. I remembered I was born around here. I knew no other bit of France, and I didn't care to go any further. Nobody came to look for me."

"No, not here. I suppose they thought it was too near. They did look for you, a little, but they gave it up. Perhaps if they had persevered and made an admiral of you we would not have been beaten at Aboukir."

At the mention of that name Peyrol shook his fist at the serene Mediterranean sky. "And yet we were no worse men than the English," he cried, "and there are no such ships as ours in the world. You see, Lieutenant, the Republican god of these talkers would never give us seamen a chance of fair play."

The lieutenant looked round in surprise. "What do you know about a Republican god?" he asked. "What on earth do you mean?"

"I have heard of and seen more gods than you could ever dream of in a long night's sleep, in every corner of the earth, in the very heart of forests, which is an inconceivable thing. Figures, stones, sticks. There must be something in the idea. . . . And what I meant," he continued in a resentful tone, "is that their Republican god, which is neither stick nor stone, but seems to be some kind of lubber, has never given us seamen a chief like that one the soldiers have got ashore."

Lieutenant Réal looked at Peyrol with unsmiling attention, then remarked quietly, "Well, the god of the aristocrats is coming back again and it looks as if he were bringing an emperor along with him. You've heard something of that, you people in the farmhouse? Haven't you?"

"No," said Peyrol. "I have heard no talk of an emperor. But what does it matter? Under one name or another a chief can be no more than a chief, and that general whom they have been calling consul is a good chief—nobody can deny that."

After saying those words in a dogmatic tone, Peyrol looked up at the sun and suggested that it was time to go down to the farmhouse *"pour manger la soupe."* With a suddenly gloomy face Réal moved off, followed by Peyrol. At the first turn of the path they got the view of the Escampobar buildings with the pigeons still walking on the ridges of the roofs, of the sunny orchards and yards without a living soul in them. Peyrol remarked that everybody no doubt was in the kitchen waiting for his and the lieutenant's return. He himself was properly hungry. "And you, Lieutenant?"

The lieutenant was not hungry. Hearing this declaration made in a peevish tone, Peyrol gave a sagacious movement of his head behind the lieutenant's back. Well, whatever happened, a man had to eat. He, Peyrol, knew what it was to be altogether without food; but even half-rations was a poor show, very poor show for anybody who had to work or to fight. For himself he couldn't imagine any conjuncture that would prevent him having a meal as long as there was something to eat within reach.

His unwonted garrulity provoked no response, but Peyrol continued to talk in that strain as though his thoughts were concentrated on food, while his eyes roved here and there and his ears were open for the slightest sound. When they arrived in front of the house Peyrol stopped to glance anxiously down the path to the coast, letting the lieutenant enter the café. The Mediterranean, in that part which could be seen from the door of the café, was as empty of all sail as a yet undiscovered sea. The dull tinkle of a cracked bell on the neck of some wandering cow was the only sound that reached him, accentuating the Sunday peace of the farm. Two goats were lying down on the western slope of the hill. It all had a very reassuring effect and the anxious expression on Peyrol's face was passing away when suddenly one of the goats leaped to its feet. The rover gave a start and became rigid in a pose of tense apprehension. A man who is in such a frame of mind that a leaping goat makes him start cannot be happy. However, the other goat remained lying down. There was really no reason for alarm, and Peyrol, composing his features as near as possible to their usual placid expression, followed the lieutenant into the house.

CHAPTER VII

A SINGLE COVER having been laid at the end of a long table in the *salle* for the lieutenant, he had his meal there while the others sat down to theirs in the kitchen, the usual strangely assorted company served by the anxious and silent Catherine. Peyrol, thoughtful and hungry, faced Citizen Scevola in his working clothes and very much withdrawn within himself. Scevola's aspect was more feverish than usual, with the red patches on his cheekbones very marked above the thick beard. From time to time the mistress of the farm would get up from her place by the side of old Peyrol and go out into the *salle* to attend to the lieutenant. The other three people seemed unconscious of her absences. Towards the end of the meal Peyrol leaned back in his wooden chair and let his gaze rest on the ex-terrorist who had not finished yet, and was still busy over his plate with the air of a man who had done a long morning's work. The door leading from the kitchen to the *salle* stood wide open, but no sound of voices ever came from there.

Till lately Peyrol had not concerned himself very much with the mental states of the people with whom he lived. Now, however, he wondered to himself what could be the thoughts of the ex-terrorist patriot, that sanguinary and extremely poor creature occupying the position of master of the Escampobar Farm. But when Citizen Scevola raised his head at last to take a long drink of wine there was nothing new on that face which in its high colour resembled so much a painted mask. Their eyes met.

"*Sacrebleu!*" exclaimed Peyrol at last. "If you never say anything to anybody like this you will forget how to speak at last."

The patriot smiled from the depths of his beard, a smile which Peyrol for some reason, mere prejudice perhaps, always thought resembled the defensive grin of some small wild animal afraid of being cornered.

"What is there to talk about?" he retorted. "You live with us; you haven't budged from here; I suppose you have counted the bunches of grapes in the enclosure and the figs on the fig-tree on the west wall many times over. . . ." He paused to lend an ear to the dead silence in the *salle*, and then said with a slight rise of tone, "You and I know everything that is going on here."

Peyrol wrinkled the corners of his eyes in a keen, searching glance. Catherine clearing the table bore herself as if she had been completely deaf. Her face, of a walnut colour, with sunken cheeks and lips, might have been a carving in the marvellous immobility of its fine wrinkles. Her carriage was upright and her hands swift in their movements. Peyrol said: "We don't want to talk about the farm. Haven't you heard any news lately?"

The patriot shook his head violently. Of public news he had a horror. Everything was lost. The country was ruled by perjurers and renegades. All the patriotic virtues were dead. He struck the table with his fist and then remained listening as though the blow could have roused an echo in the silent house. Not the faintest sound came from anywhere. Citizen Scevola sighed. It seemed to him that he was the only patriot left, and even in his retirement his life was not safe.

"I know," said Peyrol. "I saw the whole affair out of the window. You can run like a hare, citizen."

"Was I to allow myself to be sacrificed by those superstitious brutes?" argued Citizen Scevola in a high-pitched voice and with genuine indignation which Peyrol watched coldly. He could hardly catch the mutter of "Perhaps it would have been just as well if I had let those reactionary dogs kill me that time."

The old woman washing up at the sink glanced uneasily towards the door of the *salle*.

"No!" shouted the lonely sans-culotte. "It isn't possible! There must be plenty of patriots left in France. The sacred fire is not burnt out yet."

For a short time he presented the appearance of a man who is sitting with ashes on his head and desolation in his heart. His almond-shaped eyes looked dull, extinguished. But after a moment he gave a sidelong look at Peyrol as if to watch the effect and began declaiming in a low voice and apparently as if rehearsing a speech to himself: "No, it isn't possible. Some day tyranny will stumble and then it will be time to pull it down again. We will come out in our thousands and—*ça ira!*"

Those words, and even the passionate energy of the tone, left Peyrol unmoved. With his head sustained by his thick brown hand he was thinking of something else so obviously as to depress again the feebly struggling spirit of terrorism in the lonely breast of Citizen Scevola. The glow of reflected sunlight in the kitchen became darkened by the body of the fisherman of the lagoon, mumbling a shy greeting to the company from the frame of the doorway. Without altering his position Peyrol turned his eyes on him curiously. Catherine, wiping her hands on her apron, remarked: "You come late for your dinner, Michel." He stepped in then, took from the old woman's hand an earthenware pot and a large hunk of bread and carried them out at once into the yard. Peyrol and the sans-culotte got up from the table. The latter, after hesitating like somebody who has lost his way, went brusquely into the passage, while Peyrol, avoiding Catherine's anxious stare, made for the back-yard. Through the open door of the salle he obtained a glimpse of Arlette sitting upright with her hands in her lap gazing at somebody he could not see, but who could be no other than Lieutenant Réal.

In the blaze and heat of the yard the chickens, broken up into small groups, were having their siesta in patches of shade. But Peyrol cared nothing for the sun. Michel, who was eating his dinner under the pent roof of the cart shed, put the earthenware pot down on the ground and joined his master at the well encircled by a low wall of stones and topped by an arch of wrought iron on which a wild fig-tree had twined a slender offshoot. After his dog's death the fisherman had abandoned the salt lagoon, leaving his rotting punt exposed on the dismal shore and his miserable nets shut up in the dark hut. He did not care for another dog, and besides, who was there to give him a dog? He was the last of men. Somebody must be last. There was no place for him in the life of the village. So one fine morning he had walked up to the farm in order to see Peyrol. More correctly, perhaps, to let himself be seen by Peyrol. That was exactly Michel's only hope.

He sat down on a stone outside the gate with a small bundle, consisting mainly of an old blanket, and a crooked stick lying on the ground near him, and looking the most lonely, mild, and harmless creature on this earth. Peyrol had listened gravely to his confused tale of the dog's death. He, personally, would not have made a friend of a dog like Michel's dog, but he understood perfectly the sudden breaking up of the establishment on the shore of the lagoon. So when Michel had concluded with the words, "I thought I would come up here," Peyrol, without waiting for a plain request, had said: "*Très bien.* You will be my crew," and had pointed down the path leading to the seashore. And as Michel, picking up his bundle and stick, started off, waiting for no further directions, he had shouted after him: "You will find a loaf of bread and a bottle of wine in a locker aft, to break your fast on."

These had been the only formalities of Michel's engagement to serve as "crew" on board Peyrol's boat. The rover indeed had tried without loss of time to carry out his purpose of getting something of his own that would float. It was not so easy to find anything worthy. The miserable population of Madrague, a tiny fishing hamlet facing towards Toulon, had nothing to sell. Moreover, Peyrol looked with contempt on all their possessions. He would have as soon bought a catamaran of three logs of wood tied together with rattans as one of their boats; but lonely and prominent on the beach, lying on her side in weather-beaten melancholy, there was a two-masted tartane with her sun-whitened cordage hanging in festoons and her dry masts showing long cracks. No man was ever seen dozing under the shade of her hull on which the Mediterranean gulls made themselves very much at home. She looked a wreck thrown high up on the land by a disdainful sea. Peyrol, having surveyed her from a distance, saw that the rudder still hung in its place. He ran his eye along her body and said to himself that a craft with such lines would sail well. She was much bigger than anything he had thought of, but in her size, too, there was a fascination. It seemed to bring all the shores of the Mediterranean within his reach, Baleares and Corsica, Barbary and Spain. Peyrol had sailed over hundreds of leagues of ocean in craft that were no bigger. At his back in silent wonder a knot of fishermen's wives, bareheaded and lean, with a swarm of ragged children clinging to their skirts, watched the first stranger they had seen for years.

Peyrol borrowed a short ladder in the hamlet (he knew better than to trust his weight to any of the ropes hanging over the side) and carried it down to the beach followed at a respectful distance by the staring women and children: a phenomenon and a wonder to the natives, as it had happened to him before on more than one island in distant seas. He clambered on board the neglected tartane and stood on the decked forepart, the centre of all eyes. A gull flew away with an angry scream. The bottom of the open hold contained nothing but a little sand, a few broken pieces of wood, a rusty hook, and some few stalks of straw which the wind must have carried for miles before they found their rest in there. The decked after-part had a small skylight and a companion, and Peyrol's eyes rested fascinated on an enormous padlock which secured its sliding door. It was as if there had been secrets or treasures inside—and yet most probably it was empty. Peyrol turned his head away and with the whole strength of his lungs shouted in the direction of the fishermen's wives who had been joined by two very old men and a hunchbacked cripple swinging between two crutches:

"Is there anybody looking after this tartane, a caretaker?"

At first the only answer was a movement of recoil. Only the hunchback held his ground and shouted back in an unexpectedly strong voice:

"You are the first man that has been on board her for years."

The wives of the fishermen admired his boldness, for Peyrol indeed appeared to them a very formidable being.

"I might have guessed that," thought Peyrol. "She is in a dreadful mess." The disturbed gull had brought some friends as indignant as itself and they circled at different levels uttering wild cries over Peyrol's head. He shouted again:

"Who does she belong to?"

The being on crutches lifted a finger towards the circling birds and answered in a deep tone:

"They are the only ones I know." Then, as Peyrol gazed down at him over the side, he went on: "This craft used to belong to Escampobar. You know Escampobar? It's a house in the hollow between the hills there."

"Yes, I know Escampobar," yelled Peyrol, turning away and leaning against the mast in a pose which he did not change for a long time. His immobility tired out the crowd. They moved slowly in a body towards their hovels, the hunchback bringing up the rear with long swings between his crutches, and Peyrol remained alone with the angry gulls. He lingered on board the tragic craft which had taken Arlette's parents to their death in the vengeful massacre of Toulon and had brought the youthful Arlette and Citizen Scevola back to Escampobar where old Catherine, left alone at that time, had waited for days for somebody's return. Days of anguish and prayer, while she listened to the booming of guns about Toulon and with an almost greater but different terror to the dead silence which ensued.

Peyrol, enjoying the sensation of some sort of craft under his feet, indulged in no images of horror connected with that desolate tartane. It was late in the evening before he returned to the farm, so that he had to have his supper alone. The women had retired, only the sans-culotte, smoking a short pipe out of doors, had followed him into the kitchen and asked where he had been and whether he had lost his way. This question gave Peyrol an opening. He had been to Madrague and had seen a very fine tartane lying perishing on the beach.

"They told me down there that she belonged to you, *citoyen*."

At this the terrorist only blinked.

"What's the matter? Isn't she the craft you came here in? Won't you sell her to me?" Peyrol waited a little. "What objection can you have?"

It appeared that the patriot had no positive objections. He mumbled something about the tartane being very dirty. This caused Peyrol to look at him with intense astonishment.

"I am ready to take her off your hands as she stands."

"I will be frank with you, *citoyen*. You see, when she lay at the quay in Toulon a lot of fugitive traitors, men and women, and children too, swarmed on board of her, and cut the ropes with a view of escaping, but the avengers were not far behind and made short work of them. When we discovered her behind the Arsenal, I and another man, we had to throw a lot of bodies overboard, out of the hold and the cabin. You will find her very dirty all over. We had no time to clear up." Peyrol felt inclined to laugh. He had seen decks swimming in blood and had himself helped to throw dead bodies overboard after a fight; but he eyed the citizen with an unfriendly eye. He thought to himself: "He had a hand in that massacre, no doubt," but he made no audible remark. He only thought of the enormous padlock securing that emptied charnel house at the stern. The terrorist insisted. "We really had not a moment to clean her up. The circumstances were such that it was necessary for me to get away quickly lest some of the false patriots should do me some carmagnole or other. There had been bitter quarrelling in my section. I was not alone in getting away, you know."

Peyrol waved his arm to cut short the explanation. But before he and the terrorist had parted for the night Peyrol could regard himself as the owner of the tragic tartane.

Next day he returned to the hamlet and took up his quarters there for a time. The awe he had inspired wore off, though no one cared to come very near the tartane. Peyrol did not want any help. He wrenched off the enormous padlock himself with a bar of iron and let the light of day into the little cabin which did indeed bear the traces of the massacre in the stains of blood on its woodwork, but contained nothing else except a wisp of long hair and a woman's earring, a cheap thing which Peyrol picked up and looked at for a long time. The associations of such finds were not foreign to his past. He could without very strong emotion figure to himself the little place choked with corpses. He sat down and looked about at the stains and splashes which had been untouched by sunlight for years. The cheap little earring lay before him on the rough-hewn table between the lockers, and he shook his head at it weightily. He, at any rate, had never been a butcher.

Peyrol unassisted did all the cleaning. Then he turned con amore to the fitting out of the tartane. The habits of activity still clung to him. He welcomed something to do; this congenial task had all the air of preparation for a voyage, which was a pleasing dream, and it brought every evening the satisfaction of something achieved to that illusory end. He rove new gear, scraped the masts himself, did all the sweeping, scrubbing and painting single-handed, working steadily and hopefully as though he had been preparing his escape from a desert island; and directly he had cleaned and renovated the dark little hole of a cabin he took to sleeping on board. Once only he went up on a visit to the farm for a couple of days, as if to give himself a holiday. He passed them mostly in observing Arlette. She was perhaps the first problematic human being he had ever been in contact with. Peyrol had no contempt for women. He had seen them love, suffer, endure, riot, and even fight for their own hand, very much like men. Generally with men and women you had to be on your guard, but in some ways women were more to be trusted. As a matter of fact, his country-women were to him less known than any other kind. From his experience of many different races, however, he had a vague idea that women were very much alike everywhere. This one was a lovable creature. She produced on him the effect of a child, aroused a kind of intimate emotion which he had not known before to exist by itself in a man. He was startled by its detached character. "Is it that I am getting old?" he asked himself suddenly one evening, as he sat on the bench against the wall looking straight before him, after she had crossed his line of sight.

He felt himself an object of observation to Catherine, whom he used to detect peeping at him round corners or through half-opened doors. On his part he would stare at her openly—aware of the impression he produced on her: mingled curiosity and awe. He had the idea she did not disapprove of his presence at the farm, where, it was plain to him, she had a far from easy life. This had no relation to the fact that she did all the household work. She was a woman of about his own age, straight as a dart but with a wrinkled face. One evening as they were sitting alone in the kitchen Peyrol said to her: "You must have been a handsome girl in your day, Catherine. It's strange you never got married."

She turned to him under the high mantel of the fireplace and seemed struck all of a heap, unbelieving, amazed, so that Peyrol was quite provoked. "What's the matter? If the old moke in the yard had spoken you could not look more surprised. You can't deny that you were a handsome girl."

She recovered from her scare to say: "I was born here, grew up here, and early in my life I made up my mind to die here."

"A strange notion," said Peyrol, "for a young girl to take into her head."

"It's not a thing to talk about," said the old woman, stooping to get a pot out of the warm ashes. "I did not think, then," she went on, with her back to Peyrol, "that I would live long. When I was eighteen I fell in love with a priest."

"Ah, bah!" exclaimed Peyrol under his breath.

"That was the time when I prayed for death," she pursued in a quiet voice. "I spent nights on my knees upstairs in that room where you sleep now. I shunned everybody. People began to say I was crazy. We have always been hated by the rabble about here. They have poisonous tongues. I got the nickname of *'la fiancée du prêtre.'* Yes, I was handsome, but who would have looked at me if I had wanted to be looked at? My only luck was to have a fine man for a brother. He understood. No word passed his lips, but sometimes when we were alone and not even his wife was by, he would lay his hand on my shoulder gently. From that time to this I have not been to church and I never will go. But I have no quarrel with God now."

There were no signs of watchfulness and care in her bearing now. She stood straight as an arrow before Peyrol and looked at him with a confident air. The rover was not yet ready to speak. He only nodded twice and Catherine turned away to put the pot to cool in the sink. "Yes, I wished to die. But I did not, and now I have got something to do," she said, sitting down near the fireplace and taking her chin in her hand. "And I daresay you know what that is," she added.

Peyrol got up deliberately.

"Well! *bonsoir,*" he said. "I am off to Madrague. I want to begin work again on the tartane at daylight."

"Don't talk to me about the tartane! She took my brother away for ever. I stood on the shore watching her sails growing smaller and smaller. Then I came up alone to this farmhouse."

Moving calmly her faded lips which no lover or child had ever kissed, old Catherine told Peyrol of the days and nights of waiting, with the distant growl of the big guns in her ears. She used to sit outside on the bench longing for news, watching the flickers in the sky and listening to heavy bursts of gunfire coming over the water. Then came a night as if the world were coming to an end. All the sky was lighted up, the earth shook to its foundations, and she felt the house rock, so that jumping up from the bench she screamed with fear. That night she never went to bed. Next morning she saw the sea covered with sails, while a black and yellow cloud of smoke hung over Toulon. A man coming up from Madrague told her that he believed that the whole town had been blown up. She gave him a bottle of wine and he helped her to feed the stock that evening. Before going home he expressed the opinion that there could not be a soul left alive in Toulon, because the few that survived would have gone away in the English ships. Nearly a week later she was dozing by the fire when voices outside woke her up, and she beheld standing in the middle of the *salle,* pale like a corpse out of a grave, with a blood-soaked blanket over her shoulders and a red cap on her head, a ghastly looking young girl in whom she suddenly recognized her niece. She screamed in her terror: "François, François!" This was her brother's name, and she thought he was outside. Her scream scared the girl, who ran out of the door. All was still outside. Once more she screamed "François!" and, tottering as far as the door, she saw her niece clinging to a strange man in a red cap and with a sabre by his side who yelled excitedly: "You won't see François again. *Vive la République!*"

"I recognized the son Bron," went on Catherine. "I knew his parents. When the troubles began he left his home to follow the Revolution. I walked straight up to him and took the girl away from his side. She didn't want much coaxing. The child always loved me," she continued, getting up from the stool and moving a little closer to Peyrol. "She remembered her Aunt Catherine. I tore the horrid blanket off her shoulders. Her hair was clotted with blood and her clothes all stained with it. I took her upstairs. She was as helpless as a little child. I undressed her and examined her all over. She had no hurt anywhere. I was sure of that—but of what more could I be sure? I couldn't make sense of the things she babbled at me. Her very voice distracted me. She fell asleep directly I had put her into my bed, and I stood there looking down at her, nearly going out of my mind with the thought of what that child may have been dragged through. When I went downstairs I found that good-for-nothing inside the house. He was ranting up and down the *salle*, vapouring and boasting till I thought all this must be an awful dream. My head was in a whirl. He laid claim to her, and God knows what. I seemed to understand things that made my hair stir on my head. I stood there clasping my hands with all the strength I had, for fear I should go out of my senses."

"He frightened you," said Peyrol, looking at her steadily. Catherine moved a step nearer to him.

"What? The son Bron, frighten me! He was the butt of all the girls, mooning about amongst the people outside the church on feast days in the time of the king. All the countryside knew about him. No. What I said to myself was that I mustn't let him kill me. There upstairs was the child I had just got away from him, and there was I, all alone with that man with the sabre and unable to get hold of a kitchen knife even."

"And so he remained," said Peyrol.

"What would you have had me to do?" asked Catherine steadily. "He had brought the child back out of those shambles. It was a long

time before I got an idea of what had happened. I don't know everything even yet and I suppose I will never know. In a very few days my
mind was more at ease about Arlette, but it was a long time before she
would speak and then it was never anything to the purpose. And
what could I have done single-handed? There was nobody I would
condescend to call to my help. We of the Escampobar have never been
in favour with the peasants here," she said, proudly. "And this is all I
can tell you."

Her voice faltered, she sat down on the stool again and took her
chin in the palm of her hand. As Peyrol left the house to go to the
hamlet he saw Arlette and the patron come round the corner of the
yard wall walking side by side but as if unconscious of each other.

That night he slept on board the renovated tartane and the rising
sun found him at work about the hull. By that time he had ceased to be
the object of awed contemplation to the inhabitants of the hamlet who
still, however, kept up a mistrustful attitude. His only intermediary
for communicating with them was the miserable cripple. He was
Peyrol's only company, in fact, during his period of work on the tartane. He had more activity, audacity, and intelligence, it seemed to
Peyrol, than all the rest of the inhabitants put together. Early in the
morning he could be seen making his way on his crutches with a pen-
dulum motion towards the hull on which Peyrol would have been
already an hour or so at work. Peyrol then would throw him over a
sound rope's end and the cripple, leaning his crutches against the side
of the tartane, would pull his wretched little carcass, all withered
below the waist, up the rope, hand over hand, with extreme ease.
There, sitting on the small foredeck, with his back against the mast
and his thin, twisted legs folded in front of him, he would keep Peyrol
company, talking to him along the whole length of the tartane in a
strained voice and sharing his midday meal, as of right, since it was he
generally who brought the provisions slung round his neck in a
quaint flat basket. Thus were the hours of labour shortened for Peyrol
by shrewd remarks and bits of local gossip. How the cripple got hold
of it it was difficult to imagine, and the rover had not enough knowledge of European superstitions to suspect him of flying through the
night on a broomstick like a sort of male witch—for there was a manliness in that twisted scrap of humanity which struck Peyrol from the
first. His very voice was manly and the character of his gossip was not
feminine. He did indeed mention to Peyrol that people used to take

him about the neighbourhood in carts for the purpose of playing a fiddle at weddings and other festive occasions; but this seemed hardly adequate, and even he himself confessed that there was not much of that sort of thing going on during the Revolution when people didn't like to attract attention and everything was done in a hole-and-corner manner. There were no priests to officiate at weddings, and if there were no ceremonies how could there be rejoicings? Of course children were born as before, but there were no christenings—and people got to look funny somehow or other. Their countenances got changed somehow; the very boys and girls seemed to have something on their minds.

Peyrol, busy about one thing and another, listened without appearing to pay much attention to the story of the Revolution, as if to the tale of an intelligent islander on the other side of the world talking of bloody rites and amazing hopes of some religion unknown to the rest of mankind. But there was something biting in the speech of that cripple which confused his thoughts a little. Sarcasm was a mystery which he could not understand. On one occasion he remarked to his friend the cripple as they sat together on the foredeck munching the bread and figs of their midday meal:

"There must have been something in it. But it doesn't seem to have done much for you people here."

"To be sure," retorted the scrap of man vivaciously, "it hasn't straightened my back or given me a pair of legs like yours."

Peyrol, whose trousers were rolled up above the knee because he had been washing the hold, looked at his calves complacently. "You could hardly have expected that," he remarked with simplicity.

"Ah, but you don't know what people with properly made bodies expected or pretended to," said the cripple. "Everything was going to be changed. Everybody was going to tie up his dog with a string of sausages for the sake of principles." His long face which, in repose, had an expression of suffering peculiar to cripples, was lighted up by an enormous grin. "They must feel jolly well sold by this time," he added. "And of course that vexes them, but I am not vexed. I was never vexed with my father and mother. While the poor things were alive I never went hungry—not very hungry. They couldn't have been very proud of me." He paused and seemed to contemplate himself mentally. "I don't know what I would have done in their place. Something very different. But then, don't you see, I know what it means to be like I am. Of course they couldn't know, and I don't suppose the poor people had very much sense. A priest from Almanarre—Almanarre is a sort of village up there where there is a church. . . ."

Peyrol interrupted him by remarking that he knew all about Almanarre. This, on his part, was a simple delusion because in reality he knew much less of Almanarre than of Zanzibar or any pirate village from there up to Cape Guardafui. And the cripple contemplated him with his brown eyes which had an upward cast naturally.

"You know . . . ! For me," he went on, in a tone of quiet decision, "you are a man fallen from the sky. Well, a priest from Almanarre came to bury them. A fine man with a stern face. The finest man I have seen from that time till you dropped on us here. There was a story of a girl having fallen in love with him some years before. I was old enough then to have heard something of it, but that's neither here nor there. Moreover, many people wouldn't believe the tale."

Peyrol, without looking at the cripple, tried to imagine what sort of child he might have been—what sort of youth? The rover had seen staggering deformities, dreadful mutilations which were the cruel work of man; but it was amongst people with dusky skins. And that made a great difference. But what he had heard and seen since he had come back to his native land, the tales, the facts, and also the faces, reached his sensibility with a particular force, because of that feeling that came to him so suddenly after a whole lifetime spent amongst Indians, Malagashes, Arabs, blackamoors of all sorts, that he belonged there, to this land, and had escaped all those things by a mere hair's breadth. His companion completed his significant silence, which seemed to have been occupied with thoughts very much like his own, by saying:

"All this was in the king's time. They didn't cut off his head till several years afterwards. It didn't make my life any easier for me, but since those Republicans had deposed God and flung Him out of all the churches I have forgiven Him all my troubles."

"Spoken like a man," said Peyrol. Only the misshapen character of the cripple's back prevented Peyrol from giving him a hearty slap. He got up to begin his afternoon's work. It was a bit of inside painting and from the foredeck the cripple watched him at it with dreamy eyes and something ironic on his lips.

It was not till the sun had travelled over Cape Cicié, which could be seen across the water like dark mist in the glare, that he opened his lips to ask: "And what do you propose to do with this tartane, *citoyen*?"

Peyrol answered simply that the tartane was fit to go anywhere now, the very moment she took the water.

"You could go as far as Genoa and Naples and even further," suggested the cripple.

"Much further," said Peyrol.

"And you have been fitting her out like this for a voyage?"

"Certainly," said Peyrol, using his brush steadily.

"Somehow I fancy it will not be a long one."

Peyrol never checked the to-and-fro movement of his brush, but it was with an effort. The fact was that he had discovered in himself a distinct reluctance to go away from the Escampobar Farm. His desire to have something of his own that could float was no longer associated with any desire to wander. The cripple was right. The voyage of the renovated tartane would not take her very far. What was surprising was the fellow being so very positive about it. He seemed able to read people's thoughts.

The dragging of the renovated tartane into the water was a great affair. Everybody in the hamlet, including the women, did a full day's work and there was never so much coin passed from hand to hand in the hamlet in all the days of its obscure history. Swinging between his crutches on a low sand-ridge the cripple surveyed the whole of the beach. It was he that had persuaded the villagers to lend a hand and had arranged the terms for their assistance. It was he also who through a very miserable-looking pedlar (the only one who frequented the peninsula) had got in touch with some rich persons in Fréjus who had changed for Peyrol a few of his gold pieces for current money. He had expedited the course of the most exciting and interesting experience of his life, and now planted on the sand on his two sticks in the manner of a beacon he watched the last operation. The rover, as if about to launch himself upon a track of a thousand miles, walked up to shake hands with him and look once more at the soft eyes and the ironic smile.

"There is no denying it—you are a man."

"Don't talk like this to me, *citoyen*," said the cripple in a trembling voice. Till then, suspended between his two sticks and with his shoulders as high as his ears, he had not looked towards the approaching Peyrol. "This is too much of a compliment!"

"I tell you," insisted the rover roughly, and as if the insignificance of mortal envelopes had presented itself to him for the first time at the end of his roving life, "I tell you that there is that in you which would make a chum one would like to have alongside one in a tight place."

As he went away from the cripple towards the tartane, while the whole population of the hamlet disposed around her waited for his word, some on land and some waist-deep in the water holding ropes in their hands, Peyrol had a slight shudder at the thought: "Suppose I had been born like that." Ever since he had put his foot on his native land such thoughts had haunted him. They would have been impossible anywhere else. He could not have been like any blackamoor, good, bad, or indifferent, hale or crippled, king or slave; but here, on this southern shore that had called to him irresistibly as he had approached the Strait of Gibraltar on what he had felt to be his last voyage, any woman, lean and old enough, might have been his mother; he might have been any Frenchman of them all, even one of those he pitied, even one of those he despised. He felt the grip of his origins from the crown of his head to the soles of his feet while he clambered on board the tartane as if for a long and distant voyage. As a matter of fact he knew very well that with a bit of luck it would be over in about an hour. When the tartane took the water the feeling of being afloat plucked at his very heart. Some Madrague fishermen had been persuaded by the cripple to help old Peyrol to sail the tartane round to the cove below the Escampobar Farm. A glorious sun shone upon that short passage and the cove itself was full of sparkling light when they arrived. The few Escampobar goats wandering on the hillside pretending to feed where no grass was visible to the naked eye never even raised their heads. A gentle breeze drove the tartane, as fresh as paint could make her, opposite a narrow crack in the cliff which gave admittance to a tiny basin, no bigger than a village pond, concealed at the foot of the southern hill. It was there that old Peyrol, aided by the Madrague men, who had their boat with them, towed his ship, the first really that he ever owned.

Once in, the tartane nearly filled the little basin, and the fishermen, getting into their boat, rowed away for home. Peyrol, by spending the afternoon in dragging ropes ashore and fastening them to various boulders and dwarf trees, moored her to his complete satisfaction. She was as safe from the tempests there as a house ashore.

After he had made everything fast on board and had furled

the sails neatly, a matter of some time for one man, Peyrol contemplated his arrangements which savoured of rest much more than of
wandering, and found them good. Though he never meant to
abandon his room at the farmhouse he felt that his true home was in
the tartane, and he rejoiced at the idea that it was concealed from all
eyes except perhaps the eyes of the goats when their arduous feeding
took them on the southern slope. He lingered on board, he even threw
open the sliding door of the little cabin, which now smelt of fresh
paint, not of stale blood. Before he started for the farm the sun had
travelled far beyond Spain and all the sky to the west was yellow,
while on the side of Italy it presented a sombre canopy pierced here
and there with the light of stars. Catherine put a plate on the table, but
nobody asked him any questions.

He spent a lot of his time on board, going down early, coming up at
midday *"pour manger la soupe,"* and sleeping on board almost every
night. He did not like to leave the tartane alone for so many hours.
Often, having climbed a little way up to the house, he would turn
round for a last look at her in the gathering dusk, and actually would
go back again. After Michel had been enlisted for a crew and had
taken his abode on board for good, Peyrol found it a much easier
matter to spend his nights in the lantern-like room at the top of the
farmhouse.

Often waking up at night he would get up to look at the starry sky
out of all his three windows in succession, and think: "Now there is
nothing in the world to prevent me getting out to sea in less than an
hour." As a matter of fact it was possible for two men to manage the
tartane. Thus Peyrol's thought was comfortingly true in every way,
for he loved to feel himself free, and Michel of the lagoon, after the
death of his depressed dog, had no tie on earth. It was a fine thought
which somehow made it quite easy for Peyrol to go back to his four-
poster and resume his slumbers.

CHAPTER VIII

~

PERCHED SIDEWAYS ON the circular wall bordering the well, in the full blaze of the midday sun, the rover of the distant seas and the fisherman of the lagoon, sharing between them a most surprising secret, had the air of two men conferring in the dark. The first word that Peyrol said was, "Well?"

"All quiet," said the other.

"Have you fastened the cabin door properly?"

"You know what the fastenings are like."

Peyrol could not deny that. It was a sufficient answer. It shifted the responsibility on to his shoulders and all his life he had been accustomed to trust to the work of his own hands, in peace and in war. Yet he looked doubtfully at Michel before he remarked:

"Yes, but I know the man, too."

There could be no greater contrast than those two faces: Peyrol's clean, like a carving of stone, and only very little softened by time, and that of the owner of the late dog, hirsute, with many silver threads, with something elusive in the features and the vagueness of expression of a baby in arms. "Yes, I know the man," repeated Peyrol. Michel's mouth fell open at this, a small oval set a little crookedly in the innocent face.

"He will never wake," he suggested timidly.

The possession of a common and momentous secret drawing men together, Peyrol condescended to explain.

"You don't know the thickness of his skull. I do."

He spoke as though he had made it himself. Michel, who in the face of that positive statement had forgotten to shut his mouth, had nothing to say.

"He breathes all right?" asked Peyrol.

"Yes. After I got out and locked the door I listened for a bit and I thought I heard him snore."

Peyrol looked interested and also slightly anxious.

"I had to come up and show myself this morning as if nothing had happened," he said. "The officer has been here for two days and he might have taken it into his head to go down to the tartane. I have been on the stretch all the morning. A goat jumping up was enough to give me a turn. Fancy him running up here with his broken head all bandaged up, with you after him."

This seemed to be too much for Michel. He said almost indignantly:

"The man's half killed."

"It takes a lot to even half kill a Brother of the Coast. There are men and men. You, for instance," Peyrol continued placidly, "you would have been altogether killed if it had been your head that got in the way. And there are animals, beasts twice your size, regular monsters, that may be killed with nothing more than just a tap on the nose. That's well known. I was really afraid he would overcome you in some way or other. . . ."

"Come, *maître*! One isn't a little child," protested Michel against this accumulation of improbabilities. He did it, however, only in a whisper and with childlike shyness. Peyrol folded his arms on his breast:

"Go, finish your soup," he commanded in a low voice, "and then go down to the tartane. You locked the cabin door properly, you said?"

"Yes, I have," protested Michel, staggered by this display of anxiety. "He could sooner burst the deck above his head, as you know."

"All the same, take a small spar and shore up that door against the heel of the mast. And then watch outside. Don't you go in to him on any account. Stay on deck and keep a lookout for me. There is a tangle here that won't be easily cleared and I must be very careful. I will try to slip away and get down as soon as I get rid of that officer."

The conference in the sunshine being ended, Peyrol walked leisurely out of the yard gate, and protruding his head beyond the corner of the house, saw Lieutenant Réal sitting on the bench. This he had expected to see. But he had not expected to see him there alone. It was just like this: wherever Arlette happened to be, there were worrying possibilities. But she might have been helping her aunt in the kitchen with her sleeves rolled up on such white arms as Peyrol had never seen on any woman before. The way she had taken to dressing her hair in a plait with a broad black velvet ribbon and an Arlesian cap was very becoming. She was wearing now her mother's clothes of which there were chestfuls, altered for her of course. The late mistress of the Escampobar Farm had been an Arlésienne. Well-to-do, too. Yes, even for women's clothes the Escampobar natives could do without intercourse with the outer world. It was quite time that this confounded lieutenant went back to Toulon. This was the third day. His short leave must be up. Peyrol's attitude towards naval officers had been always guarded and suspicious. His relations with them had been very mixed. They had been his enemies and his superiors. He had been chased by them. He had been trusted by them. The Revolution had made a clean cut across the consistency of his wild life— Brother of the Coast and gunner in the national navy—and yet he was always the same man. It was like that, too, with them. Officers of the King, officers of the Republic, it was only changing the skin. All alike looked askance at a free rover. Even this one could not forget his epaulettes when talking to him. Scorn and mistrust of epaulettes were rooted deeply in old Peyrol. Yet he did not absolutely hate Lieutenant Réal. Only the fellow's coming to the farm was generally a curse and his presence at that particular moment a confounded nuisance and to a certain extent even a danger. "I have no mind to be hauled to Toulon by the scruff of my neck," Peyrol said to himself. There was no trusting those epaulette-wearers. Any one of them was capable of jumping on his best friend on account of some officerlike notion or other.

Peyrol, stepping round the corner, sat down by the side of Lieutenant Réal with the feeling somehow of coming to grips with a slippery customer. The lieutenant, as he sat there, unaware of Peyrol's survey of his person, gave no notion of slipperiness. On the contrary, he looked rather immovably established. Very much at home. Too much at home. Even after Peyrol sat down by his side he continued to look immovable—or at least difficult to get rid of. In the still noonday heat the faint shrilling of cicadas was the only sound of life heard for quite a long time. Delicate, evanescent, cheerful, careless sort of life, yet not without passion. A sudden gloom seemed to be cast over the joy of the cicadas by the lieutenant's voice though the words were the most perfunctory possible.

"*Tiens! Vous voilà.*"

In the stress of the situation Peyrol at once asked himself: "Now why does he say that? Where did he expect me to be?" The lieutenant need not have spoken at all. He had known him now for about two years off and on, and it had happened many times that they had sat side by side on that bench in a sort of "at arm's length" equality without exchanging a single word. And why could he not have kept quiet now? That naval officer never spoke without an object, but what could one make of words like that? Peyrol achieved an insincere yawn and suggested mildly:

"A bit of siesta wouldn't be amiss. What do you think, Lieutenant?"

And to himself he thought: "No fear, he won't go to his room." He would stay there and thereby keep him, Peyrol, from going down to the cove. He turned his eyes on that naval officer, and if extreme and concentrated desire and mere force of will could have had any effect Lieutenant Réal would certainly have been removed suddenly from that bench. But he didn't move. And Peyrol was astonished to see that man smile, but what astonished him still more was to hear him say:

"The trouble is that you have never been frank with me, Peyrol."

"Frank with you," repeated the rover. "You want me to be frank with you? Well, I have wished you to the devil many times."

"That's better," said Lieutenant Réal. "But why? I never tried to do you any harm."

"Me harm," cried Peyrol, "to me . . . ?" But he faltered in his indignation as if frightened at it and ended in a very quiet tone: "You have been nosing in a lot of dirty papers to find something against a man who was not doing *you* any harm and was a seaman before you were born."

"Quite a mistake. There was no nosing amongst papers. I came on them quite by accident. I won't deny I was *intrigué* finding a man of your sort living in this place. But don't be uneasy. Nobody would trouble his head about you. It's a long time since you have been forgotten. Have no fear."

"You! You talk to me of fear . . . ? No," cried the rover, "it's enough to turn a fellow into a sans-culotte if it weren't for the sight of that specimen sneaking around here."

The lieutenant turned his head sharply, and for a moment the naval officer and the free sea-rover looked at each other gloomily. When Peyrol spoke again he had changed his mood.

"Why should I fear anybody? I owe nothing to anybody. I have given them up the prize ship in order and everything else, except my luck; and for that I account to nobody," he added darkly.

"I don't know what you are driving at," the lieutenant said after a moment of thought. "All I know is that you seem to have given up your share of the prize money. There is no record of you ever claiming it."

Peyrol did not like the sarcastic tone. "You have a nasty tongue," he said, "with your damned trick of talking as if you were made of different clay."

"No offence," said the lieutenant, grave but a little puzzled. "Nobody will drag out that against you. It has been paid years ago to the Invalides' fund. All this is buried and forgotten."

Peyrol was grumbling and swearing to himself with such concentration that the lieutenant stopped and waited till he had finished.

"And there is no record of desertion or anything like that," he continued then. "You stand there as *disparu*. I believe that after searching for you a little they came to the conclusion that you had come by your death somehow or other."

"Did they? Well perhaps old Peyrol is dead. At any rate he has buried himself here." The rover suffered from great instability of feelings for he passed in a flash from melancholy into fierceness. "And he was quiet enough till you came sniffing around this hole. More than once in my life I had occasion to wonder how soon the jackals would have a chance to dig up my carcass; but to have a naval officer come scratching round here was the last thing. . . ." Again a change came over him. "What can you want here?" he whispered, suddenly depressed.

The lieutenant fell into the humour of that discourse. "I don't want to disturb the dead," he said, turning full to the rover who after his last words had fixed his eyes on the ground. "I want to talk to the gunner Peyrol."

Peyrol, without raising his eyes from the ground, growled: "He isn't here. He is *disparu*. Go and look at the papers again. Vanished. Nobody here."

"That," said Lieutenant Réal, in a conversational tone, "that is a lie. He was talking to me this morning on the hillside as we were looking at the English ship. He knows all about her. He told me he spent nights making plans for her capture. He seemed to be a fellow with his heart in the right place. *Un homme de cœur.* You know him."

Peyrol raised his big head slowly and looked at the lieutenant.

"Humph," he grunted. A heavy, noncommittal grunt. His old heart was stirred, but the tangle was such that he had to be on his guard with any man who wore epaulettes. His profile preserved the immobility of a head struck on a medal while he listened to the lieutenant assuring him that this time he had come to Escampobar on purpose to speak with the gunner Peyrol. That he had not done so before was because it was a very confidential matter. At this point the lieutenant stopped and Peyrol made no sign. Inwardly he was asking himself what the lieutenant was driving at. But the lieutenant seemed to have shifted his ground. His tone, too, was slightly different. More practical.

"You say you have made a study of that English ship's movements. Well, for instance, suppose a breeze springs up, as it very likely will towards the evening, could you tell me where she will be to-night? I mean, what her captain is likely to do."

"No, I couldn't," said Peyrol.

"But you said you have been observing him minutely for weeks. There aren't so many alternatives, and taking the weather and everything into consideration, you can judge almost with certainty."

"No," said Peyrol again. "It so happens that I can't."

"Can't you? Then you are worse than any of the old admirals that you think so little of. Why can't you?"

"I will tell you why," said Peyrol after a pause and with a face more like a carving than ever. "It's because the fellow has never come so far this way before. Therefore I don't know what he has got in his mind, and in consequence I can't guess what he will do next. I may be able to tell you some other day but not to-day. Next time when you come . . . to see the old gunner."

"No, it must be this time."

"Do you mean you are going to stay here to-night?"

"Did you think I was here on leave? I tell you I am on service. Don't you believe me?"

Peyrol let out a heavy sigh. "Yes, I believe you. And so they are thinking of catching her alive. And you are sent on service. Well, that doesn't make it any easier for me to see you here."

"You are a strange man, Peyrol," said the lieutenant. "I believe you wish me dead."

"No. Only out of this. But you are right, Peyrol is no friend either to your face or to your voice. They have done harm enough already."

They had never attained to such intimate terms before. There was no need for them to look at each other. The lieutenant thought: "Ah! He can't keep his jealousy in." There was no scorn or malice in that thought. It was much more like despair. He said mildly:

"You snarl like an old dog, Peyrol."

"I have felt sometimes as if I could fly at your throat," said Peyrol in a sort of calm whisper. "And it amuses you the more."

"Amuses me? Do I look light-hearted?"

Again Peyrol turned his head slowly for a long, steady stare. And again the naval officer and the rover gazed at each other with a searching and sombre frankness. This new-born intimacy could go no further.

"Listen to me, Peyrol. . . ."

"No," said the other. "If you want to talk, talk to the gunner."

Though he seemed to have adopted the notion of a double personality the rover did not seem to be much easier in one character than in the other. Furrows of perplexity appeared on his brow, and as the lieutenant did not speak at once Peyrol the gunner asked impatiently:

"So they are thinking of catching her alive?" It did not please him to hear the lieutenant say that it was not exactly this that the chiefs in Toulon had in their minds. Peyrol at once expressed the opinion that of all the naval chiefs that ever were, Citizen Renaud was the only one that was worth anything. Lieutenant Réal, disregarding the challenging tone, kept to the point.

"What they want to know is whether that English corvette interferes much with the coast traffic."

"No, she doesn't," said Peyrol; "she leaves poor people alone, unless, I suppose, some craft acts suspiciously. I have seen her give chase to one or two. But even those she did not detain. Michel—you know Michel—has heard from the mainland people that she has captured several at various times. Of course, strictly speaking, nobody is safe."

"Well, no. I wonder now what that Englishman would call 'acting suspiciously.' "

"Ah, now you are asking something. Don't you know what an Englishman is? One day easy and casual, next day ready to pounce on you like a tiger. Hard in the morning, careless in the afternoon, and only reliable in a fight, whether with or against you, but for the rest perfectly fantastic. You might think a little touched in the head, and there again it would not do to trust to that notion either."

The lieutenant lending an attentive ear, Peyrol smoothed his brow and discoursed with gusto of Englishmen as if they had been a strange, very little-known tribe. "In a manner of speaking," he concluded, "the oldest bird of them all can be caught with chaff, but not every day." He shook his head, smiling to himself faintly as if remembering a quaint passage or two.

"You didn't get all that knowledge of the English while you were a gunner," observed the lieutenant dryly.

"There you go again," said Peyrol. "And what's that to you where I learned it all? Suppose I learned it all from a man who is dead now. Put it down to that."

"I see. It amounts to this, that one can't get at the back of their minds very easily."

"No," said Peyrol, then added grumpily, "and some Frenchmen are not much better. I wish I could get at the back of your mind."

"You would find a service matter there, gunner, that's what you would find there, and a matter that seems nothing much at first sight, but when you look into it, is about as difficult to manage properly as anything you ever undertook in your life. It puzzled all the big-wigs. It must have, since I was called in. Of course I work on shore at the Admiralty and I was in the way. They showed me the order from Paris and I could see at once the difficulty of it. I pointed it out and I was told. . . ."

"To come here," struck in Peyrol.

"No. To make arrangements to carry it out."

"And you began by coming here. You are always coming here."

"I began by looking for a man," said the naval officer with emphasis.

Peyrol looked at him searchingly. "Do you mean to say that in the whole fleet you couldn't have found a man?"

"I never attempted to look for one there. My chief agreed with me that it isn't a service for navy men."

"Well, it must be something nasty for a naval man to admit that much. What is the order? I don't suppose you came over here without being ready to show it to me."

The lieutenant plunged his hand into the inside pocket of his naval jacket and then brought it out empty.

"Understand, Peyrol," he said earnestly, "this is not a service of fighting. Good men are plentiful for that. The object is to play the enemy a trick."

"Trick?" said Peyrol in a judicial tone, "that's all right. I have seen in the Indian Seas Monsieur Surcouf play tricks on the English . . . seen them with my own eyes, deceptions, disguises, and suchlike. . . . That's quite sound in war."

"Certainly. The order for this one comes from the first consul himself, for it is no small matter. It's to deceive the English admiral."

"What—that Nelson? Ah! but he is a cunning one."

After expressing that opinion the old rover pulled out a red bandana handkerchief and after rubbing his face with it repeated his opinion deliberately: *"Celui-là est un malin."*

This time the lieutenant really brought out a paper from his pocket and saying, "I have copied the order for you to see," handed it to the rover, who took it from him with a doubtful air.

Lieutenant Réal watched old Peyrol handling it at arm's length, then with his arm bent trying to adjust the distance to his eyesight, and wondered whether he had copied it in a hand big enough to be read easily by the gunner Peyrol. The order ran like this: "You will make up a packet of dispatches and pretended private letters as if from officers, containing a clear statement besides hints calculated to convince the enemy that the destination of the fleet now fitting in Toulon is for Egypt and generally for the East. That packet you will send by sea in some small craft to Naples, taking care that the vessel shall fall into the enemy's hands." The Préfet Maritime had called Réal, had shown him the paragraph of the letter from Paris, had turned the page over and laid his finger on the signature, "Bonaparte." Then after giving him a meaning glance, the admiral locked up the paper in a drawer and put the key in his pocket. Lieutenant Réal had written the passage down from memory directly the notion of consulting Peyrol had occurred to him.

The rover, screwing his eyes and pursing his lips, had come to the end of it. The lieutenant extended his hand negligently and took the paper away: "Well, what do you think?" he asked. "You understand that there can be no question of any ship of war being sacrificed to that dodge. What do you think of it?"

"Easier said than done," opined Peyrol curtly.

"That's what I told my admiral."

"Is he a lubber, so that you had to explain it to him?"

"No, gunner, he is not. He listened to me, nodding his head."

"And what did he say when you finished?"

"He said: '*Parfaitement*. Have you got any ideas about it?' And I said—listen to me, gunner—I said: '*Oui, Amiral*, I think I've got a man,' and the admiral interrupted me at once: 'All right, you don't want to talk to me about him. I put you in charge of that affair and give you a week to arrange it. When it's done report to me. Meantime you may just as well take this packet.' They were already prepared, Peyrol, all those faked letters and dispatches. I carried it out of the admiral's room, a parcel done up in sail-cloth, properly corded and sealed. I have had it in my possession for three days. It's upstairs in my valise."

"That doesn't advance you very much," growled old Peyrol.

"No," admitted the lieutenant. "I can also dispose of a few thousand francs."

"Francs," repeated Peyrol. "Well, you had better get back to Toulon and try to bribe some man to put his head into the jaws of the English lion."

Réal reflected, then said slowly, "I wouldn't tell any man that. Of course a service of danger, that would be understood."

"It would be. And if you could get a fellow with some sense in his caboche, he would naturally try to slip past the English fleet and maybe do it, too. And then where's your trick?"

"We could give him a course to steer."

"Yes. And it may happen that your course would just take him clear of all Nelson's fleet, for you never can tell what the English are doing. They might be watering in Sardinia."

"Some cruisers are sure to be out and pick him up."

"Maybe. But that's not doing the job, that's taking a chance. Do you think you are talking to a toothless baby—or what?"

"No, my gunner. It will take a strong man's teeth to undo that knot." A moment of silence followed. Then Peyrol assumed a dogmatic tone.

"I will tell you what it is, Lieutenant. This seems to me just the sort of order that a landlubber would give to good seamen. You daren't deny that."

"I don't deny it," the lieutenant admitted. "And look at the whole difficulty. For supposing even that the tartane blunders right into the English fleet, as if it had been indeed arranged, they would just look into her hold or perhaps poke their noses here and there, but it would never occur to them to search for dispatches, would it? Our man, of course, would have them well hidden, wouldn't he? He is not to know. And if he were ass enough to leave them lying about the decks the English would at once smell a rat there. But what I think he would do would be to throw the dispatches overboard."

"Yes—unless he is told the nature of the job," said Peyrol.

"Evidently. But where's the bribe big enough to induce a man to taste of the English pontoons?"

"The man will take the bribe all right and then will do his best not to be caught; and if he can't avoid that, he will take jolly good care that the English should find nothing on board his tartane. Oh no, Lieutenant, any damn scallywag that owns a tartane will take a couple of thousand francs from your hand as tame as can be; but as to deceiving the English admiral, it's the very devil of an affair. Didn't you think of all that before you spoke to the big epaulettes that gave you the job?"

"I did see it, and I put it all before him," the lieutenant said, lowering his voice still more, for their conversation had been carried on in undertones though the house behind them was silent and solitude reigned round the approaches of Escampobar Farm. It was the hour of siesta—for those that could sleep. The lieutenant, edging closer towards the old man, almost breathed the words in his ear.

"What I wanted was to hear you say all those things. Do you understand now what I meant this morning on the lookout? Don't you remember what I said?"

Peyrol, gazing into space, spoke in a level murmur.

"I remember a naval officer trying to shake old Peyrol off his feet and not managing to do it. I may be *disparu* but I am too solid yet for any *blanc-bec* that loses his temper, devil only knows why. And it's a good thing that you didn't manage it, else I would have taken you down with me, and we would have made our last somersault together for the amusement of an English ship's company. A pretty end that!"

"Don't you remember me saying, when you mentioned that the English would have sent a boat to go through our pockets, that this would have been the perfect way?" In his stony immobility with the other man leaning towards his ear, Peyrol seemed a mere insensible receptacle for whispers, and the lieutenant went on forcibly: "Well, it was in allusion to this affair, for, look here, gunner, what could be more convincing, if they had found the packet of dispatches on me! What would have been their surprise, their wonder! Not the slightest doubt could enter their heads. Could it, gunner? Of course it couldn't. I can imagine the captain of that corvette crowding sail on her to get this packet into the admiral's hands. The secret of the Toulon fleet's destination found on the body of a dead officer. Wouldn't they have exulted at their enormous piece of luck! But they wouldn't have called it accidental. Oh, no! They would have called it providential. I know the English a little, too. They like to have God on their side—the only ally they never need pay a subsidy to. Come, gunner, would it not have been a perfect way?"

Lieutenant Réal threw himself back and Peyrol, still like a carven image of grim dreaminess, growled softly:

"Time yet. The English ship is still in the Passe." He waited a little in his uncanny living-statue manner before he added viciously: "You don't seem in a hurry to go and take that leap."

"Upon my word, I am almost sick enough of life to do it," the lieutenant said in a conversational tone.

"Well, don't forget to run upstairs and take that packet with you before you go," said Peyrol as before. "But don't wait for me; I am not sick of life. I am *disparu*, and that's good enough. There's no need for me to die."

And at last he moved in his seat, swung his head from side to side as if to make sure that his neck had not been turned to stone, emitted a short laugh, and grumbled: "*Disparu! Hein!* Well, I am damned!" as if the word "vanished" had been a gross insult to enter against a man's name in a register. It seemed to rankle, as Lieutenant Réal observed with some surprise; or else it was something inarticulate that rankled, manifesting itself in that funny way. The lieutenant, too, had a moment of anger which flamed and went out at once in the deadly cold philosophic reflection: "We are victims of the destiny which has brought us together." Then again his resentment flamed. Why should he have stumbled against that girl or that woman, he didn't know how he must think of her, and suffer so horribly for it? He who had endeavoured almost from a boy to destroy all the softer feelings within himself. His changing moods of distaste, of wonder at himself and at the unexpected turns of life, wore the aspect of profound abstraction from which he was recalled by an outburst of Peyrol's, not loud but fierce enough.

"No," cried Peyrol, "I am too old to break my bones for the sake of a lubberly soldier in Paris who fancies he has invented something clever."

"I don't ask you to," the lieutenant said, with extreme severity, in what Peyrol would call an epaulette-wearer's voice. "You old sea-bandit. And it wouldn't be for the sake of a soldier anyhow. You and I are Frenchmen after all."

"You have discovered that, have you?"

"Yes," said Réal. "This morning, listening to your talk on the hill-side with that English corvette within one might say a stone's throw."

"Yes," groaned Peyrol. "A French-built ship!" He struck his breast a resounding blow. "It hurts one there to see her. It seemed to me I could jump down on her deck single-handed."

"Yes, there you and I understood each other," said the lieutenant. "But look here, this affair is a much bigger thing than getting back a captured corvette. In reality it is much more than merely playing a trick on an admiral. It's a part of a deep plan, Peyrol! It's another stroke to help us on the way towards a great victory at sea."

"Us!" said Peyrol. "I am a sea-bandit and you are a sea-officer. What do you mean by us?"

"I mean all Frenchmen," said the lieutenant. "Or, let us say simply France, which you too have served."

Peyrol, whose stone-effigy bearing had become humanized almost against his will, gave an appreciative nod, and said: "You've got something in your mind. Now what is it? If you will trust a sea-bandit."

"No, I will trust a gunner of the Republic. It occurred to me that for this great affair we could make use of this corvette that you have been observing so long. For to count on the capture of any old tartane by the fleet in a way that would not arouse suspicion is no use."

"A lubberly notion," assented Peyrol, with more heartiness than he had ever displayed towards Lieutenant Réal.

"Yes, but there's that corvette. Couldn't something be arranged to make them swallow the whole thing, somehow, some way? You laugh . . . Why?"

"I laugh because it would be a great joke," said Peyrol, whose hilarity was very short-lived. "That fellow on board, he thinks himself very clever. I never set my eyes on him, but I used to feel that I knew him as if he were my own brother; but now . . ."

He stopped short. Lieutenant Réal, after observing the sudden change on his countenance, said in an impressive manner:

"I think you have just had an idea."

"Not the slightest," said Peyrol, turning suddenly into stone as if by enchantment. The lieutenant did not feel discouraged and he was not surprised to hear the effigy of Peyrol pronounce: "All the same one could see." Then very abruptly: "You meant to stay here to-night?"

"Yes. I will only go down to Madrague and leave word with the sailing barge which was to come to-day from Toulon to go back without me."

"No, Lieutenant. You must return to Toulon to-day. When you get there you must turn out some of those damned quill-drivers at the Port Office if it were midnight and have papers made out for a tartane—oh, any name you like. Some sort of papers. And then you must come back as soon as you can. Why not go down to Madrague now and see whether the barge isn't already there? If she is, then by starting at once you may get back here some time about midnight."

He got up impetuously and the lieutenant stood up too. Hesitation was imprinted on his whole attitude. Peyrol's aspect was not animated, but his Roman face with its severe aspect gave him a great air of authority.

"Won't you tell me something more?" asked the lieutenant.

"No," said the rover. "Not till we meet again. If you return during the night don't you try to get into the house. Wait outside. Don't rouse anybody. I will be about, and if there is anything to say I will say it to you then. What are you looking about you for? You don't want to go up for your valise. Your pistols up in your room, too? What do you want with pistols, only to go to Toulon and back with a naval boat's crew?" He actually laid his hand on the lieutenant's shoulder and impelled him gently towards the track leading to Madrague. Réal turned his head at the touch and their eyes met with the strained closeness of a wrestler's hug. It was the lieutenant who gave way before the unflinchingly direct stare of the old Brother of the Coast. He gave way under the cover of a sarcastic smile and a very airy, "I see

you want me out of the way for some reason or other," which produced not the slightest effect upon Peyrol, who stood with his arm
pointing towards Madrague. When the lieutenant turned his back on
him Peyrol's pointing arm fell down by his side; but he watched the
lieutenant out of sight before he turned too and moved in a contrary
direction.

CHAPTER IX

O N LOSING SIGHT of the perplexed lieutenant, Peyrol discovered that his own mind was a perfect blank. He started
to get down to his tartane after one sidelong look at the face
of the house which contained quite a different problem. Let that wait.
His head feeling strangely empty, he felt the pressing necessity of fur-
nishing it with some thought without loss of time. He scrambled
down steep places, caught at bushes, stepped from stone to stone,
with the assurance of long practice, with mechanical precision and
without for a moment relaxing his efforts to capture some definite
scheme which he could put into his head. To his right the cove lay full
of pale light, while the rest of the Mediterranean extended beyond it
in a dark, unruffled blue. Peyrol was making for the little basin where
his tartane had been hidden for years, like a jewel in a casket meant
only for the secret rejoicing of his eye, of no more practical use than a
miser's hoard—and as precious! Coming upon a hollow in the ground
where grew a few bushes and even a few blades of grass, Peyrol sat
down to rest. In that position his visible world was limited to a stony
slope, a few boulders, the bush against which he leaned and the vista
of a piece of empty sea-horizon. He perceived that he detested that
lieutenant much more when he didn't see him. There was something
in the fellow. Well, at any rate he had got rid of him for say eight or ten
hours. An uneasiness came over the old rover, a sense of the endan-
gered stability of things, which was anything but welcome. He won-

dered at it and the thought "I am growing old," intruded on him again. And yet he was aware of his sturdy body. He could still creep stealthily like an Indian and with his trusty cudgel knock a man over with a certain aim at the back of his head, and with force enough to fell him like a bullock. He had done that thing no further back than two o'clock the night before, not twelve hours ago, as easy as easy and without an undue sense of exertion. This fact cheered him up. But still he could not find an idea for his head. Not what one could call a real idea. It wouldn't come. It was no use sitting there.

He got up and after a few strides came to a stony ridge from which he could see the two white blunt mastheads of his tartane. Her hull was hidden from him by the formation of the shore, in which the most prominent feature was a big flat piece of rock. That was the spot on which not twelve hours before Peyrol, unable to rest in his bed and coming to seek sleep in his tartane, had seen by moonlight a man standing above his vessel and looking down at her, a characteristic forked black shape that certainly had no business to be there. Peyrol, by a sudden and logical deduction, had said to himself: "Landed from an English boat." Why, how, wherefore, he did not stay to consider. He acted at once like a man accustomed for many years to meet emergencies of the most unexpected kind. The dark figure, lost in a sort of attentive amazement, heard nothing, suspected nothing. The impact of the thick end of the cudgel came down on its head like a thunderbolt from the blue. The sides of the little basin echoed the crash. But he could not have heard it. The force of the blow flung the senseless body over the edge of the flat rock and down headlong into the open hold of the tartane, which received it with the sound of a muffled drum. Peyrol could not have done the job better at the age of twenty. No. Not so well. There was swiftness, mature judgment—and the sound of the muffled drum was followed by a perfect silence, without a sigh, without a moan. Peyrol ran round a little promontory to where the shore shelved down to the level of the tartane's rail and got on board. And still the silence remained perfect in the cold moonlight and amongst the deep shadows of the rocks. It remained perfect because Michel, who always slept under the half-deck forward, being wakened by the thump which had made the whole tartane tremble, had lost the power of speech. With his head just protruding from under the half-deck, arrested on all fours and shivering violently like a dog that had been washed with hot water, he was kept from advancing further by his terror of this bewitched corpse that had come on board flying through the air. He would not have touched it for anything.

The "You there, Michel," pronounced in an undertone, acted like a moral tonic. This then was not the doing of the Evil One; it was no sorcery! And even if it had been, now that Peyrol was there, Michel had lost all fear. He ventured not a single question while he helped Peyrol to turn over the limp body. Its face was covered with blood from the cut on the forehead which it had got by striking the sharp edge of the keelson. What accounted for the head not being completely smashed and for no limbs being broken was the fact that on its way through the air the victim of undue curiosity had come in contact with and had snapped like a carrot one of the foremast shrouds. Raising his eyes casually Peyrol noticed the broken rope, and at once put his hand on the man's breast.

"His heart beats yet," he murmured. "Go and light the cabin lamp, Michel."

"You going to take that thing into the cabin?"

"Yes," said Peyrol. "The cabin is used to that kind of thing," and suddenly he felt very bitter. "It has been a death-trap for better people than this fellow, whoever he is."

While Michel was away executing that order Peyrol's eyes roamed all over the shores of the basin, for he could not divest himself of the idea that there must be more Englishmen dodging about. That one of the corvette's boats was still in the cove he had not the slightest doubt. As to the motive of her coming, it was incomprehensible. Only that senseless form lying at his feet could perhaps have told him: but Peyrol had little hope that it would ever speak again. If his friends started to look for their shipmate there was just a bare chance that they would not discover the existence of the basin. Peyrol stooped and felt the body all over. He found no weapon of any kind on it. There was only a common clasp-knife on a lanyard round its neck.

That soul of obedience, Michel, returning from aft, was directed to throw a couple of bucketfuls of salt water upon the bloody head with its face upturned to the moon. The lowering of the body down into the cabin was a matter of some little difficulty. It was heavy. They laid it full length on a locker and after Michel with a strange tidiness had arranged its arms along its sides it looked incredibly rigid. The dripping head with soaked hair was like the head of a drowned man with a gaping pink gash on the forehead.

"Go on deck to keep a lookout," said Peyrol. "We may have to fight yet before the night's out."

After Michel left him Peyrol began by flinging off his jacket and, without a pause, dragging his shirt off over his head. It was a very fine shirt. The Brothers of the Coast in their hours of ease were by no means a ragged crowd, and Peyrol the gunner had preserved a taste for fine linen. He tore the shirt into long strips, sat down on the locker and took the wet head on his knees. He bandaged it with some skill, working as calmly as though he had been practising on a dummy. Then the experienced Peyrol sought the lifeless hand and felt the pulse. The spirit had not fled yet. The rover, stripped to the waist, his powerful arms folded on the grizzled pelt of his bare breast, sat gazing down at the inert face in his lap with the eyes closed peacefully under the white band covering the forehead. He contemplated the heavy jaw combined oddly with a certain roundness of cheek, the noticeably broad nose with a sharp tip and a faint dent across the bridge, either natural or the result of some old injury. A face of brown clay, roughly modelled, with a lot of black eyelashes stuck on the closed lids and looking artificially youthful on that physiognomy forty years old or more. And Peyrol thought of his youth. Not his own youth; that he was never anxious to recapture. It was of that man's youth that he thought, of how that face had looked twenty years ago. Suddenly he shifted his position, and putting his lips to the ear of that inanimate head, yelled with all the force of his lungs:

"Hullo! Hullo! Wake up, shipmate!"

It seemed enough to wake up the dead. A faint *"Voilà! Voilà!"* was the answer from a distance, and presently Michel put his head into the cabin with an anxious grin and a gleam in the round eyes.

"You called, *maître?*"

"Yes," said Peyrol. "Come along and help me to shift him."

"Overboard?" murmured Michel readily.

"No," said Peyrol, "into that bunk. Steady! Don't bang his head," he cried with unexpected tenderness. "Throw a blanket over him. Stay in the cabin and keep his bandages wetted with salt water. I don't think anybody will trouble you to-night. I am going to the house."

"The day is not very far off," remarked Michel.

This was one reason the more why Peyrol was in a hurry to get back to the house and steal up to his room unseen. He drew on his jacket over his bare skin, picked up his cudgel, recommended Michel not to let that strange bird get out of the cabin on any account. As Michel was convinced that the man would never walk again in his life, he received those instructions without particular emotion.

The dawn had broken some time before Peyrol, on his way up to Escampobar, happened to look round and had the luck to actually see with his own eyes the English man-of-war's boat pulling out of the cove. This confirmed his surmises but did not enlighten him a bit as to the causes. Puzzled and uneasy, he approached the house through the farmyard. Catherine, always the first up, stood at the open kitchen door. She moved aside and would have let him pass without remark, if Peyrol himself had not asked in a whisper: "Anything new?" She answered him in the same tone: "She has taken to roaming at night." Peyrol stole silently up to his bedroom, from which he descended an hour later as though he had spent all the night in his bed up there.

It was this nocturnal adventure which had affected the character of Peyrol's forenoon talk with the lieutenant. What with one thing and another he found it very trying. Now that he had got rid of Réal for several hours, the rover had to turn his attention to that other invader of the strained, questionable, and ominous in its origins, peace of the Escampobar Farm. As he sat on the flat rock with his eyes fixed idly on the few drops of blood betraying his last night's work to the high heaven, and trying to get hold of something definite that he could think about, Peyrol became aware of a faint thundering noise. Faint as it was it filled the whole basin. He soon guessed its nature, and his face lost its perplexity. He picked up his cudgel, got on his feet briskly, muttering to himself: "He's anything but dead," and hurried on board the tartane.

On the after-deck Michel was keeping a lookout. He had carried out the orders he had received by the well. Besides being secured by the very obvious padlock, the cabin door was shored up by a spar which made it stand as firm as a rock. The thundering noise seemed to issue from its immovable substance magically. It ceased for a moment, and a sort of distracted continuous growling could be heard. Then the thundering began again. Michel reported:

"This is the third time he starts this game."

"Not much strength in this," remarked Peyrol gravely.

"That he can do it at all is a miracle," said Michel, showing a certain excitement. "He stands on the ladder and beats the door with his fists. He is getting better. He began about half an hour after I got back on board. He drummed for a bit and then fell off the ladder. I heard him. I had my ear against the scuttle. He lay there and talked to himself for a long time. Then he went at it again." Peyrol approached the scuttle while Michel added his opinion: "He will go on like that for ever. You can't stop him."

"Easy there," said Peyrol in a deep authoritative voice. "Time you finish that noise."

These words brought instantly a deathlike silence. Michel ceased to grin. He wondered at the power of these few words of a foreign language.

Peyrol himself smiled faintly. It was ages since he had uttered a sentence of English. He waited complacently until Michel had unbarred and unlocked the door of the cabin. After it was thrown open he boomed out a warning: "Stand clear!" and, turning about, went down with great deliberation, ordering Michel to go forward and keep a lookout.

Down there the man with the bandaged head was hanging on to the table and swearing feebly without intermission. Peyrol, after listening for a time with an air of interested recognition as one would to a tune heard many years ago, stopped it by a deep-voiced:

"That will do." After a short silence he added: "You look *bien malade, hein*? What you call sick," in a tone which if not tender was certainly not hostile. "We will remedy that."

"Who are you?" asked the prisoner, looking frightened and throwing his arm up quickly to guard his head against the coming blow. But Peyrol's uplifted hand fell only on his shoulder in a hearty slap which made him sit down suddenly on a locker in a partly collapsed attitude and unable to speak. But though very much dazed he was able to watch Peyrol open a cupboard and produce from there a small demijohn and two tin cups. He took heart to say plaintively: "My throat's like tinder," and then suspiciously: "Was it you who broke my head?"

"It was me," admitted Peyrol, sitting down on the opposite side of the table and leaning back to look at his prisoner comfortably.

"What the devil did you do that for?" inquired the other with a sort of faint fierceness which left Peyrol unmoved.

"Because you put your nose where you have no business. Understand? I see you there under the moon, *penché*, eating my tartane with your eyes. You never hear me, *hein*?"

"I believe you walked on air. Did you mean to kill me?"

"Yes, in preference to letting you go and make a story of it on board your cursed corvette."

"Well then, now's your chance to finish me. I am as weak as a kitten."

"How did you say that? Kitten? Ha, ha, ha!" laughed Peyrol. "You make a nice *petit chat*." He seized the demijohn by the neck and filled the mugs. "There," he went on, pushing one towards the prisoner— "it's good drink—that."

Symons' state was as though the blow had robbed him of all power of resistance, of all faculty of surprise, and generally of all the means by which a man may assert himself except bitter resentment. His head was aching, it seemed to him enormous, too heavy for his neck and as if full of hot smoke. He took a drink under Peyrol's fixed gaze and with uncertain movements put down the mug. He looked drowsy for a moment. Presently a little colour deepened his bronze; he hitched himself up on the locker and said in a strong voice:

"You played a damned dirty trick on me. Call yourself a man, walking on air behind a fellow's back and felling him like a bullock?"

Peyrol nodded calmly and sipped from his mug.

"If I had met you anywhere else but looking at my tartane I would have done nothing to you. I would have permitted you to go back to your boat. Where was your damned boat?"

"How can I tell you? I can't tell where I am. I've never been here before. How long have I been here?"

"Oh, about fourteen hours," said Peyrol.

"My head feels as if it would fall off if I moved," grumbled the other. . . . "You are a damned bungler, that's what you are."

"What for—bungler?"

"For not finishing me off at once."

He seized the mug and emptied it down his throat. Peyrol drank, too, observing him all the time. He put the mug down with extreme gentleness and said slowly:

"How could I know it was you? I hit hard enough to crack the skull of any other man."

"What do you mean? What do you know about my skull? What are you driving at? I don't know you, you white-headed villain, going about at night knocking people on the head from behind. Did you do for our officer, too?"

"Oh yes! Your officer. What was he up to? What trouble did you people come to make here, anyhow?"

"Do you think they tell a boat's crew? Go and ask our officer. He went up the gully and our coxswain got the jumps. He says to me: 'You are light-footed, Sam,' says he; 'you just creep round the head of the cove and see if our boat can be seen across from the other side.' Well, I couldn't see anything. That was all right. But I thought I would climb a little higher amongst the rocks. . . ."

He paused drowsily.

"That was a silly thing to do," remarked Peyrol in an encouraging voice.

"I would've sooner expected to see an elephant inland than a craft lying in a pool that seemed no bigger than my hand. Could not understand how she got there. Couldn't help going down to find out—and the next thing I knew I was lying on my back with my head tied up, in a bunk in this kennel of a cabin here. Why couldn't you have given me a hail and engaged me properly, yardarm to yardarm? You would have got me all the same, because all I had in the way of weapons was the clasp-knife which you have looted off me."

"Up on the shelf there," said Peyrol, looking round. "No, my friend, I wasn't going to take the risk of seeing you spread your wings and fly."

"You need not have been afraid for your tartane. Our boat was after no tartane. We wouldn't have taken your tartane for a gift. Why, we see them by dozens every day—those tartanes."

Peyrol filled the two mugs again. "Ah," he said, "I daresay you see many tartanes, but this one is not like the others. You a sailor—and you couldn't see that she was something extraordinary."

"Hellfire and gunpowder!" cried the other. "How can you expect me to have seen anything? I just noticed that her sails were bent before your club hit me on the head." He raised his hands to his head and groaned. "Oh Lord, I feel as though I had been drunk for a month."

Peyrol's prisoner did look somewhat as though he had got his head broken in a drunken brawl. But to Peyrol his appearance was not repulsive. The rover preserved a tender memory of his freebooter's life with its lawless spirit and its spacious scene of action, before the change in the state of affairs in the Indian Ocean, the astounding rumours from the outer world, made him reflect on its precarious character. It was true that he had deserted the French flag when quite

a youngster; but at that time the flag was white; and now it was a flag
of three colours. He had known the practice of liberty, equality and
fraternity as understood in the haunts open or secret of the Brotherhood of the Coast. So the change, if one could believe what people
talked about, could not be very great. The rover had also his own positive notions as to what these three words were worth. Liberty—to
hold your own in the world if you could. Equality—yes! But no body
of men ever accomplished anything without a chief. All this was
worth what it was worth. He regarded fraternity somewhat differ-
ently. Of course brothers would quarrel amongst themselves; it was
during a fierce quarrel that flamed up suddenly in a company of
Brothers that he had received the most dangerous wound of his life.
But for that Peyrol nursed no grudge against anybody. In his view the
claim of the Brotherhood was a claim for help against the outside
world. And here he was sitting opposite a Brother whose head he had
broken on sufficient grounds. There he was across the table looking
dishevelled and dazed, uncomprehending and aggrieved, and that
head of his proved as hard as ages ago when the nickname of Testa
Dura had been given to him by a Brother of Italian origin on some
occasion or other, some butting match no doubt; just as he, Peyrol
himself, was known for a time on both sides of the Mozambique
Channel as Poigne-de-Fer, after an incident when in the presence of
the Brothers he played at arm's length with the windpipe of an
obstreperous negro sorcerer with an enormous girth of chest. The villagers brought out food with alacrity, and the sorcerer was never the
same man again. It had been a great display.

Yes, no doubt it was Testa Dura; the young neophyte of the order
(where and how picked up Peyrol never heard), strange to the camp,
simple-minded and much impressed by the swaggering cosmopolitan company in which he found himself. He had attached himself
to Peyrol in preference to some of his own countrymen of whom there
were several in that band, and used to run after him like a little dog
and certainly had acted a good shipmate's part on the occasion of that
wound which had neither killed nor cowed Peyrol but merely had
given him an opportunity to reflect at leisure on the conduct of his
own life.

The first suspicion of that amazing fact had intruded on Peyrol
while he was bandaging that head by the light of the smoky lamp.
Since the fellow still lived, it was not in Peyrol to finish him off or let

him lie unattended like a dog. And then this was a sailor. His being English was no obstacle to the development of Peyrol's mixed feelings in which hatred certainly had no place. Amongst the members of the Brotherhood it was the Englishmen whom he preferred. He had also found amongst them that particular and loyal appreciation, which a Frenchman of character and ability will receive from Englishmen sooner than from any other nation. Peyrol had at times been a leader, without ever trying for it very much, for he was not ambitious. The lead used to fall to him mostly at a time of crisis of some sort; and when he had got the lead it was on the Englishmen that he used to depend most.

And so that youngster had turned into this English man-of-war's man! In the fact itself there was nothing impossible. You found Brothers of the Coast in all sorts of ships and in all sorts of places. Peyrol had found one once in a very ancient and hopeless cripple practising the profession of a beggar on the steps of Manila cathedral; and had left him the richer by two broad gold pieces to add to his secret hoard. There was a tale of a Brother of the Coast having become a mandarin in China, and Peyrol believed it. One never knew where and in what position one would find a Brother of the Coast. The wonderful thing was that this one should have come to seek him out, to put himself in the way of his cudgel. Peyrol's greatest concern had been all through that Sunday morning to conceal the whole adventure from Lieutenant Réal. As against a wearer of epaulettes, mutual protection was the first duty between Brothers of the Coast. The unexpectedness of that claim coming to him after twenty years invested it with an extraordinary strength. What he would do with the fellow he didn't know. But since that morning the situation had changed. Peyrol had received the lieutenant's confidence and had got on terms with him in a special way. He fell into profound thought.

"*Sacrée tête dure,*" he muttered without rousing himself. Peyrol was annoyed a little at not having been recognized. He could not conceive how difficult it would have been for Symons to identify this portly deliberate person with a white head of hair as the object of his youthful admiration, the black-ringleted French Brother in the prime of life of whom everybody thought so much. Peyrol was roused by hearing the other declare suddenly:

"I am an Englishman, I am. I am not going to knuckle under to anybody. What are you going to do with me?"

"I will do what I please," said Peyrol, who had been asking himself exactly the same question.

"Well, then, be quick about it, whatever it is. I don't care a damn what you do, but—be—quick—about it."

He tried to be emphatic; but as a matter of fact the last words came out in a faltering tone. And old Peyrol was touched. He thought that if he were to let him drink the mugful standing there, it would make him dead drunk. But he took the risk. So he said only:

"*Allons.* Drink." The other did not wait for a second invitation but could not control very well the movements of his arm extended towards the mug. Peyrol raised his on high.

"*Trinquons*, eh?" he proposed. But in his precarious condition the Englishman remained unforgiving.

"I'm damned if I do," he said indignantly, but so low that Peyrol had to turn his ear to catch the words. "You will have to explain to me first what you meant by knocking me on the head."

He drank, staring all the time at Peyrol in a manner which was meant to give offence but which struck Peyrol as so childlike that he burst into a laugh.

"*Sacré imbécile, va!* Did I not tell you it was because of the tartane? If it hadn't been for the tartane I would have hidden from you. I would have crouched behind a bush like a—what do you call them?—*lièvre*."

The other, who was feeling the effect of the drink, stared with frank incredulity.

"You are of no account," continued Peyrol. "Ah! if you had been an officer I would have gone for you anywhere. Did you say your officer went up the gully?"

Symons sighed deeply and easily. "That's the way he went. We had heard on board of a house thereabouts."

"Oh, he went to the house!" said Peyrol. "Well, if he did get there he must be very sorry for himself. There is half a company of infantry billeted in the farm."

This inspired fib went down easily with the English sailor. Soldiers were stationed in many parts of the coast as any seaman of the blockading fleet knew very well. To the many expressions which had passed over the face of that man recovering from a long period of unconsciousness, there was added the shade of dismay.

"What the devil have they stuck soldiers on this piece of rock for?" he asked.

"Oh, signalling post and things like that. I am not likely to tell you everything. Why! you might escape."

That phrase reached the soberest spot in the whole of Symons' individuality. Things were happening, then. Mr. Bolt was a prisoner. But the main idea evoked in his confused mind was that he would be given up to those soldiers before very long. The prospect of captivity made his heart sink and he resolved to give as much trouble as he could.

"You will have to get some of these soldiers to carry me up. I won't walk. I won't. Not after having had my brains nearly knocked out from behind. I tell you straight! I won't walk. Not a step. They will have to carry me ashore."

Peyrol only shook his head deprecatingly.

"Now you go and get a corporal with a file of men," insisted Symons obstinately. "I want to be made a proper prisoner of. Who the devil are you? You had no right to interfere. I believe you are a civilian. A common *marinero*, whatever you may call yourself. You look to me a pretty fishy *marinero* at that. Where did you learn English? In prison— eh? You ain't going to keep me in this damned dog-hole, on board your rubbishy tartane. Go and get that corporal, I tell you."

He looked suddenly very tired and only murmured: "I am an Englishman, I am."

Peyrol's patience was positively angelic.

"Don't you talk about the tartane," he said impressively, making his words as distinct as possible. "I told you she was not like the other tartanes. That is because she is a courier boat. Every time she goes to sea she makes a *pied-de-nez*, what you call thumb to the nose, to all your English cruisers. I do not mind telling you because you are my prisoner. You will soon learn French now."

"Who are you? The caretaker of this thing or what?" asked the undaunted Symons. But Peyrol's mysterious silence seemed to intimidate him at last. He became dejected and began to curse in a languid tone all boat expeditions, the coxswain of the gig, and his own infernal luck.

Peyrol sat alert and attentive like a man interested in an experiment, while after a moment Symons' face began to look as if he had been hit with a club again, but not as hard as before. A film came over his round eyes and the words "fishy *marinero*" made their way out of his lips in a sort of death-bed voice. Yet such was the hardness of his

head that he actually rallied enough to address Peyrol in an ingrati-
ating tone.

"Come, Grandfather!" He tried to push the mug across the table
and upset it. "Come! Let us finish what's in that tiny bottle of yours."

"No," said Peyrol, drawing the demijohn to his side of the table
and putting the cork in.

"No?" repeated Symons in an unbelieving voice and looking at
the demijohn fixedly . . . "You must be a tinker . . ." He tried to say
something more under Peyrol's watchful eyes, failed once or twice,
and suddenly pronounced the word "*cochon*" so correctly as to make
old Peyrol start. After that it was no use looking at him any more.
Peyrol busied himself in locking up the demijohn and the mugs.
When he turned round most of his prisoner's body was extended over
the table and no sound came from it, not even a snore.

When Peyrol got outside, pulling to the door of the cuddy behind
him, Michel hastened from forward to receive the master's orders. But
Peyrol stood so long on the after-deck meditating profoundly with his
hand over his mouth that Michel became fidgety and ventured a
cheerful: "It looks as if he were not going to die."

"He is dead," said Peyrol with grim jocularity. "Dead drunk. And
you very likely will not see me till to-morrow sometime."

"But what am I to do?" asked Michel timidly.

"Nothing," said Peyrol. "Of course you must not let him set fire to
the tartane."

"But suppose," insisted Michel, "he should give signs of
escaping."

"If you see him trying to escape," said Peyrol with mock solemnity, "then, Michel, it will be a sign for you to get out of his way as
quickly as you can. A man who would try to escape with a head like
this on him would just swallow you at one mouthful."

He picked up his cudgel and, stepping ashore, went off without as
much as a look at his faithful henchman. Michel listened to him
scrambling amongst the stones and his habitual amiably vacant face
acquired a sort of dignity from the utter and absolute blankness that
came over it.

CHAPTER X

I T WAS ONLY after reaching the level ground in front of the farmhouse that Peyrol took time to pause and resume his contact
with the exterior world.

While he had been closeted with his prisoner the sky had got covered with a thin layer of cloud, in one of those swift changes of
weather that are not unusual in the Mediterranean. This grey vapour,
drifting high up, close against the disc of the sun, seemed to enlarge
the space behind its veil, add to the vastness of a shadowless world no
longer hard and brilliant but all softened in the contours of its masses
and in the faint line of the horizon, as if ready to dissolve in the
immensity of the Infinite.

Familiar and indifferent to his eyes, material and shadowy, the
extent of the changeable sea had gone pale under the pale sun in a
mysterious and emotional response. Mysterious too was the great
oval patch of dark water to the west; and also a broad blue lane traced
on the dull silver of the waters in a parabolic curve described magis-
trally by an invisible finger for a symbol of endless wandering. The
face of the farmhouse might have been the face of a house from which
all the inhabitants had fled suddenly. In the high part of the building
the window of the lieutenant's room remained open, both glass and
shutter. By the door of the *salle* the stable fork leaning against the wall
seemed to have been forgotten by the sans-culotte. This aspect of
abandonment struck Peyrol with more force than usual. He had been

thinking so hard of all these people, that to find no one about seemed unnatural and even depressing. He had seen many abandoned places in his life, grass huts, mud forts, kings' palaces—temples from which every white-robed soul had fled. Temples, however, never looked quite empty. The gods clung to their own. Peyrol's eyes rested on the bench against the wall of the *salle*. In the usual course of things it should have been occupied by the lieutenant who had the habit of sitting there with hardly a movement, for hours, like a spider watching for the coming of a fly. This paralyzing comparison held Peyrol motionless with a twisted mouth and a frown on his brow, before the evoked vision, coloured and precise, of the man more troubling than the reality had ever been.

He came to himself with a start. What sort of occupation was this, *'cré nom de nom,* staring at a silly bench with no one on it? Was he going wrong in his head? Or was it that he was getting really old? He had noticed old men losing themselves like that. But he had something to do. First of all he had to go and see what the English sloop in the Passe was doing.

While he was making his way towards the lookout on the hill where the inclined pine hung peering over the cliff as if an insatiable curiosity were holding it in that precarious position, Peyrol had another view from above of the farmyard and of the buildings and was again affected by their deserted appearance. Not a soul, not even an animal seemed to have been left; only on the roofs the pigeons walked with smart elegance. Peyrol hurried on and presently saw the English ship well over on the Porquerolles side with her yards braced up and her head to the southward. There was a little wind in the Passe, while the dull silver of the open had a darkling rim of rippled water far away to the east in that quarter where, far or near, but mostly out of sight, the British fleet kept its endless watch. Not a shadow of a spar or gleam of sail on the horizon betrayed its presence; but Peyrol would not have been surprised to see a crowd of ships surge up, people the horizon with hostile life, come in running, and dot the sea with their ordered groups all about Cape Cicié, parading their damned impudence. Then indeed that corvette, the big factor of everyday life on that stretch of coast, would become very small potatoes indeed; and the man in command of her (he had been Peyrol's personal adversary in many imaginary encounters fought to a finish in the room upstairs), then indeed that Englishman, would have to mind his steps. He would be ordered to come within hail of the admiral, be sent here and there, made to run like a little dog and as likely as not get called on board the flagship and get a dressing down for something or other.

Peyrol thought for a moment that the impudence of this Englishman was going to take the form of running along the peninsula and looking into the very cove; for the corvette's head was falling off slowly. A fear for his tartane clutched Peyrol's heart till he remembered that the Englishman did not know of her existence. Of course not. His cudgel had been absolutely effective in stopping that bit of information. The only Englishman who knew of the existence of the tartane was that fellow with the broken head. Peyrol actually laughed at his momentary scare. Moreover, it was evident that the Englishman did not mean to parade in front of the peninsula. He did not mean to be impudent. The sloop's yards were swung right round and she came again to the wind but now heading to the northward back from where she came. Peyrol saw at once that the Englishman meant to pass to windward of Cape Esterel, probably with the intention of anchoring for the night off the long white beach which in a regular curve closes the roadstead of Hyères on that side.

Peyrol pictured her to himself, on the clouded night, not so very dark since the full moon was but a day old, lying at anchor within hail of the low shore, with her sails furled and looking profoundly asleep, but with the watch on deck lying by the guns. He gnashed his teeth. It had come to this at last, that the captain of the *Amelia* could do nothing with his ship without putting Peyrol into a rage. Oh, for forty Brothers, or sixty, picked ones, he thought, to teach the fellow what it might cost him taking liberties along the French coast! Ships had been carried by surprise before, on nights when there was just light enough to see the whites of each other's eyes in a close tussle. And what would be the crew of that Englishman? Something between ninety and a hundred altogether, boys and landsmen included. . . . Peyrol shook his fist for a good-bye, just when Cape Esterel shut off the English sloop from his sight. But in his heart of hearts that seaman of cosmopolitan associations knew very well that no forty or sixty, not any given hundred Brothers of the Coast would have been enough to capture that corvette making herself at home within ten miles of where he had first opened his eyes to the world.

He shook his head dismally at the leaning pine, his only companion. The disinherited soul of that rover ranging for so many years a lawless ocean with the coasts of two continents for a raiding ground, had come back to its crag, circling like a sea-bird in the dusk and longing for a great sea victory for its people: that inland multitude of which Peyrol knew nothing except the few individuals on that peninsula cut off from the rest of the land by the dead water of a salt lagoon; and where only a strain of manliness in a miserable cripple and an unaccountable charm of a half-crazed woman had found response in his heart.

This scheme of false dispatches was but a detail in a plan for a great, a destructive victory. Just a detail, but not a trifle all the same. Nothing connected with the deception of an admiral could be called trifling. And such an admiral too. It was, Peyrol felt vaguely, a scheme that only a confounded landsman would invent. It behoved the sailors, however, to make a workable thing of it. It would have to be worked through that corvette.

And here Peyrol was brought up by the question that all his life had not been able to settle for him—and that was whether the English were really very stupid or very acute. That difficulty had presented itself with every fresh case. The old rover had enough genius in him to have arrived at a general conclusion that if they were to be deceived at all it could not be done very well by words but rather by deeds; not by mere wriggling, but by deep craft concealed under some sort of straightforward action. That conviction, however, did not take him forward in this case, which was one in which much thinking would be necessary.

The *Amelia* had disappeared behind Cape Esterel, and Peyrol wondered with a certain anxiety whether this meant that the Englishman had given up his man for good. "If he has," said Peyrol to himself, "I am bound to see him pass out again from beyond Cape Esterel before it gets dark." If, however, he did not see the ship again within the next hour or two, then she would be anchored off the beach, to wait for the night before making some attempt to discover what had become of her man. This could be done only by sending out one or two boats to explore the coast, and no doubt to enter the cove—perhaps even to land a small search party.

After coming to this conclusion Peyrol began deliberately to charge his pipe. Had he spared a moment for a glance inland he might have caught a whisk of a black skirt, the gleam of a white fichu— Arlette running down the faint track leading from Escampobar to the village in the hollow; the same track in fact up which Citizen Scevola, while indulging in the strange freak to visit the church, had been chased by the incensed faithful. But Peyrol, while charging and lighting his pipe, had kept his eyes fastened on Cape Esterel. Then, throwing his arm affectionately over the trunk of the pine, he had settled himself to watch. Far below him the roadstead, with its play of grey and bright gleams, looked like a plaque of mother-of-pearl in a frame of yellow rocks and dark green ravines set off inland by the masses of the hills displaying the tint of the finest purple; while above his head the sun, behind a cloud-veil, hung like a silver disc.

That afternoon, after waiting in vain for Lieutenant Réal to appear outside in the usual way, Arlette, the mistress of Escampobar, had gone unwillingly into the kitchen where Catherine sat upright in a heavy capacious wooden armchair, the back of which rose above the top of her white muslin cap. Even in her old age, even in her hours of ease, Catherine preserved the upright carriage of the family that had held Escampobar for so many generations. It would have been easy to believe that, like some characters famous in the world, Catherine would have wished to die standing up and with unbowed shoulders.

With her sense of hearing undecayed she detected the light footsteps in the *salle* long before Arlette entered the kitchen. That woman, who had faced alone and unaided (except for her brother's comprehending silence) the anguish of passion in a forbidden love, and of terrors comparable to those of the Judgment Day, neither turned her face, quiet without serenity, nor her eyes, fearless but without fire, in the direction of her niece.

Arlette glanced on all sides, even at the walls, even at the mound of ashes under the big overmantel, nursing in its heart a spark of fire, before she sat down and leaned her elbow on the table.

"You wander about like a soul in pain," said her aunt, sitting by the hearth like an old queen on her throne.

"And you sit here eating your heart out."

"Formerly," remarked Catherine, "old women like me could always go over their prayers, but now . . ."

"I believe you have not been to church for years. I remember Scevola telling me that a long time ago. Was it because you didn't like people's eyes? I have fancied sometimes that most people in the world must have been massacred long ago."

Catherine turned her face away. Arlette rested her head on her half-closed hand, and her eyes, losing their steadiness, began to tremble amongst cruel visions. She got up suddenly and caressed the thin, half-averted, withered cheek with the tips of her fingers, and in a low voice, with that marvellous cadence that plucked at one's heart-strings, she said coaxingly:

"Those were dreams, weren't they?"

In her immobility the old woman called with all the might of her will for the presence of Peyrol. She had never been able to shake off a superstitious fear of that niece restored to her from the terrors of a Judgment Day in which the world had been given over to the devils. She was always afraid that this girl, wandering about with restless eyes and a dim smile on her silent lips, would suddenly say something atrocious, unfit to be heard, calling for vengeance from heaven, unless Peyrol were by. That stranger come from *"par delà les mers"* was out of it altogether, cared probably for no one in the world but had struck her imagination by his massive aspect, his deliberation suggesting a mighty force like the reposeful attitude of a lion. Arlette desisted from caressing the irresponsive cheek, exclaimed petulantly: "I am awake now!" and went out of the kitchen without having asked her aunt the question she had meant to ask, which was whether she knew what had become of the lieutenant.

Her heart had failed her. She let herself drop on the bench outside the door of the *salle*. "What is the matter with them all?" she thought. "I can't make them out. What wonder is it that I have not been able to sleep?" Even Peyrol, so different from all mankind, who from the first moment when he stood before her had the power to soothe her aimless unrest, even Peyrol would now sit for hours with the lieutenant on the bench, gazing into the air and keeping him in talk about things without sense, as if on purpose to prevent him from thinking of her. Well, he could not do that. But the enormous change implied in the fact that every day had a to-morrow now, and that all the people around her had ceased to be mere phantoms for her wandering glances to glide over without concern, made her feel the need of support from somebody, from somewhere. She could have cried aloud for it.

She sprang up and walked along the whole front of the farm building. At the end of the wall enclosing the orchard she called out in a modulated undertone: "Eugène," not because she hoped that the lieutenant was anywhere within earshot, but for the pleasure of hearing the sound of the name uttered for once above a whisper. She turned about and at the end of the wall on the yard side she repeated her call, drinking in the sound that came from her lips. "Eugène, Eugène," with a sort of half-exulting despair. It was in such dizzy moments that she wanted a steadying support. But all was still. She heard no friendly murmur, not even a sigh. Above her head under the thin grey sky a big mulberry tree stirred no leaf. Step by step, as if unconsciously, she began to move down the track. At the end of fifty yards she opened the inland view, the roofs of the village between the green tops of the platanes overshadowing the fountain, and just beyond the flat blue-grey level of the salt lagoon, smooth and dull like a slab of lead. But what drew her on was the church-tower, where, in a round arch, she could see the black speck of the bell which escaping the requisitions of the Republican wars, and dwelling mute above the locked-up empty church, had only lately recovered its voice. She ran on, but when she had come near enough to make out the figures moving about the village fountain, she checked herself, hesitated a moment, and then took the footpath leading to the presbytery.

She pushed open the little gate with the broken latch. The humble building of rough stones, from between which much mortar had crumbled out, looked as though it had been sinking slowly into the ground. The beds of the plot in front were choked with weeds, because the abbé had no taste for gardening. When the heiress of Escampobar opened the door, he was walking up and down the largest room which was his bedroom and sitting room and where he also took his meals. He was a gaunt man with a long, as if convulsed, face. In his young days he had been tutor to the sons of a great noble, but he did not emigrate with his employer. Neither did he submit to the Republic. He had lived in his native land like a hunted wild beast, and there had been many tales of his activities, warlike and others. When the hierarchy was re-established he found no favour in the eyes of his superiors. He had remained too much of a Royalist. He had accepted, without a word, the charge of this miserable parish, where he had acquired influence quickly enough. His sacerdotalism lay in him like a cold passion. Though accessible enough, he never walked abroad without his breviary, acknowledging the solemnly bared heads by a curt nod. He was not exactly feared, but some of the oldest inhabitants who remembered the previous incumbent, an old man who died in the garden after having been dragged out of bed by some patriots anxious to take him to prison in Hyères, jerked their heads sideways in a knowing manner when their curé was mentioned.

On seeing this apparition in an Arlesian cap and silk skirt, a white fichu, and otherwise as completely different as any princess could be from the rustics with whom he was in daily contact, his face expressed the blankest astonishment. Then—for he knew enough of the gossip of his community—his straight, thick eyebrows came together inimically. This was no doubt the woman of whom he had heard his parishioners talk with bated breath as having given herself and her property up to a Jacobin, a Toulon sans-culotte who had either delivered her parents to execution or had murdered them himself during the first three days of massacres. No one was very sure which it was, but the rest was current knowledge. The abbé, though persuaded that any amount of moral turpitude was possible in a godless country, had not accepted all that tale literally. No doubt those people were Republican and impious, and the state of affairs up there was scandalous and horrible. He struggled with his feelings of repulsion and managed to smooth his brow and waited. He could not imagine what that woman with mature form and a youthful face could want at the presbytery. Suddenly it occurred to him that perhaps she wanted to thank him—it was a very old occurrence—for interposing between the fury of the villagers and that man. He couldn't call him, even in his thoughts, her husband, for apart from all other circumstances, that connection could not imply any kind of marriage to a priest, even had there been legal form observed. His visitor was apparently disconcerted by the expression of his face, the austere aloofness of his attitude, and only a low murmur escaped her lips. He bent his head and was not very certain what he had heard.

"You come to seek my aid?" he asked in a doubting tone.

She nodded slightly, and the abbé went to the door she had left half open and looked out. There was not a soul in sight between the presbytery and the village, or between the presbytery and the church. He went back to face her, saying:

"We are as alone as we can well be. The old woman in the kitchen is as deaf as a post."

Now that he had been looking at Arlette closer the abbé felt a sort of dread. The carmine of those lips, the pellucid, unstained, unfathomable blackness of those eyes, the pallor of her cheeks, suggested to him something provokingly pagan, something distastefully different from the common sinners of this earth. And now she was ready to speak. He arrested her with a raised hand.

"Wait," he said. "I have never seen you before. I don't even know properly who you are. None of you belong to my flock—for you are from Escampobar, are you not?" Sombre under their bony arches, his eyes fastened on her face, noticed the delicacy of features, the naïve pertinacity of her stare. She said:

"I am the daughter."

"The daughter . . . ! Oh! I see . . . Much evil is spoken of you."

She said a little impatiently: "By that rabble?" and the priest remained mute for a moment. "What do they say? In my father's time they wouldn't have dared to say anything. The only thing I saw of them for years and years was when they were yelping like curs on the heels of Scevola."

The absence of scorn in her tone was perfectly annihilating. Gentle sounds flowed from her lips and a disturbing charm from her strange equanimity. The abbé frowned heavily at these fascinations, which seemed to have in them something diabolic.

"They are simple souls, neglected, fallen back into darkness. It isn't their fault. They have natural feelings of humanity which were outraged. I saved him from their indignation. There are things that must be left to divine justice."

He was exasperated by the unconsciousness of that fair face.

"That man whose name you have just pronounced and which I have heard coupled with the epithet of 'blood-drinker' is regarded as the master of Escampobar Farm. He has been living there for years. How is that?"

"Yes, it is a long time ago since he brought me back to the house. Years ago. Catherine let him stay."

"Who is Catherine?" the abbé asked harshly.

"She is my father's sister who was left at home to wait. She had given up all hope of seeing any of us again, when one morning Scevola came with me to the door. Then she let him stay. He is a poor creature. What else could Catherine have done? And what is it to us up there how the people in the village regard him?" She dropped her eyes and seemed to fall into deep thought, then added, "It was only later that I discovered that he was a poor creature, even quite lately. They call him 'blood-drinker,' do they? What of that? All the time he was afraid of his own shadow."

She ceased but did not raise her eyes.

"You are no longer a child," began the abbé in a severe voice, frowning at her downcast eyes, and he heard a murmur: "Not very long." He disregarded it and continued: "I ask you, is this all that you have to tell me about that man? I hope that at least you are no hypocrite."

"Monsieur l'Abbé," she said, raising her eyes fearlessly, "what more am I to tell you about him? I can tell you things that will make your hair stand on end, but it wouldn't be about him."

For all answer the abbé made a weary gesture and turned away to walk up and down the room. His face expressed neither curiosity nor pity, but a sort of repugnance which he made an effort to overcome. He dropped into a deep and shabby old armchair, the only object of luxury in the room, and pointed to a wooden straight-backed stool. Arlette sat down on it and began to speak. The abbé listened, but looking far away; his big bony hands rested on the arms of the chair. After the first words he interrupted her: "This is your own story you are telling me."

"Yes," said Arlette.

"Is it necessary that I should know?"

"Yes, Monsieur l'Abbé."

"But why?"

He bent his head a little, without, however, ceasing to look far away. Her voice now was very low. Suddenly the abbé threw himself back.

"You want to tell me your story because you have fallen in love with a man?"

"No, because that has brought me back to myself. Nothing else could have done it."

He turned his head to look at her grimly, but he said nothing and looked away again. He listened. At the beginning he muttered once or twice, "Yes, I have heard that," and then kept silent, not looking at her at all. Once he interrupted her by a question: "You were confirmed before the convent was forcibly entered and the nuns dispersed?"

"Yes," she said, "a year before that or more."

"And then two of those ladies took you with them towards Toulon."

"Yes, the other girls had their relations near by. They took me with them thinking to communicate with my parents, but it was difficult. Then the English came and my parents sailed over to try and get some news of me. It was safe for my father to be in Toulon then. Perhaps you think that he was a traitor to his country?" she asked, and waited with parted lips. With an impassible face the abbé murmured: "He was a good Royalist," in a tone of bitter fatalism, which seemed to absolve that man and all the other men of whose actions and errors he had ever heard.

For a long time, Arlette continued, her father could not discover the house where the nuns had taken refuge. He only obtained some information on the very day before the English evacuated Toulon. Late in the day he appeared before her and took her away. The town was full of retreating foreign troops. Her father left her with her mother and went out again to make preparations for sailing home that very night; but the tartane was no longer in the place where he had left her lying. The two Madrague men that he had for a crew had disappeared also. Thus the family was trapped in that town full of tumult and confusion. Ships and houses were bursting into flames. Appalling explosions of gunpowder shook the earth. She spent that night on her knees with her face hidden in her mother's lap, while her father kept watch by the barricaded door with a pistol in each hand.

In the morning the house was filled with savage yells. People were heard rushing up the stairs, and the door was burst in. She jumped up at the crash and flung herself down on her knees in a corner with her face to the wall. There was a murderous uproar, she heard two shots fired, then somebody seized her by the arm and pulled her up to her feet. It was Scevola. He dragged her to the door. The bodies of her father and mother were lying across the doorway. The room was full of gunpowder smoke. She wanted to fling herself on the bodies and cling to them, but Scevola took her under the arms and lifted her over them. He seized her hand and made her run with him, or rather dragged her downstairs. Outside on the pavement some dreadful men and many fierce women with knives joined them. They ran along the streets brandishing pikes and sabres, pursuing other groups of unarmed people, who fled round corners with loud shrieks.

"I ran in the midst of them, Monsieur l'Abbé," Arlette went on in a breathless murmur. "Whenever I saw any water I wanted to throw myself into it, but I was surrounded on all sides, I was jostled and pushed and most of the time Scevola held my hand very tight. When they stopped at a wine shop, they would offer me some wine. My tongue stuck to the roof of my mouth and I drank. The wine, the pavements, the arms and faces, everything was red. I had red splashes all over me. I had to run with them all day, and all the time I felt as if I were falling down, and down, and down. The houses were nodding at me. The sun would go out at times. And suddenly I heard myself yelling exactly like the others. Do you understand, Monsieur l'Abbé? The very same words!"

The eyes of the priest in their deep orbits glided towards her and then resumed their far-away fixity. Between his fatalism and his faith he was not very far from the belief of Satan taking possession of rebellious mankind, exposing the nakedness of hearts like flint and of the homicidal souls of the Revolution.

"I have heard something of that," he whispered stealthily.

She affirmed with quiet earnestness: "Yet at that time I resisted with all my might."

That night Scevola put her under the care of a woman called Perose. She was young and pretty and was a native of Arles, her mother's country. She kept an inn. That woman locked her up in her own room, which was next to the room where the patriots kept on shouting, singing and making speeches far into the night. Several times the woman would look in for a moment, make a hopeless gesture at her with both arms, and vanish again. Later, on many other nights when all the band lay asleep on benches and on the floor, Perose would steal into the room, fall on her knees by the bed on which Arlette sat upright, open-eyed, and raving silently to herself, embrace her feet and cry herself to sleep. But in the morning she would jump up briskly and say: "Come. The great affair is to keep our life in our bodies. Come along to help in the work of justice"; and they would join the band that was making ready for another day of traitor hunting. But after a time the victims, of which the streets were full at first, had to be sought for in back-yards, ferreted out of their hiding-places, dragged up out of the cellars, or down from the garrets of the houses, which would be entered by the band with howls of death and vengeance.

"Then, Monsieur l'Abbé," said Arlette, "I let myself go at last. I could resist no longer. I said to myself: 'If it is so then it must be right.' But most of the time I was like a person half asleep and dreaming things that it is impossible to believe. About that time, I don't know why, the woman Perose hinted to me that Scevola was a poor creature. Next night while all the band lay fast asleep in the big room Perose and Scevola helped me out of the window into the street and led me to the quay behind the arsenal. Scevola had found our tartane lying at the pontoon and one of the Madrague men with her. The other had disappeared. Perose fell on my neck and cried a little. She gave me a kiss and said: "My time will come soon. You, Scevola, don't you show yourself in Toulon, because nobody believes in you any more. *Adieu*, Arlette. *Vive la Nation!*" and she vanished in the night. I waited on the pontoon shivering in my torn clothes, listening to Scevola and the man throwing dead bodies overboard out of the tartane. Splash, splash, splash. And suddenly I felt I must run away, but they were after me in a moment, dragged me back and threw me down into that cabin which smelt of blood. But when I got back to the farm all feeling had left me. I did not feel myself exist. I saw things round me here and there, but I couldn't look at anything for long. Something was gone out of me. I know now that it was not my heart, but then I didn't mind what it was. I felt light and empty, and a little cold all the time, but I could smile at people. Nothing could matter. Nothing could mean anything. I cared for no one. I wanted nothing. I wasn't alive at all, Monsieur l'Abbé. People seemed to see me and would talk to me, and it seemed funny—till one day I felt my heart beat."

"Why precisely did you come to me with this tale?" asked the abbé in a low voice.

"Because you are a priest. Have you forgotten that I have been brought up in a convent? I have not forgotten how to pray. But I am afraid of the world now. What must I do?"

"Repent!" thundered the abbé, getting up. He saw her candid gaze uplifted and lowered his voice forcibly. "You must look with fearless sincerity into the darkness of your soul. Remember whence the only true help can come. Those whom God has visited by a trial such as yours can not be held guiltless of their enormities. Withdraw from the world. Descend within yourself and abandon the vain thoughts of what people call happiness. Be an example to yourself of the sinfulness of our nature and of the weakness of our humanity. You may have been possessed. What do I know? Perhaps it was permitted in order to lead your soul to saintliness through a life of seclusion and prayer. To that it would be my duty to help you. Meantime you must pray to be given strength for a complete renunciation."

Arlette, lowering her eyes slowly, appealed to the abbé as a symbolic figure of spiritual mystery. "What can be God's designs on this creature?" he asked himself.

"Monsieur le Curé," she said quietly, "I felt the need to pray to-day for the first time in many years. When I left home it was only to go to your church."

"The church stands open to the worst of sinners," said the abbé.

"I know. But I would have had to pass before all those villagers: and you, abbé, know well what they are capable of."

"Perhaps," murmured the abbé, "it would be better not to put their charity to the test."

"I must pray before I go back again. I thought you would let me come in through the sacristy."

"It would be inhuman to refuse your request," he said, rousing himself and taking down a key that hung on the wall. He put on his broad-brimmed hat and without a word led the way through the wicket gate and along the path which he always used himself and which was out of sight of the village fountain. After they had entered the damp and dilapidated sacristy he locked the door behind them and only then opened another, a smaller one, leading into the church. When he stood aside, Arlette became aware of the chilly odour as of freshly turned-up earth mingled with a faint scent of incense. In the deep dusk of the nave a single little flame glimmered before an image of the virgin. The abbé whispered as she passed on:

"There before the great altar abase yourself and pray for grace and strength and mercy in this world full of crimes against God and men."

She did not look at him. Through the thin soles of her shoes she could feel the chill of the flagstones. The abbé left the door ajar, sat down on a rush-bottomed chair, the only one in the sacristy, folded his arms, and let his chin fall on his breast. He seemed to be sleeping profoundly, but at the end of half an hour he got up and, going to the doorway, stood looking at the kneeling figure sunk low on the altar steps. Arlette's face was buried in her hands in a passion of piety and prayer. The abbé waited patiently for a good many minutes more, before he raised his voice in a grave murmur which filled the whole dark place.

"It is time for you to leave. I am going to ring for vespers."

The view of her complete absorption before the Most High had touched him. He stepped back into the sacristy and after a time heard the faintest possible swish of the black silk skirt of the Escampobar daughter in her Arlesian costume. She entered the sacristy lightly with shining eyes, and the abbé looked at her with some emotion.

"You have prayed well, my daughter," he said. "No forgiveness will be refused to you, for you have suffered much. Put your trust in the grace of God."

She raised her head and stayed her footsteps for a moment. In the dark little place he could see the gleam of her eyes swimming in tears.

"Yes, Monsieur l'Abbé," she said in her clear seductive voice. "I have prayed and I feel answered. I entreated the merciful God to keep the heart of the man I love always true to me or else to let me die before I set my eyes on him again."

The abbé paled under his tan of a village priest and leaned his shoulders against the wall without a word.

CHAPTER XI

A FTER LEAVING THE church by the sacristy door Arlette never looked back. The abbé saw her flit past the presbytery, and the building hid her from his sight. He did not accuse her of duplicity. He had deceived himself. A heathen. White as her skin was, the blackness of her hair and of her eyes, the dusky red of her lips, suggested a strain of Saracen blood. He gave her up without a sigh.

Arlette walked rapidly towards Escampobar as if she could not get there soon enough; but as she neared the first enclosed field her steps became slower and after hesitating awhile she sat down between two olive trees, near a wall bordered by a growth of thin grass at the foot. "And if I have been possessed," she argued to herself, "as the abbé said, what is it to me as I am now? That evil spirit cast my true self out of my body and then cast away the body too. For years I have been living empty. There has been no meaning in anything."

But now her true self had returned matured in its mysterious exile, hopeful and eager for love. She was certain that it had never been far away from that outcast body which Catherine had told her lately was fit for no man's arms. That was all that old woman knew about it, thought Arlette, not in scorn but rather in pity. She knew better, she had gone to heaven for truth in that long prostration with its ardent prayers and its moment of ecstasy before an unlighted altar.

She knew its meaning well, and also the meaning of another—of a terrestrial revelation which had come to her that day at noon while she waited on the lieutenant. Everybody else was in the kitchen; she and Réal were as much alone together as had ever happened to them in their lives. That day she could not deny herself the delight to be near him, to watch him covertly, to hear him perhaps utter a few words, to experience that strange satisfying consciousness of her own existence which nothing but Réal's presence could give her; a sort of unimpassioned but all-absorbing bliss, warmth, courage, confidence . . . ! She backed away from Réal's table, seated herself facing him and cast down her eyes. There was a great stillness in the *salle* except for the murmur of the voices in the kitchen. She had at first stolen a glance or two and then peeping again through her eyelashes, as it were, she saw his eyes rest on her with a peculiar meaning. This had never happened before. She jumped up, thinking that he wanted something, and while she stood in front of him with her hand resting on the table he stooped suddenly, pressed it to the table with his lips, and began kissing it passionately without a sound, endlessly. . . . More startled than surprised at first, then infinitely happy, she was beginning to breathe quickly, when he left off and threw himself back in the chair. She walked away from the table and sat down again to gaze at him openly, steadily, without a smile. But he was not looking at her. His passionate lips were set hard now and his face had an expression of stern despair. No word passed between them. Brusquely he got up with averted eyes and went outside, leaving the food before him unfinished.

In the usual course of things, on any other day, she would have got up and followed him, for she had always yielded to the fascination that had first roused her faculties. She would have gone out just to pass in front of him once or twice. But this time she had not obeyed what was stronger than fascination, something within herself which at the same time prompted and restrained her. She only raised her arm and looked at her hand. It was true. It had happened. He had kissed it. Formerly she cared not how gloomy he was as long as he remained somewhere where she could look at him—which she would do at every opportunity with an open and unbridled innocence. But now she knew better than to do that. She had got up, had passed through the kitchen, meeting without embarrassment Catherine's inquisitive glance, and had gone upstairs. When she came down after a time, he was nowhere to be seen, and everybody else, too, seemed to have gone into hiding; Michel, Peyrol, Scevola.... But if she had met Scevola she would not have spoken to him. It was now a very long time since she had volunteered a conversation with Scevola. She guessed, however, that Scevola had simply gone to lie down in his lair, a narrow shabby room lighted by one glazed little window high up in the end wall. Catherine had put him in there on the very day he had brought her niece home and he had retained it for his own ever since. She could even picture him to herself in there stretched on his pallet. She was capable of that now. Formerly, for years after her return, people that were out of her sight were out of her mind also. Had they run away and left her she would not have thought of them at all. She would have wandered in and out of the empty house and round the empty fields without giving anybody a thought. Peyrol was the first human being she had noticed for years. Peyrol, since he had come, had always existed for her. And as a matter of fact the rover was generally very much in evidence about the farm. That afternoon, however, even Peyrol was not to be seen. Her uneasiness began to grow, but she felt a strange reluctance to go into the kitchen where she knew her aunt would be sitting in the armchair like a presiding genius of the house taking its rest, and unreadable in her immobility. And yet she felt she must talk about Réal to somebody. This was how the idea of going down to the church had come to her. She would talk of him to the priest and to God. The force of old associations asserted itself. She had been taught to believe that one could tell everything to a priest, and that the omnipotent God who knew everything could be prayed to, asked for grace, for strength, for mercy, for protection, for pity. She had done it and felt she had been heard.

HER HEART HAD quietened down while she rested under the wall. Pulling out a long stalk of grass she twined it round her fingers absently. The veil of cloud had thickened over her head, early dusk had descended upon the earth, and she had not found out what had become of Réal. She jumped to her feet wildly. But directly she had done that she felt the need of self-control. It was with her usual light step that she approached the front of the house and for the first time in her life perceived how barren and sombre it looked when Réal was not about. She slipped in quietly through the door of the main building and ran upstairs. It was dark on the landing. She passed by the door leading into the room occupied by her aunt and herself. It had been her father and mother's bedroom. The other big room was the lieutenant's during his visits to Escampobar. Without even a rustle of her dress, like a shadow, she glided along the passage, turned the handle without noise, and went in. After shutting the door behind her she listened. There was no sound in the house. Scevola was either already down in the yard or still lying open-eyed on his tumbled pallet in raging sulks about something. She had once accidentally caught him at it, down on his face, one eye and cheek of which were buried in the pillow, the other eye glaring savagely, and had been scared away by a thick mutter: "Keep off. Don't approach me." And all this had meant nothing to her then.

Having ascertained that the inside of the house was as still as the grave, Arlette walked across to the window, which when the lieutenant was occupying the room stood always open and with the shutter pushed right back against the wall. It was of course uncurtained, and as she came near to it Arlette caught sight of Peyrol coming down the hill on his return from the lookout. His white head gleamed like silver against the slope of the ground and by and by passed out of her sight, while her ear caught the sound of his footsteps below the window. They passed into the house, but she did not hear him come upstairs. He had gone into the kitchen. To Catherine. They would talk about her and Eugène. But what would they say? She was so new to life that everything appeared dangerous: talk, attitudes, glances. She felt frightened at the mere idea of silence between those two. It was possible. Suppose they didn't say anything to each other. That would be awful.

Yet she remained calm like a sensible person, who knows that rushing about in excitement is not the way to meet unknown dangers. She swept her eyes over the room and saw the lieutenant's valise in a corner. That was really what she had wanted to see. He wasn't gone then. But it didn't tell her, though she opened it, what had become of him. As to his return, she had no doubt whatever about that. He had always returned. She noticed particularly a large packet sewn up in sail-cloth and with three large red seals on the seam. It didn't, however, arrest her thoughts. Those were still hovering about Catherine and Peyrol downstairs. How changed they were. Had they ever thought that she was mad? She became indignant. "How could I have prevented that?" she asked herself with despair. She sat down on the edge of the bed in her usual attitude, her feet crossed, her hands lying in her lap. She felt on one of them the impress of Réal's lips, soothing, reassuring like every certitude, but she was aware of a still remaining confusion in her mind, an indefinite weariness like the strain of an imperfect vision trying to discern shifting outlines, floating shapes, incomprehensible signs. She could not resist the temptation of resting her tired body, just for a little while.

She lay down on the very edge of the bed, the kissed hand tucked under her cheek. The faculty of thinking abandoned her altogether, but she remained open-eyed, wide awake. In that position, without hearing the slightest sound, she saw the door handle move down as far as it would go, perfectly noiseless, as though the lock had been oiled not long before. Her impulse was to leap right out into the middle of the room, but she restrained herself and only swung herself into a sitting posture. The bed had not creaked. She lowered her feet gently to the ground, and by the time when holding her breath she put her ear against the door, the handle had come back into position. She had detected no sound outside. Not the faintest. Nothing. It never occurred to her to doubt her own eyes, but the whole thing had been so noiseless that it could not have disturbed the lightest sleeper. She was sure that had she been lying on her other side, that is with her back to the door, she would have known nothing. It was some time before she walked away from the door and sat on a chair which stood near a heavy and much-carved table, an heirloom more appropriate to a château than to a farmhouse. The dust of many months covered its smooth oval surface of dark, finely grained wood.

"It must have been Scevola," thought Arlette. It could have been no one else. What could he have wanted? She gave herself up to thought, but really she did not care. The absent Réal occupied all her mind. With an unconscious slowness her finger traced in the dust on the table the initials E A and achieved a circle round them. Then she jumped up, unlocked the door, and went downstairs. In the kitchen, as she fully expected, she found Scevola with the others. Directly she appeared he got up and ran upstairs, but returned almost immediately looking as if he had seen a ghost, and when Peyrol asked him some insignificant question his lips and even his chin trembled before he could command his voice. He avoided looking anybody in the face. The others too seemed shy of meeting each other's eyes, and the evening meal of the Escampobar seemed haunted by the absent lieutenant. Peyrol, besides, had his prisoner to think of. His existence presented a most interesting problem, and the proceedings of the English ship were another, closely connected with it and full of dangerous possibilities. Catherine's black and ungleaming eyes seemed to have sunk deeper in their sockets, but her face wore its habitual severe aloofness of expression. Suddenly Scevola spoke as if in answer to some thought of his own.

"What has lost us was moderation."

Peyrol swallowed the piece of bread and butter which he had been masticating slowly, and asked:

"What are you alluding to, *citoyen*?"

"I am alluding to the Republic," answered Scevola, in a more assured tone than usual. "Moderation I say. We patriots held our hand too soon. All the children of the ci-devants and all the children of traitors should have been killed together with their fathers and mothers. Contempt for civic virtues and love of tyranny were inborn in them all. They grow up and trample on all the sacred principles. . . . The work of the Terror is undone!"

"What do you propose to do about it?" growled Peyrol. "No use declaiming here or anywhere for that matter. You wouldn't find anybody to listen to you—you cannibal," he added in a good-humoured tone. Arlette, leaning her head on her left hand, was tracing with the forefinger of her right invisible initials on the table-cloth. Catherine, stooping to light a four-beaked oil lamp mounted on a brass pedestal, turned her finely carved face over her shoulder. The sans-culotte jumped up, flinging his arms about. His hair was tousled from his sleepless tumbling on his pallet. The unbuttoned sleeves of his shirt flapped against his thin hairy forearms. He no longer looked as though he had seen a ghost. He opened a wide black mouth, but Peyrol raised his finger at him calmly.

"No, no. The time when your own people up La Boyère way—don't they live up there?—trembled at the idea of you coming to visit them with a lot of patriot scallywags at your back is past. You have nobody at your back; and if you started spouting like this at large, people would rise up and hunt you down like a mad dog."

Scevola, who had shut his mouth, glanced over his shoulder, and as if impressed by his unsupported state went out of the kitchen, reeling, like a man who had been drinking. He had drunk nothing but water. Peyrol looked thoughtfully at the door which the indignant sans-culotte had slammed after him. During the colloquy between the two men, Arlette had disappeared into the *salle*. Catherine, straightening her long back, put the oil lamp with its four smoky flames on the table. It lighted her face from below. Peyrol moved it slightly aside before he spoke.

"It was lucky for you," he said, gazing upwards, "that Scevola hadn't even one other like himself when he came here."

"Yes," she admitted. "I had to face him alone from first to last. But can you see me between him and Arlette? In those days he raved terribly, but he was dazed and tired out. Afterwards I recovered myself and I could argue with him firmly. I used to say to him, 'Look, she is so young and she has no knowledge of herself.' Why, for months the only thing she would say that one could understand was 'Look how it spurts, look how it splashes!' He talked to me of his Republican virtue. He was not a profligate. He could wait. She was, he said, sacred to him, and things like that. He would walk up and down for hours talking of her and I would sit there listening to him with the key of the room the child was locked in, in my pocket. I temporized, and, as you say yourself, it was perhaps because he had no one at his back that he did not try to kill me, which he might have done any day. I temporized. And after all, why should he want to kill me? He told me more than once he was sure to have Arlette for his own. Many a time he made me shiver explaining why it must be so. She owed her life to him. Oh! that dreadful crazy life. You know he is one of those men that can be patient as far as women are concerned."

Peyrol nodded understandingly. "Yes, some are like that. That kind is more impatient sometimes to spill blood. Still I think that your life was one long narrow escape, at least till I turned up here."

"Things had settled down, somehow," murmured Catherine. "But all the same I was glad when you appeared here, a grey-headed man, serious."

"Grey hairs will come to any sort of man," observed Peyrol acidly, "and you did not know me. You don't know anything of me even now."

"There have been Peyrols living less than half a day's journey from here," observed Catherine in a reminiscent tone.

"That's all right," said the rover in such a peculiar tone that she asked him sharply: "What's the matter? Aren't you one of them? Isn't Peyrol your name?"

"I have had many names and this was one of them. So this name and my grey hair pleased you, Catherine? They gave you confidence in me, *hein*?"

"I wasn't sorry to see you come. Scevola, too, I believe. He heard that patriots were being hunted down, here and there, and he was growing quieter every day. You roused the child wonderfully."

"And did that please Scevola too?"

"Before you came she never spoke to anybody unless first spoken to. She didn't seem to care where she was. At the same time," added Catherine after a pause, "she didn't care what happened to her either. Oh, I have had some heavy hours thinking it all over, in the daytime doing my work, and at night while I lay awake, listening to her breathing. And I growing older all the time, and, who knows, with my last hour ready to strike. I often thought that when I felt it coming I would speak to you as I am speaking to you now."

"Oh, you did think," said Peyrol in an undertone. "Because of my grey hairs, I suppose."

"Yes. And because you came from beyond the seas," Catherine said with unbending mien and in an unflinching voice. "Don't you know that the first time Arlette saw you she spoke to you and that it was the first time I heard her speak of her own accord since she had been brought back by that man, and I had to wash her from head to foot before I put her into her mother's bed."

"The first time," repeated Peyrol.

"It was like a miracle happening," said Catherine, "and it was you that had done it."

"Then it must be that some Indian witch has given me the power," muttered Peyrol, so low that Catherine could not hear the words. But she did not seem to care, and presently went on again:

"And the child took to you wonderfully. Some sentiment was aroused in her at last."

"Yes," assented Peyrol grimly. "She did take to me. She learned to talk to—the old man."

"It's something in you that seems to have opened her mind and unloosed her tongue," said Catherine, speaking with a sort of regal composure down at Peyrol, like a chieftainess of a tribe. "I often used to look from afar at you two talking and wonder what she . . ."

"She talked like a child," struck in Peyrol abruptly. "And so you were going to speak to me before your last hour came. Why, you are not making ready to die yet?"

"Listen, Peyrol. If anybody's last hour is near it isn't mine. You just look about you a little. It was time I spoke to you."

"Why, I am not going to kill anybody," muttered Peyrol. "You are getting strange ideas into your head."

"It is as I said," insisted Catherine without animation. "Death seems to cling to her skirts. She has been running with it madly. Let us keep her feet out of more human blood."

Peyrol, who had let his head fall on his breast, jerked it up suddenly. "What on earth are you talking about?" he cried angrily. "I don't understand you at all."

"You have not seen the state she was in when I got her back into my hands," remarked Catherine. . . . "I suppose you know where the lieutenant is. What made him go off like that? Where did he go to?"

"I know," said Peyrol. "And he may be back tonight."

"You know where he is! And of course you know why he has gone away and why he is coming back," pronounced Catherine in an ominous voice. "Well, you had better tell him that unless he has a pair of eyes at the back of his head he had better not return here—not return at all; for if he does, nothing can save him from a treacherous blow."

"No man was ever safe from treachery," opined Peyrol after a moment's silence. "I won't pretend not to understand what you mean."

"You heard as well as I what Scevola said just before he went out. The lieutenant is the child of some ci-devant and Arlette of a man they called a traitor to his country. You can see yourself what was in his mind."

"He is a chicken-hearted spouter," said Peyrol contemptuously, but it did not affect Catherine's attitude of an old sibyl risen from the tripod to prophesy calmly atrocious disasters. "It's all his Republicanism," commented Peyrol with increased scorn. "He has got a fit of it on."

"No, that's jealousy," said Catherine. "Maybe he has ceased to care for her in all these years. It is a long time since he has left off worrying me. With a creature like that I thought that if I let him be master here . . . But no! I know that after the lieutenant started coming here his awful fancies have come back. He is not sleeping at night. His Republicanism is always there. But don't you know, Peyrol, that there may be jealousy without love?"

"You think so," said the rover profoundly. He pondered full of his own experience. "And he has tasted blood, too," he muttered after a pause. "You may be right."

"I may be right," repeated Catherine in a slightly indignant tone. "Every time I see Arlette near him I tremble lest it should come to words and to a bad blow. And when they are both out of my sight it is still worse. At this moment I am wondering where they are. They may be together and I daren't raise my voice to call her away for fear of rousing his fury."

"But it's the lieutenant he is after," observed Peyrol in a lowered voice. "Well, I can't stop the lieutenant coming back."

"Where is she? Where is he?" whispered Catherine in a tone betraying her secret anguish.

Peyrol rose quietly and went into the salle, leaving the door open. Catherine heard the latch of the outer door being lifted cautiously. In a few moments Peyrol returned as quietly as he had gone out.

"I stepped out to look at the weather. The moon is about to rise and the clouds have thinned down. One can see a star here and there." He lowered his voice considerably. "Arlette is sitting on the bench humming a little song to herself. I really wonder whether she knew I was standing within a few feet of her."

"She doesn't want to hear or see anybody except one man," affirmed Catherine, now in complete control of her voice. "And she was humming a song, did you say? She who would sit for hours without making a sound. And God knows what song it could have been!"

"Yes, there's a great change in her," admitted Peyrol with a heavy sigh. "This lieutenant," he continued after a pause, "has always behaved coldly to her. I noticed him many times turn his face away when he saw her coming towards us. You know what these epaulette-wearers are, Catherine. And then this one has some worm of his own that is gnawing at him. I doubt whether he has ever forgotten that he was a ci-devant boy. Yet I do believe that she does not want to see and hear anybody but him. Is it because she has been deranged in her head for so long?"

"No, Peyrol," said the old woman. "It isn't that. You want to know how I can tell? For years nothing could make her either laugh or cry. You know that yourself. You have seen her every day. Would you believe that within the last month she has been both crying and laughing on my breast without knowing why?"

"This I don't understand," said Peyrol.

"But I do. That lieutenant has got only to whistle to make her run after him. Yes, Peyrol. That is so. She has no fear, no shame, no pride. I myself have been nearly like that." Her fine brown face seemed to grow more impassive before she went on much lower and as if arguing with herself: "Only I at least was never blood-mad. I was fit for any man's arms. . . . But then that man is not a priest."

The last words made Peyrol start. He had almost forgotten that story. He said to himself: "She knows, she has had the experience."

"Look here, Catherine," he said decisively, "the lieutenant is coming back. He will be here probably about midnight. But one thing I can tell you: he is not coming back to whistle her away. Oh, no! It is not for her sake that he will come back."

"Well, if it isn't for her that he is coming back then it must be because death has beckoned to him," she announced in a tone of solemn unemotional conviction. "A man who has received a sign from death—nothing can stop him!"

Peyrol, who had seen death face to face many times, looked at Catherine's fine brown profile curiously.

"It is a fact," he murmured, "that men who rush out to seek death do not often find it. So one must have a sign? What sort of sign would it be?"

"How is anybody to know?" asked Catherine, staring across the kitchen at the wall. "Even those to whom it is made do not recognize it for what it is. But they obey all the same. I tell you, Peyrol, nothing can stop them. It may be a glance, or a smile, or a shadow on the water, or a thought that passes through the head. For my poor brother and sister-in-law it was the face of their child."

Peyrol folded his arms on his breast and dropped his head. Melancholy was a sentiment to which he was a stranger; for what has melancholy to do with the life of a sea-rover, a Brother of the Coast, a simple, venturesome, precarious life, full of risks and leaving no time for introspection or for that momentary self-forgetfulness which is called gaiety. Sombre fury, fierce merriment, he had known in passing gusts, coming from outside; but never this intimate inward sense of the vanity of all things, that doubt of the power within himself.

"I wonder what the sign for me will be," he thought; and concluded with self-contempt that for him there would be no sign, that he would have to die in his bed like an old yard dog in his kennel. Having reached that depth of despondency, there was nothing more before him but a black gulf into which his consciousness sank like a stone.

The silence which had lasted perhaps a minute after Catherine had finished speaking was traversed suddenly by a clear high voice saying:

"What are you two plotting here?"

Arlette stood in the doorway of the *salle*. The gleam of light in the whites of her eyes set off her black and penetrating glance. The surprise was complete. The profile of Catherine, who was standing by the table, became if possible harder; a sharp carving of an old prophetess of some desert tribe. Arlette made three steps forward. In Peyrol even extreme astonishment was deliberate. He had been famous for never looking as though he had been caught unprepared. Age had accentuated that trait of a born leader. He only slipped off the edge of the table and said in his deep voice:

"Why, *patronne*! We haven't said a word to each other for ever so long."

Arlette moved nearer still. "I know," she cried. "It was horrible. I have been watching you two. Scevola came and dumped himself on the bench close to me. He began to talk to me, and so I went away. That man bores me. And here I find you people saying nothing. It's insupportable. What has come to you both? Say, you, Papa Peyrol—don't you like me any more?" Her voice filled the kitchen. Peyrol went to the *salle* door and shut it. While coming back he was staggered by the brilliance of life within her that seemed to pale the flames of the lamp. He said half in jest:

"I don't know whether I didn't like you better when you were quieter."

"And you would like best to see me still quieter in my grave."

She dazzled him. Vitality streamed out of her eyes, her lips, her whole person, enveloped her like a halo and . . . yes, truly, the faintest possible flush had appeared on her cheeks, played on them faintly rosy like the light of a distant flame on the snow. She raised her arms up in the air and let her hands fall from on high on Peyrol's shoulders, captured his desperately dodging eyes with her black and compelling glance, put out all her instinctive seduction—while he felt a growing fierceness in the grip of her fingers.

"No! I can't hold it in! Monsieur Peyrol, Papa Peyrol, old gunner, you horrid sea-wolf, be an angel and tell me where he is."

The rover, whom only that morning the powerful grasp of Lieutenant Réal found as unshakable as a rock, felt all his strength vanish under the hands of that woman. He said thickly:

"He has gone to Toulon. He had to go."

"What for? Speak the truth to me!"

"Truth is not for everybody to know," mumbled Peyrol, with a sinking sensation as though the very ground were going soft under his feet. "On service," he added in a growl.

Her hands slipped suddenly from his big shoulders. "On service?" she repeated. "What service?" Her voice sank and the words "Oh, yes! His service" were hardly heard by Peyrol, who as soon as her hands had left his shoulders felt his strength returning to him and the yielding earth grow firm again under his feet. Right in front of him Arlette, silent, with her arms hanging down before her with entwined fingers, seemed stunned because Lieutenant Réal was not free from all earthly connections, like a visiting angel from heaven depending only on God to whom she had prayed. She had to share him with some service that could order him about. She felt in herself a strength, a power, greater than any service.

"Peyrol," she cried low, "don't break my heart, my new heart, that has just begun to beat. Feel how it beats. Who could bear it?" She seized the rover's thick hairy paw and pressed it hard against her breast. "Tell me when he will be back."

"Listen, patronne, you had better go upstairs," began Peyrol with a great effort and snatching his captured hand away. He staggered backwards a little while Arlette shouted at him:

"You can't order me about as you used to do." In all the changes from entreaty to anger she never struck a false note, so that her emotional outburst had the heart-moving power of inspired art. She turned round with a tempestuous swish to Catherine who had neither stirred nor emitted a sound: "Nothing you two can do will make any difference now." The next moment she was facing Peyrol again. "You frighten me with your white hairs. Come! . . . am I to go on my knees to you . . . ? There!"

The rover caught her under the elbows, swung her up clear of the ground, and set her down on her feet as if she had been a child. Directly he had let her go, she stamped her foot at him.

"Are you stupid?" she cried. "Don't you understand that something has happened to-day?"

Through all this scene Peyrol had kept his head as creditably as could have been expected, in the manner of a seaman caught by a white squall in the tropics. But at those words a dozen thoughts tried to rush together through his mind, in chase of that startling declaration. Something had happened! Where? How? Whom to? What thing? It couldn't be anything between her and the lieutenant. He had, it seemed to him, never lost sight of the lieutenant from the first hour when they met in the morning till he had sent him off to Toulon by an actual push on the shoulder; except while he was having his dinner in the next room with the door open, and for the few minutes spent in talking with Michel in the yard. But that was only a very few minutes, and directly afterwards the first sight of the lieutenant sitting gloomily on the bench like a lonely crow did not suggest either elation or excitement or any emotion connected with a woman. In the face of these difficulties Peyrol's mind became suddenly a blank.

"*Voyons, patronne*," he began, unable to think of anything else to say. "What's all this fuss about? I expect him to be back here about midnight."

He was extremely relieved to notice that she believed him. It was the truth. For indeed he did not know what he could have invented on the spur of the moment that would get her out of the way and induce her to go to bed. She treated him to a sinister frown and a terribly menacing, "If you have lied . . . Oh!"

He produced an indulgent smile. "Compose yourself. He will be here soon after midnight. You may go to sleep with an easy mind."

She turned her back on him contemptuously, and said curtly, "Come along, Aunt," and went to the door leading to the passage. There she turned for a moment with her hand on the door handle.

"You are changed. I can't trust either of you. You are not the same people."

She went out. Only then did Catherine detach her gaze from the wall to meet Peyrol's eyes. "Did you hear what she said? We! Changed! It is she herself . . ."

Peyrol nodded twice and there was a long pause, during which even the flames of the lamp did not stir.

"Go after her, Mademoiselle Catherine," he said at last with a shade of sympathy in his tone. She did not move. "*Allons— du courage*," he urged her deferentially as it were. "Try to put her to sleep."

CHAPTER XII

U PRIGHT AND DELIBERATE, Catherine left the kitchen, and in the passage outside found Arlette waiting for her with a lighted candle in her hand. Her heart was filled with sudden desolation by the beauty of that young face enhaloed in the patch of light, with the profound darkness as of a dungeon for a background. At once her niece led the way upstairs muttering savagely through her pretty teeth: "He thinks I could go to sleep. Old imbecile!"

Peyrol did not take his eyes off Catherine's straight back till the door had closed after her. Only then he relieved himself by letting the air escape through his pursed lips and rolling his eyes freely about. He picked up the lamp by the ring on the top of the central rod and went into the *salle,* closing behind him the door of the dark kitchen. He stood the lamp on the very table on which Lieutenant Réal had had his midday meal. A small white cloth was still spread on it and there was his chair askew as he had pushed it back when he got up. Another of the many chairs in the *salle* was turned round conspicuously to face the table. These things made Peyrol remark to himself bitterly: "She sat and stared at him as if he had been gilt all over, with three heads and seven arms on his body"—a comparison reminiscent of certain idols he had seen in an Indian temple. Though not an iconoclast, Peyrol felt positively sick at the recollection, and hastened to step outside. The great cloud had broken up and the mighty fragments were moving to the westward in stately flight before the rising moon. Scevola, who had been lying extended full length on the bench, swung himself up suddenly, very upright.

"Had a little nap in the open?" asked Peyrol, letting his eyes roam through the luminous space under the departing rearguard of the clouds jostling each other up there.

"I did not sleep," said the sans-culotte. "I haven't closed my eyes—not for one moment."

"That must be because you weren't sleepy," suggested the deliberate Peyrol, whose thoughts were far away with the English ship. His mental eye contemplated her black image against the white beach of the Salins describing a sparkling curve under the moon, and meantime he went on slowly: "For it could not have been noise that kept you awake." On the level of Escampobar the shadows lay long on the ground while the side of the lookout hill remained yet black but edged with an increasing brightness. And the amenity of the stillness was such that it softened for a moment Peyrol's hard inward attitude towards all mankind, including even the captain of the English ship. The old rover savoured a moment of serenity in the midst of his cares.

"This is an accursed spot," declared Scevola suddenly.

Peyrol, without turning his head, looked at him sideways. Though he had sprung up from his reclining posture smartly enough, the citizen had gone slack all over and was sitting all in a heap. His shoulders were hunched up, his hands reposed on his knees. With his staring eyes he resembled a sick child in the moonlight.

"It's the very spot for hatching treacheries. One feels steeped in them up to the neck."

He shuddered and yawned a long irresistible nervous yawn with the gleam of unexpected long canines in a retracted, gaping mouth giving away the restless panther lurking in the man.

"Oh, yes, there's treachery about right enough. You couldn't conceive that, *citoyen*?"

"Of course I couldn't," assented Peyrol with serene contempt. "What is this treachery that you are concocting?" he added carelessly, in a social way, while enjoying the charm of a moonlit evening. Scevola, who did not expect that turn, managed, however, to produce a rattling sort of laugh almost at once.

"That's a good one. Ha! ha! ha! . . . Me! . . . Concocting! . . . Why me?"

"Well," said Peyrol carelessly, "there are not many of us to carry out treacheries about here. The women are gone upstairs; Michel is down at the tartane. There's me, and you would not dare suspect me of treachery. Well, there remains only you."

Scevola roused himself. "This is not much of a jest," he said. "I have been a treason-hunter. I . . ."

He checked that strain. He was full of purely emotional suspicions. Peyrol was talking like this only to annoy him and to get him out of the way; but in the particular state of his feelings Scevola was acutely aware of every syllable of these offensive remarks. "Aha," he thought to himself, "he doesn't mention the lieutenant." This omission seemed to the patriot of immense importance. If Peyrol had not mentioned the lieutenant it was because those two had been plotting some treachery together, all the afternoon on board that tartane. That's why nothing had been seen of them for the best part of the day. As a matter of fact, Scevola, too, had observed Peyrol returning to the farm in the evening, only he had observed him from another window than Arlette. This was a few minutes before his attempt to open the lieutenant's door, in order to find out whether Réal was in his room. He had tiptoed away, uncertain, and going into the kitchen had found only Catherine and Peyrol there. Directly Arlette joined them a sudden inspiration made him run upstairs and try the door again. It was open now! A clear proof that it was Arlette who had been locked up in there. The discovery that she made herself at home like this in the lieutenant's room gave Scevola such a sickening shock that he thought he would die of it. It was beyond doubt now that the lieutenant had been conspiring with Peyrol down on board that tartane; for what else could they have been doing there? "But why had not Réal come up in the evening with Peyrol?" Scevola asked himself, sitting on the bench with his hands clasped between his knees. . . . "It's their cunning," he concluded suddenly. "Conspirators always avoid being seen together. Ha!"

It was as if somebody had let off a lot of fireworks in his brain. He was illuminated, dazzled, confused, with a hissing in his ears and showers of sparks before his eyes. When he raised his head he saw he was alone. Peyrol had vanished. Scevola seemed to remember that he had heard somebody pronounce the word "good-night" and the door of the *salle* slam. And sure enough the door of the *salle* was shut now. A dim light shone in the window that was next to it. Peyrol had extinguished three of the lamp flames and was now reclining on one of the long tables with that faculty of accommodating himself to a plank an old sea-dog never loses. He had decided to remain below simply to be handy, and he didn't lie down on one of the benches along the wall because they were too narrow. He left one wick burning, so that the lieutenant should know where to look for him, and he was tired enough to think that he would snatch a couple of hours' sleep before Réal could return from Toulon. He settled himself with one arm under his head as if he were on the deck of a privateer, and it never occurred to him that Scevola was looking through the panes; but they were so small and dusty that the patriot could see nothing. His movement had been purely instinctive. He wasn't even aware that he had looked in. He went away from there, walked to the end of the building, spun round and walked back again to the other end; and it was as if he had been afraid of going beyond the wall against which he reeled sometimes. "Conspiracy, conspiracy," he thought. He was now absolutely certain that the lieutenant was still hiding in that tartane, and was only waiting till all was quiet to sneak back to his room in which Scevola had proof positive that Arlette was in the habit of making herself at home. To rob him of his right to Arlette was part of the conspiracy no doubt.

"Have I been a slave to those two women, have I waited all those years, only to see that corrupt creature go off infamously with a ci-devant, with a conspiring aristocrat?"

He became giddy with virtuous fury. There was enough evidence there for any revolutionary tribunal to cut all their heads off. Tribunal! There was no tribunal! No revolutionary justice! No patriots! He hit his shoulder against the wall in his distress with such force that he rebounded. This world was no place for patriots.

"If I had betrayed myself in the kitchen they would have murdered me in there."

As it was he thought that he had said too much. Too much. "Prudence! Caution!" he repeated to himself, gesticulating with both arms. Suddenly he stumbled and there was an amazing metallic clatter made by something that fell at his feet.

"They are trying to kill me now," he thought, shaking with fright. He gave himself up for dead. Profound silence reigned all round. Nothing more happened. He stooped fearfully to look and recognized his own stable fork lying on the ground. He remembered he had left it at noon leaning against the wall. His own foot had made it fall. He threw himself upon it greedily. "Here's what I need," he muttered feverishly. "I suppose that by now the lieutenant would think I am gone to bed."

He flattened himself upright against the wall with the fork held along his body like a grounded musket. The moon clearing the hill-top flooded suddenly the front of the house with its cold light, but he didn't know it; he imagined himself still to be ambushed in the shadow and remained motionless, glaring at the path leading towards the cove. His teeth chattered with savage impatience.

He was so plainly visible in his deathlike rigidity that Michel, coming up out of the ravine, stopped dead short, believing him an apparition not belonging to this earth. Scevola, on his side, noticed the moving shadow cast by a man—that man!—and charged forward without reflection, the prongs of the fork lowered like a bayonet. He didn't shout. He came straight on, growling like a dog, and lunged headlong with his weapon.

Michel, a primitive, untroubled by anything so uncertain as intelli-gence, executed an instantaneous sideways leap with the precision of a wild animal; but he was enough of a man to become afterwards paralyzed with astonishment. The impetus of the rush carried Scevola several yards down the hill, before he could turn round and assume an offensive attitude. Then the two adversaries recognized each other. The terrorist exclaimed: "Michel?" and Michel hastened to pick up a large stone from the ground.

"Hey, you, Scevola," he cried, not very loud but very threatening. "What are these tricks. . . ? Keep away, or I will heave that piece of rock at your head, and I am good at that."

Scevola grounded the fork with a thud. "I didn't recognize you," he said.

"That's a story. Who did you think I was? Not the other! I haven't got a bandaged head, have I?"

Scevola began to scramble up. "What's this?" he asked. "What head, did you say?"

"I say that if you come near I will knock you over with that stone," answered Michel. "You aren't to be trusted when the moon is full. Not recognize! There's a silly excuse for flying at people like this. You haven't got anything against me, have you?"

"No," said the ex-terrorist in a dubious tone and keeping a watchful eye on Michel, who was still holding the stone in his hand.

"People have been saying for years that you are a kind of lunatic," Michel criticized fearlessly, because the other's discomfiture was evident enough to put heart into the timid hare. "If a fellow cannot come up now to get a snooze in the shed without being run at with a fork, well . . ."

"I was only going to put this fork away," Scevola burst out volubly. "I had left it leaning against the wall, and as I was passing along I suddenly saw it, so I thought I would put it in the stable before I went to bed. That's all."

Michel's mouth fell open a bit.

"Now what do you think I would want with a stable fork at this time of night, if it wasn't to put it away?" argued Scevola.

"What indeed!" mumbled Michel, who began to doubt the evidence of his senses.

"You go about mooning like a fool and imagine a lot of silly things, you great, stupid imbecile. All I wanted to do was to ask whether everything was all right down there, and you, idiot, bound to one side like a goat and pick up a stone. The moon has affected your head, not mine. Now drop it."

Michel, accustomed to do what he was told, opened his fingers slowly, not quite convinced but thinking there might be something in it. Scevola, perceiving his advantage, scolded on:

"You are dangerous. You ought to have your feet and hands tied every full moon. What did you say about a head just now? What head?"

"I said that I didn't have a broken head."

"Was that all?" said Scevola. He was asking himself what on earth could have happened down there during the afternoon to cause a broken head. Clearly, it must have been either a fight or an accident, but in any case he considered that it was for him a favourable circumstance, for obviously a man with a bandaged head is at a disadvantage. He was inclined to think it must have been some silly accident, and he regretted profoundly that the lieutenant had not killed himself outright. He turned sourly to Michel.

"Now you may go into the shed. And don't try any of your tricks with me any more, because next time you pick up a stone I will shoot you like a dog."

He began to move towards the yard gate which stood always open, throwing over his shoulder an order to Michel: "Go into the *salle.* Somebody has left a light in there. They all seem to have gone crazy to-day. Take the lamp into the kitchen and put it out and see that the door into the yard is shut. I am going to bed." He passed through the gateway, but he did not penetrate into the yard very far. He stopped to watch Michel obeying the order. Scevola, advancing his head cautiously beyond the pillar of the gate, waited till he had seen Michel open the door of the *salle* and then bounded out again across the level space and down the ravine path. It was a matter of less than a minute. His fork was still on his shoulder. His only desire was not to be interfered with, and for the rest he did not care what they all did, what they would think and how they would behave. The fixed idea had taken complete possession of him. He had no plan, but he had a principle on which to act; and that was to get at the lieutenant unawares, and if the fellow died without knowing what hand had struck him, so much the better. Scevola was going to act in the cause of virtue and justice. It was not to be a matter of personal contest at all. Meantime, Michel, having gone into the *salle*, had discovered Peyrol fast asleep on a table. Though his reverence for Peyrol was unbounded, his simplicity was such that he shook his master by the shoulder as he would have done any common mortal. The rover passed from a state of inertia into a sitting posture so quickly that Michel stepped back a pace and waited to be addressed. But as Peyrol only stared at him, Michel took the initiative in a concise phrase:

"He's at it!"

Peyrol did not seem completely awake: "What is it you mean?" he asked.

"He is making motions to escape."

Peyrol was wide awake now. He even swung his feet off the table.

"Is he? Haven't you locked the cabin door?"

Michel, very frightened, explained that he had never been told to do that.

"No?" remarked Peyrol placidly. "I must have forgotten." But Michel remained agitated and murmured: "He is escaping."

"That's all right," said Peyrol. "What are you fussing about? How far can he escape, do you think?"

A slow grin appeared on Michel's face. "If he tries to scramble over the top of the rocks, he will get a broken neck in a very short time," he said. "And he certainly won't get very far, that's a fact."

"Well—you see," said Peyrol.

"And he doesn't seem strong either. He crawled out of the cabin door and got as far as the little water cask and he dipped and dipped into it. It must be half empty by now. After that he got on to his legs. I cleared out ashore directly I heard him move," he went on in a tone of intense self-approval. "I hid myself behind a rock and watched him."

"Quite right," observed Peyrol. After that word of commendation, Michel's face wore a constant grin.

"He sat on the after-deck," he went on as if relating an immense joke, "with his feet dangling down the hold, and may the devil take me if I don't think he had a nap with his back against the cask. He was nodding and catching himself up, with that big white head of his. Well, I got tired of watching that, and as you told me to keep out of his way, I thought I would come up here and sleep in the shed. That was right, wasn't it?"

"Quite right," repeated Peyrol. "Well, you go now into the shed. And so you left him sitting on the after-deck?"

"Yes," said Michel. "But he was rousing himself. I hadn't got away more than ten yards when I heard an awful thump on board. I think he tried to get up and fell down the hold."

"Fell down the hold?" repeated Peyrol sharply.

"Yes, *notre maître*. I thought at first I would go back and see, but you had warned me against him, hadn't you? And I really think that nothing can kill him."

Peyrol got down from the table with an air of concern which would have astonished Michel, if he had not been utterly incapable of observing things.

"This must be seen to," murmured the rover, buttoning the waistband of his trousers. "My cudgel there, in the corner. Now you go to the shed. What the devil are you doing at the door? Don't you know the way to the shed?" This last observation was caused by Michel remaining in the doorway of the *salle* with his head out and looking to right and left along the front of the house. "What's come to you? You don't suppose he has been able to follow you so quick as this up here?"

"Oh no, *notre maître,* quite impossible. I saw that *sacré* Scevola promenading up and down here. I don't want to meet him again."

"Was he promenading outside?" asked Peyrol, with annoyance. "Well, what do you think he can do to you? What notions have you got in your silly head? You are getting worse and worse. Out you go."

Peyrol extinguished the lamp and, going out, closed the door without the slightest noise. The intelligence about Scevola being on the move did not please him very much, but he reflected that probably the sans-culotte had fallen asleep again and after waking up was on his way to bed when Michel caught sight of him. He had his own view of the patriot's psychology and did not think the women were in any danger. Nevertheless he went to the shed and heard the rustling of straw as Michel settled himself for the night.

"*Debout*," he cried low. "Sh, don't make any noise. I want you to go into the house and sleep at the bottom of the stairs. If you hear voices, go up, and if you see Scevola about, knock him down. You aren't afraid of him, are you?"

"No, if you tell me not to be," said Michel, who, picking up his shoes, a present from Peyrol, walked barefoot towards the house. The rover watched him slipping noiselessly through the *salle* door. Having thus, so to speak, guarded his base, Peyrol proceeded down the ravine with a very deliberate caution. When he got as far as the little hollow in the ground from which the mastheads of the tartane could be seen, he squatted and waited. He didn't know what his prisoner had done or was doing and he did not want to blunder into the way of his escape. The day-old moon was high enough to have shortened the shadows almost to nothing and all the rocks were inundated by a yellow sheen, while the bushes by contrast looked very black. Peyrol reflected that he was not very well concealed. The continued silence impressed him in the end. "He has got away," he thought. Yet he was not sure. Nobody could be sure. He reckoned it was about an hour since Michel had left the tartane; time enough for a man, even on all fours, to crawl down to the shore of the cove. Peyrol wished he had not hit so hard. His object could have been attained with half the force. On the other hand all the proceedings of his prisoner, as reported by Michel, seemed quite rational. Naturally the fellow was badly shaken. Peyrol felt as though he wanted to go on board and give him some encouragement, and even active assistance.

The report of a gun from seaward cut his breath short as he lay there meditating. Within a minute there was a second report, sending another wave of deep sound among the crags and hills of the peninsula. The ensuing silence was so profound that it seemed to extend to the very inside of Peyrol's head, and lull all his thoughts for a moment. But he had understood. He said to himself that after this his prisoner, if he had life enough left in him to stir a limb, would rather die than not try to make his way to the seashore. The ship was calling to her man.

In fact those two guns had proceeded from the *Amelia*. After passing beyond Cape Esterel, Captain Vincent dropped an anchor under foot off the beach just as Peyrol had surmised he would do. From about six o'clock till nine the *Amelia* lay there with her unfurled sails hanging in the gear. Just before the moon rose the captain came up on deck and after a short conference with his first lieutenant, directed the master to get the ship under way and put her head again for the Petite Passe. Then he went below, and presently word was passed on deck that the captain wanted Mr. Bolt. When the master's mate appeared in his cabin, Captain Vincent motioned him to a chair.

"I don't think I ought to have listened to you," he said. "Still, the idea was fascinating, but how it would strike other people it is hard to say. The losing of our man is the worst feature. I have an idea that we might recover him. He may have been captured by the peasants or have met with an accident. It's unbearable to think of him lying at the foot of some rock with a broken leg. I have ordered the first and second cutters to be manned, and I propose that you should take command of them, enter the cove and, if necessary, advance a little inland to investigate. As far as we know there have never been any troops on that peninsula. The first thing you will do is to examine the coast."

He talked for some time, giving more minute instructions, and then went on deck. The *Amelia*, with the two cutters towing alongside, reached about half-way down the Passe and then the boats were ordered to proceed. Just before they shoved off, two guns were fired in quick succession.

"Like this, Bolt," explained Captain Vincent, "Symons will guess that we are looking for him; and if he is hiding anywhere near the shore he will be sure to come down where he can be seen by you."

CHAPTER XIII

THE MOTIVE FORCE of a fixed idea is very great. In the case of Scevola it was great enough to launch him down the slope and to rob him for the moment of all caution. He bounded amongst the boulders, using the handle of the stable fork for a staff. He paid no regard to the nature of the ground, till he got a fall and found himself sprawling on his face, while the stable fork went clattering down until it was stopped by a bush. It was this circumstance which saved Peyrol's prisoner from being caught unawares. Since he had got out of the little cabin, simply because after coming to himself he had perceived it was open, Symons had been greatly refreshed by long drinks of cold water and by his little nap in the fresh air. Every moment he was feeling in better command of his limbs. As to the command of his thoughts, that was coming to him too rather quickly. The advantage of having a very thick skull became evident in the fact that as soon as he had dragged himself out of that cabin he knew where he was. The next thing he did was to look at the moon, to judge of the passage of time. Then he gave way to an immense surprise at the fact of being alone aboard the tartane. As he sat with his legs dangling into the open hold he tried to guess how it came about that the cabin had been left unlocked and unguarded.

He went on thinking about this unexpected situation. What could have become of that white-headed villain? Was he dodging about somewhere watching for a chance to give him another tap on the head? Symons felt suddenly very unsafe sitting there on the after-deck in the full light of the moon. Instinct rather than reason suggested to him that he ought to get down into the dark hold. It seemed a great undertaking at first, but once he started he accomplished it with the greatest ease, though he could not avoid knocking down a small spar which was leaning up against the deck. It preceded him into the hold with a loud crash which gave poor Symons an attack of palpitation of the heart. He sat on the keelson of the tartane and gasped, but after a while reflected that all this did not matter. His head felt very big, his neck was very painful, and one shoulder was certainly very stiff. He could never stand up against that old ruffian. But what had become of him? Why! He had gone to fetch the soldiers! After that conclusion Symons became more composed. He began to try to remember things. When he had last seen that old fellow it was daylight, and now—Symons looked up at the moon again—it must be near six bells in the first watch. No doubt the old scoundrel was sitting in a wine shop drinking with the soldiers. They would be here soon enough! The idea of being a prisoner of war made his heart sink a little. His ship appeared to him invested with an extraordinary number of lovable features which included Captain Vincent and the first lieutenant. He would have been glad to shake hands even with the corporal, a surly and malicious marine acting as master-at-arms of the ship. "I wonder where she is now," he thought dismally, feeling his distaste for captivity grow with the increase of his strength.

It was at this moment that he heard the noise of Scevola's fall. It was pretty close; but afterwards he heard no voices and footsteps heralding the approach of a body of men. If this was the old ruffian coming back, then he was coming back alone. At once Symons started on all fours for the fore-end of the tartane. He had an idea that ensconced under the fore-deck he would be in a better position to parley with the enemy and that perhaps he could find there a hand-spike or some piece of iron to defend himself with. Just as he had settled himself in his hiding-place Scevola stepped from the shore on to the after-deck.

At the very first glance Symons perceived that this one was very unlike the man he expected to see. He felt rather disappointed. As Scevola stood still in the full moonlight Symons congratulated himself on having taken up a position under the fore-deck. That fellow, who had a beard, was like a sparrow in body compared with the other; but he was armed dangerously with something that looked to Symons like either a trident or fishgrains on a staff. "A devil of a weapon that," he thought, appalled. And what on earth did that beggar want on board? What could he be after?

The new-comer acted strangely at first. He stood stock-still, craning his neck here and there, peering along the whole length of the tartane, then crossing the deck he repeated all those performances on the other side. "He has noticed that the cabin door is open. He's trying to see where I've got to. He will be coming forward to look for me," said Symons to himself. "If he corners me here with that beastly pronged affair I am done for." For a moment he debated within himself whether it wouldn't be better to make a dash for it and scramble ashore; but in the end he mistrusted his strength. "He would run me down for sure," he concluded. "And he means no good, that's certain. No man would go about at night with a confounded thing like that if he didn't mean to do for somebody."

Scevola, after keeping perfectly still, straining his ears for any sound from below where he supposed Lieutenant Réal to be, stooped down to the cabin scuttle and called in a low voice: "Are you there, lieutenant?" Symons saw these motions and could not imagine their purport. That excellent able seaman of proved courage in many cutting-out expeditions broke into a slight perspiration. In the light of the moon the prongs of the fork polished by much use shone like silver, and the whole aspect of the stranger was weird and dangerous in the extreme. Whom could that man be after but him, himself?

Scevola, receiving no answer, remained in a stooping position. He could not detect the slightest sound of breathing down there. He remained in this position so long that Symons became quite interested. "He must think I am still down there," he whispered to himself. The next proceeding was quite astonishing. The man, taking up a position on one side of the cuddy scuttle and holding his horrid weapon as one would a boarding pike, uttered a terrific whoop and went on yelling in French with such volubility that he quite frightened Symons. Suddenly he left off, moved away from the scuttle, and looked at a loss what to do next. Anybody who could have seen then Symons' protruded head with his face turned aft would have seen on it an expression of horror. "The cunning beast," he thought. "If I had been down there, with the row he made I would have surely rushed on deck and then he would have had me." Symons experienced the feeling of a very narrow escape; yet it brought not much relief. It was simply a matter of time. The fellow's homicidal purpose was evident. He was bound before long to come forward. Symons saw him move, and thought, "Now he's coming," and prepared himself for a dash. "If I can dodge past those blamed prongs I might be able to take him by the throat," he reflected, without, however, feeling much confidence in himself.

But to his great relief Scevola's purpose was simply to conceal the fork in the hold in such a manner that the handle of it just reached the edge of the after-deck. In that position it was of course invisible to anybody coming from the shore. Scevola had made up his mind that the lieutenant was out of the tartane. He had wandered away along the shore and would probably be back in a moment. Meantime it had occurred to him to see if he could discover anything compromising in the cabin. He did not take the fork down with him because in that confined space it would have been useless and rather a source of embarrassment than otherwise, should the returning lieutenant find him there. He cast a circular glance around the basin and then prepared to go down.

Every movement of his was watched by Symons. He guessed Scevola's purpose by his movements and said to himself: "Here's my only chance, and not a second to be lost either." Directly Scevola turned his back on the forepart of the tartane in order to go down the little cabin ladder, Symons crawled out from his concealment. He ran along the hold on all fours for fear the other should turn his head round before disappearing below, but directly he judged that the man had touched bottom, he stood on his feet and catching hold of the main rigging swung himself on the after-deck and, as it were in the same movement, flung himself on the doors of the cabin which came together with a crash. How he could secure them he had not thought, but as a matter of fact he saw the padlock hanging on a staple on one side; the key was in it, and it was a matter of a fraction of a second to secure the doors effectually.

Almost simultaneously with the crash of the cabin door there was a shrill exclamation of surprise down there, and just as Symons had turned the key the man he had trapped made an effort to break out. That, however, did not disturb Symons. He knew the strength of that door. His first action was to get possession of the stable fork. At once he felt himself a match for any single man or even two men unless they had firearms. He had no hope, however, of being able to resist the soldiers and really had no intention of doing so. He expected to see them appear at any moment led by that confounded *marinero*. As to what the farmer man had come for on board the tartane he had not the slightest doubt about it. Not being troubled by too much imagination, it seemed to him obvious that it was to kill an Englishman and for nothing else. "Well, I am jiggered," he exclaimed mentally. "The damned savage! I haven't done anything to him. They must be a murderous lot hereabouts." He looked anxiously up the slope. He would have welcomed the arrival of soldiers. He wanted more than ever to be made a proper prisoner, but a profound stillness reigned on the shore and a most absolute silence down below in the cabin. Absolute. No word, no movement. The silence of the grave. "He's scared to death," thought Symons, hitting in his simplicity on the exact truth. "It would serve him jolly well right if I went down there and ran him through with that thing. I would do it for a shilling, too." He was getting angry. It occurred to him also that there was some wine down there, too. He discovered he was very thirsty and he felt rather faint. He sat down on the little skylight to think the matter over while awaiting the soldiers. He even gave a friendly thought to Peyrol himself. He was quite aware that he could have gone ashore and hidden himself for a time, but that meant in the end being hunted among the rocks and, certainly, captured; with the additional risk of getting a musket ball through his body.

The first gun of the *Amelia* lifted him to his feet as though he had been snatched up by the hair of his head. He intended to give a resounding cheer, but produced only a feeble gurgle in his throat. His ship was talking to him. They hadn't given him up. At the second report he scrambled ashore with the agility of a cat—in fact, with so much agility that he had a fit of giddiness. After it passed off he returned deliberately to the tartane to get hold of the stable fork. Then trembling with emotion, he staggered off quietly and resolutely with the only purpose of getting down to the seashore. He knew that as long as he kept downhill he would be all right. The ground in this part being a smooth rocky surface and Symons being barefooted, he passed at no great distance from Peyrol without being heard. When he got on rough ground he used the stable fork for a staff. Slowly as he moved he was not really strong enough to be sure-footed. Ten minutes later or so Peyrol, lying ensconced behind a bush, heard the noise of a rolling stone far away in the direction of the cove. Instantly the patient Peyrol got on his feet and started towards the cove himself. Perhaps he would have smiled if the importance and gravity of the affair in which he was engaged had not given all his thoughts a serious cast. Pursuing a higher path than the one followed by Symons, he had presently the satisfaction of seeing the fugitive, made very noticeable by the white bandages about his head, engaged in the last part of the steep descent. No nurse could have watched with more anxiety the adventure of a little boy than Peyrol the progress of his former prisoner. He was very glad to perceive that he had had the sense to take what looked like the tartane's boathook to help himself with. As Symons' figure sank lower and lower in his descent Peyrol moved on, step by step, till at last he saw him from above sitting down on the seashore, looking very forlorn and lonely, with his bandaged head between his hands. Instantly Peyrol sat down too, protected by a projecting rock. And it is safe to say that with that there came a complete cessation of all sound and movement on the lonely head of the peninsula for a full half hour.

Peyrol was not in doubt as to what was going to happen. He was as certain that the corvette's boat or boats were now on the way to the cove as though he had seen them leave the side of the *Amelia*. But he began to get a little impatient. He wanted to see the end of this episode. Most of the time he was watching Symons. "*Sacrée tête dure,*" he thought. "He has gone to sleep." Indeed Symons' immobility was so complete that he might have been dead from his exertions: only Peyrol had a conviction that his once youthful chum was not the sort of person that dies easily. The part of the cove he had reached was all right for Peyrol's purpose. But it would have been quite easy for a boat or boats to fail to notice Symons, and the consequence of that would be that the English would probably land in several parties for a search, discover the tartane. . . . Peyrol shuddered.

Suddenly he made out a boat just clear of the eastern point of the cove. Mr. Bolt had been hugging the coast and progressing very slowly, according to his instructions, till he had reached the edge of the point's shadow where it lay ragged and black on the moonlit water. Peyrol could see the oars rise and fall. Then another boat glided into view. Peyrol's alarm for his tartane grew intolerable. "Wake up, animal, wake up," he mumbled through his teeth. Slowly they glided on, and the first cutter was on the point of passing by the man on the shore when Peyrol was relieved by the hail of "Boat ahoy" reaching him faintly where he knelt leaning forward, an absorbed spectator.

He saw the boat heading for Symons, who was standing up now and making desperate signs with both arms. Then he saw him dragged in over the bows, the boat back out, and then both of them tossed oars and floated side by side on the sparkling water of the cove.

Peyrol got up from his knees. They had their man now. But perhaps they would persist in landing since there must have been some other purpose at first in the mind of the captain of the English corvette. This suspense did not last long. Peyrol saw the oars fall in the water, and in a very few minutes the boats, pulling round, disappeared one after another behind the eastern point of the cove.

"That's done," muttered Peyrol to himself. "I will never see the silly Hard-head again." He had a strange notion that those English boats had carried off something belonging to him, not a man but a part of his own life, the sensation of a regained touch with the far-off days in the Indian Ocean. He walked down quickly as if to examine the spot from which Testa Dura had left the soil of France. He was in a hurry now to get back to the farmhouse and meet Lieutenant Réal, who would be due back from Toulon. The way by the cove was as short as any other. When he got down he surveyed the empty shore and wondered at a feeling of emptiness within himself. While walking up towards the foot of the ravine he saw an object lying on the ground. It was a stable fork. He stood over it asking himself, "How on earth did this thing come here?" as though he had been too surprised to pick it up. Even after he had done so he remained motionless, meditating on it. He connected it with some activity of Scevola, since he was the man to whom it belonged, but that was no sort of explanation of its presence on that spot, unless . . .

"Could he have drowned himself?" thought Peyrol, looking at the smooth and luminous water of the cove. It could give him no answer. Then at arm's length he contemplated his find. At last he shook his head, shouldered the fork, and with slow steps continued on his way.

CHAPTER XIV

THE MIDNIGHT MEETING of Lieutenant Réal and Peyrol was perfectly silent. Peyrol, sitting on the bench outside the *salle,* had heard the footsteps coming up the Madrague track long before the lieutenant became visible. But he did not move. He did not even look at him. The lieutenant, unbuckling his sword-belt, sat down without uttering a word. The moon, the only witness of the meeting, seemed to shine on two friends so identical in thought and feeling that they could commune with each other without words. It was Peyrol who spoke first.

"You are up to time."

"I had the deuce of a job to hunt up the people and get the certificate stamped. Everything was shut up. The Port Admiral was giving a dinner-party, but he came out to speak to me when I sent in my name. And all the time, do you know, gunner, I was wondering whether I would ever see you again in my life. Even after I had the certificate, such as it is, in my pocket, I wondered whether I would."

"What the devil did you think was going to happen to me?" growled Peyrol perfunctorily. He had thrown the incomprehensible stable fork under the narrow bench, and with his feet drawn in he could feel it there, lying against the wall.

"No, the question with me was whether I would ever come here again."

Réal drew a folded paper from his pocket and dropped it on the bench. Peyrol picked it up carelessly. That thing was meant only to throw dust into Englishmen's eyes. The lieutenant, after a moment's silence, went on with the sincerity of a man who suffered too much to keep his trouble to himself.

"I had a hard struggle."

"That was too late," said Peyrol, very positively. "You had to come back here for very shame; and now you have come, you don't look very happy."

"Never mind my looks, gunner. I have made up my mind."

A ferocious, not unpleasing thought flashed through Peyrol's mind. It was that this intruder on the Escampobar sinister solitude in which he, Peyrol, kept order was under a delusion. Mind! Pah! His mind had nothing to do with his return. He had returned because in Catherine's words, "death had made a sign to him." Meantime, Lieutenant Réal raised his hat to wipe his moist brow.

"I made up my mind to play the part of dispatch-bearer. As you have said yourself, Peyrol, one could not bribe a man—I mean an honest man—so you will have to find the vessel and leave the rest to me. In two or three days . . . You are under a moral obligation to let me have your tartane."

Peyrol did not answer. He was thinking that Réal had got his sign, but whether it meant death from starvation or disease on board an English prison hulk, or in some other way, it was impossible to say. This naval officer was not a man he could trust; to whom he could, for instance, tell the story of his prisoner and what he had done with him. Indeed, the story was altogether incredible. The Englishman commanding that corvette had no visible, conceivable, or probable reason for sending a boat ashore to the cove of all places in the world. Peyrol himself could hardly believe that it had happened. And he thought: "If I were to tell that lieutenant he would only think that I was an old scoundrel who had been in treasonable communication with the English for God knows how long. No words of mine could persuade him that this was as unforeseen to me as the moon falling from the sky."

"I wonder," he burst out, but not very loud, "what made you keep on coming back here time after time!" Réal leaned his back against the wall and folded his arms in the familiar attitude of their leisurely talks.

"Ennui, Peyrol," he said in a far-away tone. "Confounded boredom."

Peyrol also, as if unable to resist the force of example, assumed the same attitude, and said:

"You seem to be a man that makes no friends."

"True, Peyrol. I think I am that sort of man."

"What, no friends at all? Not even a little friend of any sort?"

Lieutenant Réal leaned the back of his head against the wall and made no answer. Peyrol got on his legs.

"Oh, then, it wouldn't matter to anybody if you were to disappear for years in an English hulk. And so if I were to give you my tartane you would go?"

"Yes, I would go this moment."

Peyrol laughed quite loud, tilting his head back. All at once the laugh stopped short and the lieutenant was amazed to see him reel as though he had been hit in the chest. While giving way to his bitter mirth, the rover had caught sight of Arlette's face at the open window of the lieutenant's room. He sat heavily on the bench and was unable to make a sound. The lieutenant was startled enough to detach the back of his head from the wall to look at him. Peyrol stooped low suddenly, and began to drag the stable fork from its conceal-ment. Then he got on his feet and stood leaning on it, glaring down at Réal, who gazed upwards with languid surprise. Peyrol was ask-ing himself, "Shall I pick him up on that pair of prongs, carry him down, and fling him in the sea?" He felt suddenly overcome by a heaviness of arms and a heaviness of heart that made all movement impossible. His stiffened and powerless limbs refused all service. . . . Let Catherine look after her niece. He was sure that the old woman was not very far away. The lieutenant saw him absorbed in examining the points of the prongs carefully. There was something queer about all this.

"Hallo, Peyrol! What's the matter?" he couldn't help asking.

"I was just looking," said Peyrol. "One prong is chipped a little. I found this thing in a most unlikely place."

The lieutenant still gazed at him curiously.

"I know! It was under the bench."

"H'm," said Peyrol, who had recovered some self-control. "It belongs to Scevola."

"Does it?" said the lieutenant, falling back again.

His interest seemed exhausted, but Peyrol didn't move.

"You go about with a face fit for a funeral," he remarked suddenly in a deep voice. "Hang it all, Lieutenant, I have heard you laugh once or twice, but the devil take me if I ever saw you smile. It is as if you had been bewitched in your cradle."

Lieutenant Réal got up as if moved by a spring.

"Bewitched," he repeated, standing very stiff: "In my cradle, eh . . . ? No, I don't think it was so early as that."

He walked forward with a tense still face straight at Peyrol as though he had been blind. Startled, the rover stepped out of the way and, turning on his heels, followed him with his eyes. The lieutenant paced on, as if drawn by a magnet, in the direction of the door of the house. Peyrol, his eyes fastened on Réal's back, let him nearly reach it before he called out tentatively: "I say, Lieutenant!" To his extreme surprise, Réal swung round as if to a touch.

"Oh, yes," he answered, also in an undertone. "We will have to discuss that matter to-morrow."

Peyrol, who had approached him close, said in a whisper which sounded quite fierce: "Discuss? No! We will have to carry it out to-morrow. I have been waiting half the night just to tell you that."

Lieutenant Réal nodded. The expression on his face was so stony that Peyrol doubted whether he had understood. He added:

"It isn't going to be child's play." The lieutenant was about to open the door when Peyrol said: "A moment," and again the lieutenant turned about silently.

"Michel is sleeping somewhere on the stairs. Will you just stir him up and tell him I am waiting outside? We two will have to finish our night on board the tartane, and start work at break of day to get her ready for sea. Yes, Lieutenant, by noon. In twelve hours' time you will be saying good-bye to *la belle France*."

Lieutenant Réal's eyes staring over his shoulder seemed glazed and motionless in the moonlight like the eyes of a dead man. But he went in. Peyrol heard presently sounds within of somebody staggering in the passage and Michel projected himself outside headlong, but after a stumble or two pulled up, scratching his head and looking on every side in the moonlight without perceiving Peyrol, who was regarding him from a distance of five feet. At last Peyrol said:

"Come, wake up! Michel! Michel!"

"*Voilà, notre maître.*"

"Look at what I have picked up," said Peyrol. "Take it and put it away."

Michel didn't offer to touch the stable fork extended to him by Peyrol.

"What's the matter with you?" asked Peyrol.

"Nothing, nothing! Only last time I saw it, it was on Scevola's shoulder." He glanced up at the sky. "A little better than an hour ago."

"What was he doing?"

"Going into the yard to put it away."

"Well, now *you* go into the yard to put it away," said Peyrol, "and don't be long about it." He waited with his hand over his chin till his henchman reappeared before him. But Michel had not got over his surprise.

"He was going to bed, you know," he said.

"Eh, what! He was going. . . . He hasn't gone to sleep in the stable, perchance? He does sometimes, you know."

"I know. I looked. He isn't there," said Michel, very awake and round-eyed.

Peyrol started towards the cove. After three or four steps he turned round and found Michel motionless where he had left him.

"Come on," he cried, "we will have to fit the tartane for sea directly the day breaks."

Standing in the lieutenant's room just clear of the open window, Arlette listened to their voices and to the sound of their footsteps diminishing down the slope. Before they had quite died out she became aware of a light tread approaching the door of the room.

Lieutenant Réal had spoken the truth. While in Toulon he had more than once said to himself that he could never go back to that fatal farmhouse. His mental state was quite pitiable. Honour, decency, every principle forbade him to trifle with the feelings of a poor creature with her mind darkened by a very terrifying, atrocious and, as it were, guilty experience. And suddenly he had given way to a base impulse and had betrayed himself by kissing her hand! He recognized with despair that this was no trifling, but that the impulse had come from the very depths of his being. It was an awful discovery for a man who on emerging from boyhood had laid for himself a rigidly straight line of conduct amongst the unbridled passions and the clamouring falsehoods of revolution which seemed to have destroyed in him all capacity for the softer emotions. Taciturn and guarded, he had formed no intimacies. Relations he had none. He had kept clear of social connections. It was in his character. At first he visited Escampobar because when he took his leave he had no place in the world to go to, and a few days there were a complete change from the odious town. He enjoyed the sense of remoteness from ordinary mankind. He had developed a liking for old Peyrol, the only man who had nothing to do with the revolution—who had not even seen it at work. The sincere lawlessness of the ex–Brother of the Coast was refreshing. That one was neither a hypocrite nor a fool. When he robbed or killed it was not in the name of the sacred revolutionary principles or for the love of humanity.

Of course Réal had remarked at once Arlette's black, profound, and unquiet eyes and the persistent dim smile on her lips, her mysterious silences and the rare sound of her voice which made a caress of every word. He heard something of her story from the reluctant Peyrol who did not care to talk about it. It awakened in Réal more bitter indignation than pity. But it stimulated his imagination, confirmed him in that scorn and angry loathing for the revolution he had felt as a boy and had nursed secretly ever since. She attracted him by her unapproachable aspect. Later he tried not to notice that, in common parlance, she was inclined to hang about him. He used to catch her gazing at him stealthily. But he was free from masculine vanity. It was one day in Toulon that it suddenly dawned on him what her mute interest in his person might mean. He was then sitting outside a café sipping some drink or other with three or four officers, and not listening to their uninteresting conversation. He marvelled that this sort of illumination should come to him like this, under these circumstances; that he should have thought of her while seated in the street with these men round him, in the midst of more or less professional talk! And then it suddenly dawned on him that he had been thinking of nothing but that woman for days.

He got up brusquely, flung the money for his drink on the table, and without a word left his companions. But he had the reputation of an eccentric man and they did not even comment on his abrupt departure. It was a clear evening. He walked straight out of town, and that night wandered beyond the fortifications, not noticing the direction he took. All the countryside was asleep. There was not a human being stirring, and his progress in that desolate part of the country between the forts could have been traced only by the barking of dogs in the rare hamlets and scattered habitations.

"What has become of my rectitude, of my self-respect, of the firmness of my mind?" he asked himself pedantically. "I have let myself be mastered by an unworthy passion for a mere mortal envelope, stained with crime and without a mind."

His despair at this awful discovery was so profound that if he had not been in uniform he would have tried to commit suicide with the small pistol he had in his pocket. He shrank from the act, and the thought of the sensation it would produce, from the gossip and comments it would raise, the dishonouring suspicions it would provoke. "No," he said to himself, "what I will have to do is to unmark my linen, put on civilian old clothes and walk out much farther away, miles beyond the forts, hide myself in some wood or in an overgrown hollow and put an end to my life there. The gendarmes or a *garde-champêtre* discovering my body after a few days, a complete stranger without marks of identity, and being unable to find out anything about me, will give me an obscure burial in some village churchyard."

On that resolution he turned back abruptly and at daybreak found himself outside the gate of the town. He had to wait till it was opened, and then the morning was so far advanced that he had to go straight to work at his office at the Toulon Admiralty. Nobody noticed anything peculiar about him that day. He went through his routine tasks with outward composure, but all the same he never ceased arguing with himself. By the time he returned to his quarters he had come to the conclusion that as an officer in war-time he had no right to take his own life. His principles would not permit him to do that. In this reasoning he was perfectly sincere. During a deadly struggle against an irreconcilable enemy his life belonged to his country. But there were moments when his loneliness, haunted by the forbidden vision of Escampobar with the figure of that distracted girl, mysterious, awful, pale, irresistible in her strangeness, passing along the walls, appearing on the hill-paths, looking out of the window, became unbearable. He spent hours of solitary anguish shut up in his quarters, and the opinion amongst his comrades was that Réal's misanthropy was getting beyond all bounds.

One day it dawned upon him clearly that he could not stand this. It affected his power of thinking. "I shall begin to talk nonsense to people," he said to himself. "Hasn't there been once a poor devil who fell in love with a picture or a statue? He used to go and contemplate it. His misfortune cannot be compared with mine! Well, I will go to look at her as at a picture, too; a picture as untouchable as if it had been under glass." And he went on a visit to Escampobar at the very first opportunity. He made up for himself a repellent face, he clung to Peyrol for society, out there on the bench, both with their arms folded and gazing into space. But whenever Arlette crossed his line of sight it was as if something had moved in his breast. Yet these visits made life just bearable; they enabled him to attend to his work without beginning to talk nonsense to people. He said to himself that he was strong enough to rise above temptation, that he would never overstep the line; but it had happened to him upstairs in his room at the farm, to weep tears of sheer tenderness while thinking of his fate. These tears would put out for a while the gnawing fire of his passion. He assumed austerity like an armour and in his prudence he, as a matter of fact, looked very seldom at Arlette for fear of being caught in the act.

The discovery that she had taken to wandering at night had upset him all the same, because that sort of thing was unaccountable. It gave him a shock which unsettled, not his resolution, but his fortitude. That morning he had allowed himself, while she was waiting on him, to be caught looking at her and then, losing his self-control, had given her that kiss on the hand. Directly he had done it he was appalled. He had overstepped the line. Under the circumstances this was an absolute moral disaster. The full consciousness of it came to him slowly. In fact this moment of fatal weakness was one of the reasons why he had let himself be sent off so unceremoniously by Peyrol to Toulon. Even while crossing over he thought the only thing was not to come back any more. Yet while battling with himself he went on with the execution of the plan. A bitter irony presided over his dual state. Before leaving the admiral who had received him in full uniform in a room lighted by a single candle, he was suddenly moved to say: "I suppose if there is no other way I am authorized to go myself," and the admiral had answered: "I didn't contemplate that, but if you are willing I don't see any objection. I would only advise you to go in uniform in the character of an officer entrusted with dispatches. No doubt in time the Government would arrange for your exchange. But bear in mind that it would be a long captivity, and you must understand it might affect your promotion."

At the foot of the grand staircase in the lighted hall of the official building Réal suddenly thought: "And now I must go back to

Escampobar." Indeed he had to go to Escampobar because the false dispatches were there in the valise he had left behind. He couldn't go back to the admiral and explain that he had lost them. They would look on him as an unutterable idiot or a man gone mad. While walking to the quay where the naval boat was waiting for him he said to himself: "This, in truth, is my last visit for years—perhaps for life."

Going back in the boat, notwithstanding that the breeze was very light, he would not let the men take to the oars. He didn't want to return before the women had gone to bed. He said to himself that the proper and honest thing to do was not to see Arlette again. He even managed to persuade himself that his uncontrolled impulse had had no meaning for that witless and unhappy creature. She had neither started nor exclaimed; she had made no sign. She had remained passive and then she had backed away and sat down quietly. He could not even remember that she had coloured at all. As to himself, he had enough self-control to rise from the table and go out without looking at her again. Neither did she make a sign. What could startle that body without mind? She had made nothing of it, he thought with self-contempt. "Body without mind! Body without mind!" he repeated with angry derision directed at himself. And all at once he thought: "No. It isn't that. All in her is mystery, seduction, enchantment. And then—what do I care for her mind!"

This thought wrung from him a faint groan so that the coxswain asked respectfully: "Are you in pain, Lieutenant?" "It's nothing," he muttered and set his teeth with the desperation of a man under torture.

While talking with Peyrol outside the house, the words "I won't see her again," and "body without mind" rang through his head. By the time he had left Peyrol and walked up the stairs his endurance was absolutely at an end. All he wanted was to be alone. Going along the dark passage he noticed that the door of Catherine's room was standing ajar. But that did not arrest his attention. He was approaching a state of insensibility. As he put his hand on the door handle of his room he said to himself: "It will soon be over!"

He was so tired out that he was almost unable to hold up his head, and on going in he didn't see Arlette, who stood against the wall on one side of the window, out of the moonlight and in the darkest corner of the room. He only became aware of somebody's presence in the room as she flitted past him with the faintest possible rustle, when he staggered back two paces and heard behind him the key being turned in the lock. If the whole house had fallen into ruins, bringing him to the ground, he could not have been more overwhelmed and, in a manner, more utterly bereft of all his senses. The first that came back to him was the sense of touch when Arlette seized his hand. He regained his hearing next. She was whispering to him: "At last. At last! But you are careless. If it had been Scevola instead of me in this room you would have been dead now. I have seen him at work." He felt a significant pressure on his hand, but he couldn't see her properly yet, though he was aware of her nearness with every fibre of his body. "It wasn't yesterday though," she added in a low tone. Then suddenly: "Come to the window so that I may look at you."

A great square of moonlight lay on the floor. He obeyed the tug like a little child. She caught hold of his other hand as it hung by his side. He was rigid all over, without joints, and it did not seem to him that he was breathing. With her face a little below his she stared at him closely, whispering gently: "Eugène, Eugène," and suddenly the livid immobility of his face frightened her. "You say nothing. You look ill. What is the matter? Are you hurt?" She let go his insensitive hands and began to feel him all over for evidence of some injury. She even snatched off his hat and flung it away in her haste to discover that his head was unharmed; but finding no sign of bodily damage, she calmed down like a sensible, practical person. With her hands clasped round his neck she hung back a little. Her little even teeth gleamed, her black eyes, immensely profound, looked into his, not with a transport of passion or fear but with a sort of reposeful satisfaction, with a searching and appropriating expression. He came back to life with a low and reckless exclamation, felt horribly insecure at once as if he were standing on a lofty pinnacle above a noise as of breaking waves in his ears, in fear lest her fingers should part and she would fall off and be lost to him for ever. He flung his arms round her waist and hugged her close to his breast. In the great silence, in the bright moonlight falling through the window, they stood like that for a long, long time. He looked at her head resting on his shoulder. Her eyes were closed and the expression on her unsmiling face was that of a delightful dream, something infinitely ethereal, peaceful and, as it were, eternal. Its appeal pierced his heart with a pointed sweetness.

"She is exquisite. It's a miracle," he thought with a sort of terror. "It's impossible."

She made a movement to disengage herself, and instinctively he resisted, pressing her closer to his breast. She yielded for a moment and then tried again. He let her go. She stood at arm's length, her hands on his shoulders, and her charm struck him suddenly as funny in the seriousness of expression as of a very capable, practical woman.

"All this is very well," she said in a businesslike undertone. "We will have to think how to get away from here. I don't mean now, this moment," she added, feeling his slight start. "Scevola is thirsting for your blood." She detached one hand to point a finger at the inner wall of the room, and lowered her voice. "He's there, you know. Don't trust Peyrol either. I was looking at you two out there. He has changed. I can trust him no longer." Her murmur vibrated. "He and Catherine behave strangely. I don't know what came to them. He doesn't talk to me. When I sit down near him he turns his shoulder to me. . . ."

She felt Réal sway under her hands, paused in concern and said: "You are tired." But as he didn't move, she actually led him to a chair, pushed him into it, and sat on the floor at his feet. She rested her head against his knees and kept possession of one of his hands. A sigh escaped her. "I knew this was going to be," she said very low. "But I was taken by surprise."

"Oh, you knew it was going to be," he repeated faintly.

"Yes! I had prayed for it. Have you ever been prayed for, Eugène?" she asked, lingering on his name.

"Not since I was a child," answered Réal in a sombre tone.

"Oh yes! You have been prayed for to-day. I went down to the church. . . ." Réal could hardly believe his ears. . . . "The abbé let me in by the sacristy door. He told me to renounce the world. I was ready to renounce anything for you." Réal, turning his face to the darkest part of the room, seemed to see the spectre of fatality awaiting its time to move forward and crush that calm, confident joy. He shook off the dreadful illusion, raised her hand to his lips for a lingering kiss, and then asked:

"So you knew that it was going to be? Everything? Yes! And of me, what did you think?"

She pressed strongly the hand to which she had been clinging all the time. "I thought this."

"But what did you think of my conduct at times? You see, I did not know what was going to be. I . . . I was afraid," he added under his breath.

"Conduct? What conduct? You came, you went. When you were not here I thought of you, and when you were here I could look my fill at you. I tell you I knew how it was going to be. I was not afraid then."

"You went about with a little smile," he whispered, as one would mention an inconceivable marvel.

"I was warm and quiet," murmured Arlette, as if on the borders of dreamland. Tender murmurs flowed from her lips describing a state of blissful tranquillity in phrases that sounded like the veriest non-sense, incredible, convincing, and soothing to Réal's conscience.

"You were perfect," it went on. "Whenever you came near me everything seemed different."

"What do you mean? How different?"

"Altogether. The light, the very stones of the house, the hills, the little flowers amongst the rocks! Even Nanette was different."

Nanette was a white Angora with long silken hair, a pet that lived mostly in the yard.

"Oh, Nanette was different too," said Réal, whom delight in the modulations of that voice had cut him off from all reality, and even from a consciousness of himself, while he sat stooping over that head resting against his knee, the soft grip of her hand being his only con-tact with the world.

"Yes. Prettier. It's only the people. . . ." She ceased on an uncertain note. The crested wave of enchantment seemed to have passed over his head, ebbing out faster than the sea, leaving the dreary expanses of the sand. He felt a chill at the roots of his hair.

"What people?" he asked.

"They are so changed. Listen, to-night while you were away—why did you go away?—I caught those two in the kitchen, saying nothing to each other. That Peyrol—he is terrible."

He was struck by the tone of awe, by its profound conviction. He could not know that Peyrol, unforeseen, unexpected, inexplicable, had given by his mere appearance at Escampobar a moral and even a physical jolt to all her being, that he was to her an immense figure, like a messenger from the unknown entering the solitude of Escampobar; something immensely strong, with inexhaustible power, unaffected by familiarity and remaining invincible.

"He will say nothing, he will listen to nothing. He can do what he likes."

"Can he?" muttered Réal.

She sat up on the floor, moved her head up and down several times as if to say that there could be no doubt about that.

"Is he, too, thirsting for my blood?" asked Réal bitterly.

"No, no. It isn't that. You could defend yourself. I could watch over you. I have been watching over you. Only two nights ago I thought I heard noises outside and I went downstairs, fearing for you; your window was open but I could see nobody, and yet I felt. . . . No, it isn't that! It's worse. I don't know what he wants to do. I can't help being fond of him, but I begin to fear him now. When he first came here and I saw him he was just the same—only his hair was not so white—big, quiet. It seemed to me that something moved in my head. He was gentle, you know. I had to smile at him. It was as if I had recognized him. I said to myself: 'That's he, the man himself.' "

"And when I came?" asked Réal with a feeling of dismay.

"You! You were expected," she said in a low tone with a slight tinge of surprise at the question, but still evidently thinking of the Peyrol mystery. "Yes, I caught them at it last evening, he and Catherine in the kitchen, looking at each other and as quiet as mice. I told him he couldn't order me about. Oh, *mon chéri, mon chéri,* don't you listen to Peyrol—don't let him . . ."

With only a slight touch on his knee she sprang to her feet. Réal stood up, too.

"He can do nothing to me," he mumbled.

"Don't tell him anything. Nobody can guess what he thinks, and now even I cannot tell what he means when he speaks. It was as if he knew a secret." She put an accent into those words which made Réal feel moved almost to tears. He repeated that Peyrol could have no influence over him, and he felt that he was speaking the truth. He was in the power of his own word. Ever since he had left the admiral in a gold-embroidered uniform, impatient to return to his guests, he was on a service for which he had volunteered. For a moment he had the sensation of an iron hoop very tight round his chest. She peered at his face closely, and it was more than he could bear.

"All right. I'll be careful," he said. "And Catherine, is she also dangerous?"

In the sheen of the moonlight Arlette, her neck and head above the gleams of the fichu, visible and elusive, smiled at him and moved a step closer.

"Poor Aunt Catherine . . . ," she said. "Put your arm round me, Eugène. . . . She can do nothing. She used to follow me with her eyes always. She thought I didn't notice, but I did. And now she seems unable to look me in the face. Peyrol, too, for that matter. He used to follow me with his eyes. Often I wondered what made them look at me like that. Can you tell, Eugène? But it's all changed now."

"Yes, it is all changed," said Réal in a tone which he tried to make as light as possible. "Does Catherine know you are here?"

"When we went upstairs this evening I lay down all dressed on my bed and she sat on hers. The candle was out, but in the moonlight I could see her quite plainly with her hands on her lap. When I could lie still no longer I simply got up and went out of the room. She was still sitting at the foot of her bed. All I did was to put my finger on my lips and then she dropped her head. I don't think I quite closed the door. . . . Hold me tighter, Eugène, I am tired. . . . Strange, you know! Formerly, a long time ago, before I ever saw you, I never rested and never felt tired." She stopped her murmur suddenly and lifted a finger recommending silence. She listened and Réal listened too, he did not know for what; and in this sudden concentration on a point, all that had happened since he had entered the room seemed to him a dream in its improbability and in the more than lifelike force dreams have in their inconsequence. Even the woman letting herself go on his arm seemed to have no weight as it might have happened in a dream.

"She is there," breathed Arlette suddenly, rising on tiptoe to reach up to his ear. "She must have heard you go past."

"Where is she?" asked Réal with the same intense secrecy.

"Outside the door. She must have been listening to the murmur of our voices. . . ." Arlette breathed into his ear as if relating an enormity. "She told me one day that I was one of those who are fit for no man's arms."

At this he flung his other arm round her and looked into her enlarged as if frightened eyes, while she clasped him with all her strength and they stood like that a long time, lips pressed on lips without a kiss, and breathless in the closeness of their contact. To him the stillness seemed to extend to the limits of the universe. The thought "Am I going to die?" flashed through that stillness and lost itself in it like a spark flying in an everlasting night. The only result of it was the tightening of his hold on Arlette.

An aged and uncertain voice was heard uttering the word "Arlette." Catherine, who had been listening to their murmurs, could not bear the long silence. They heard her trembling tones as distinctly as though she had been in the room. Réal felt as if it had saved his life. They separated silently.

"Go away," called out Arlette.

"Arl—— . . ."

"Be quiet," she cried louder. "You can do nothing."

"Arlette," came through the door, tremulous and commanding.

"She will wake up Scevola," remarked Arlette to Réal in a conversational tone. And they both waited for sounds that did not come. Arlette pointed her finger at the wall. "He is there, you know."

"He is asleep," muttered Réal. But the thought "I am lost" which he formulated in his mind had no reference to Scevola.

"He is afraid," said Arlette contemptuously in an undertone. "But that means little. He would quake with fright one moment and rush out to do murder the next."

Slowly, as if drawn by the irresistible authority of the old woman, they had been moving towards the door. Réal thought with the sudden enlightenment of passion: "If she does not go now I won't have the strength to part from her in the morning." He had no image of death before his eyes but of a long and intolerable separation. A sigh verging upon a moan reached them from the other side of the door and made the air around them heavy with sorrow against which locks and keys will not avail.

"You had better go to her," he whispered in a penetrating tone.

"Of course I will," said Arlette with some feeling. "Poor old thing. She and I have only each other in the world, but I am the daughter here, she must do what I tell her." With one of her hands on Réal's shoulder she put her mouth close to the door and said distinctly:

"I am coming directly. Go back to your room and wait for me," as if she had no doubt of being obeyed.

A profound silence ensued. Perhaps Catherine had gone already. Réal and Arlette stood still for a whole minute as if both had been changed into stone.

"Go now," said Réal in a hoarse, hardly audible voice.

She gave him a quick kiss on the lips and again they stood like a pair of enchanted lovers bewitched into immobility.

"If she stays on," thought Réal, "I shall never have the courage to tear myself away, and then I shall have to blow my brains out." But when at last she moved he seized her again and held her as if she had been his very life. When he let her go he was appalled by hearing a very faint laugh of her secret joy.

"Why do you laugh?" he asked in a scared tone.

She stopped to answer him over her shoulder.

"I laughed because I thought of all the days to come. Days and days and days. Have you thought of them?"

"Yes," Réal faltered, like a man stabbed to the heart, holding the door half open. And he was glad to have something to hold on to.

She slipped out with a soft rustle of her silk skirt, but before he had time to close the door behind her she put back her arm for an instant. He had just time to press the palm of her hand to his lips. It was cool. She snatched it away and he had the strength of mind to shut the door after her. He felt like a man chained to the wall and dying of thirst, from whom a cold drink is snatched away. The room became dark suddenly. He thought, "A cloud over the moon, a cloud over the moon, an enormous cloud," while he walked rigidly to the window, insecure and swaying as if on a tight rope. After a moment he perceived the moon in a sky on which there was no sign of the smallest cloud anywhere. He said to himself, "I suppose I nearly died just now. But no," he went on thinking with deliberate cruelty, "Oh, no, I shall not die. I shall only suffer, suffer, suffer. . . ."

"Suffer, suffer." Only by stumbling against the side of the bed did he discover that he had gone away from the window. At once he flung himself violently on the bed with his face buried in the pillow, which he bit to restrain the cry of distress about to burst through his lips. Natures schooled into insensibility when once overcome by a mastering passion are like vanquished giants ready for despair. He, a man on service, felt himself shrinking from death and that doubt contained in itself all possible doubts of his own fortitude. The only thing he knew was that he would be gone to-morrow morning. He shuddered along his whole extended length, then lay still gripping a handful of bedclothes in each hand to prevent himself from leaping up in panicky restlessness. He was saying to himself pedantically, "I must lie down and rest, I must rest to have strength for to-morrow, I must rest," while the tremendous struggle to keep still broke out in waves of perspiration on his forehead. At last sudden oblivion must have descended on him because he turned over and sat up suddenly with the sound of the word *"Ecoutez"* in his ears.

A strange, dim, cold light filled the room; a light he did not recognize for anything he had known before, and at the foot of his bed stood a figure in dark garments with a dark shawl over its head, with a fleshless predatory face and dark hollows for its eyes, silent, expectant, implacable. . . . "Is this death?" he asked himself, staring at it terrified. It resembled Catherine. It said again: *"Ecoutez."* He took away his eyes from it and glancing down noticed that his clothes were torn open on his chest. He would not look up at that thing, whatever it was, spectre or old woman, and said:

"Yes, I hear you."

"You are an honest man." It was Catherine's unemotional voice. "The day has broken. You will go away."

"Yes," he said, without raising his head.

"She is asleep," went on Catherine or whoever it was, "exhausted, and you would have to shake her hard before she would wake. You will go. You know," the voice continued inflexibly, "she is my niece, and you know that there is death in the folds of her skirt and blood about her feet. She is for no man."

Réal felt all the anguish of an unearthly experience. This thing that looked like Catherine and spoke like a cruel fate had to be faced. He raised his head in this light that seemed to him appalling and not of this world.

"Listen well to me, you too," he said. "If she had all the madness of the world and the sin of all the murders of the Revolution on her shoulders, I would still hug her to my breast. Do you understand?"

The apparition which resembled Catherine lowered and raised its hooded head slowly. "There was a time when I could have hugged *l'enfer même* to my breast. He went away. He had his vow. You have only your honesty. You will go."

"I have my duty," said Lieutenant Réal in measured tones, as if calmed by the excess of horror that old woman inspired him with.

"Go without disturbing her, without looking at her."

"I will carry my shoes in my hand," he said. He sighed deeply and felt as if sleepy. "It is very early," he muttered.

"Peyrol is already down at the well," announced Catherine. "What can he be doing there all this time?" she added in a troubled voice. Réal, with his feet now on the ground, gave her a side glance; but she was already gliding away, and when he looked again she had vanished from the room and the door was shut.

CHAPTER XV

～

ATHERINE, GOING DOWNSTAIRS, found Peyrol still at the well. He seemed to be looking into it with extreme interest.

"Your coffee is ready, Peyrol," she shouted to him from the doorway.

He turned very sharply like a man surprised and came along smiling.

"That's pleasant news, Mademoiselle Catherine," he said. "You are down early."

"Yes," she admitted, "but you too, Peyrol. Is Michel about? Let him come and have some coffee, too."

"Michel's at the tartane. Perhaps you don't know that she is going to make a little voyage." He drank a mouthful of coffee and took a bite out of a slice of bread. He was hungry. He had been up all night and had even had a conversation with Citizen Scevola. He had also done some work with Michel after daylight; however, there had not been much to do because the tartane was always kept ready for sea. Then after having again locked up Citizen Scevola, who was extremely concerned as to what was going to happen to him but was left in a state of uncertainty, he had come up to the farm, had gone upstairs where he was busy with various things for a time, and then had stolen down very cautiously to the well, where Catherine, whom he had not expected downstairs so early, had seen him before she went into Lieutenant Réal's room. While he enjoyed his coffee he listened without

any signs of surprise to Catherine's comments upon the disappear-
ance of Scevola. She had looked into his den. He had not slept on his
pallet last night, of that she was certain, and he was nowhere to be
seen, not even in the most distant field, from the points of vantage
around the farm. It was inconceivable that he should have slipped
away to Madrague, where he disliked to go, or to the village, where he
was afraid to go. Peyrol remarked that whatever happened to him he
was no great loss, but Catherine was not to be soothed.

"It frightens a body," she said. "He may be hiding somewhere to
jump on one treacherously. You know what I mean, Peyrol."

"Well, the lieutenant will have nothing to fear, as he's going away.
As to myself, Scevola and I are good friends. I had a long talk with him
quite recently. You two women can manage him perfectly; and then,
who knows, perhaps he has gone away for good."

Catherine stared at him, if such a word as stare can be applied to a
profound contemplative gaze. "The lieutenant has nothing to fear
from him," she repeated cautiously.

"No, he is going away. Didn't you know it?" The old woman continued to look at him profoundly. "Yes, he is on service."

For another minute or so Catherine continued silent in her contemplative attitude. Then her hesitation came to an end. She could not
resist the desire to inform Peyrol of the events of the night. As she
went on Peyrol forgot the half-full bowl of coffee and his half-eaten
piece of bread. Catherine's voice flowed with austerity. She stood
there, imposing and solemn like a peasant-priestess. The relation of
what had been to her a soul-shaking experience did not take much
time, and she finished with the words, "The lieutenant is an honest
man." And after a pause she insisted further: "There is no denying it.
He has acted like an honest man."

For a moment longer Peyrol continued to look at the coffee in the
bowl, then without warning got up with such violence that the chair
behind him was thrown back upon the flagstones.

"Where is he, that honest man?" he shouted suddenly in stento-
rian tones which not only caused Catherine to raise her hands, but
frightened himself, and he dropped at once to a mere forcible utter-
ance. "Where is that man? Let me see him."

Even Catherine's hieratic composure was disturbed. "Why," she
said, looking really disconcerted, "he will be down here directly. This
bowl of coffee is for him."

Peyrol made as if to leave the kitchen, but Catherine stopped him. "For God's sake, Monsieur Peyrol," she said, half in entreaty and half in command, "don't wake up the child. Let her sleep. Oh, let her sleep! Don't wake her up. God only knows how long it is since she has slept properly. I could not tell you. I daren't think of it." She was shocked by hearing Peyrol declare: "All this is confounded nonsense." But he sat down again, seemed to catch sight of the coffee bowl, and emptied what was left in it down his throat.

"I don't want her on my hands more crazy than she has been before," said Catherine, in a sort of exasperation but in a very low tone. This phrase in its selfish form expressed a real and profound compassion for her niece. She dreaded the moment when that fatal Arlette would wake up and the dreadful complications of life which her slumbers had suspended would have to be picked up again. Peyrol fidgeted on his seat.

"And so he told you he was going? He actually did tell you that?" he asked.

"He promised to go before the child wakes up. . . . At once."

"But, *sacré nom d'un chien*, there is never any wind before eleven o'clock," Peyrol exclaimed in a tone of profound annoyance, yet trying to moderate his voice, while Catherine, indulgent to his changing moods, only compressed her lips and nodded at him soothingly. "It is impossible to work with people like that," he mumbled.

"Do you know, Monsieur Peyrol, that she has been to see the priest?" Catherine was heard suddenly, towering above her end of the table. The two women had had a talk before Arlette had been induced by her aunt to lie down. Peyrol gave a start.

"What? Priest? . . . Now look here, Catherine," he went on with repressed ferocity, "do you imagine that all this interests me in the least?"

"I can think of nothing but that niece of mine. We two have nobody but each other in the world," she went on, reproducing the very phrase Arlette had used to Réal. She seemed to be thinking aloud, but noticed that Peyrol was listening with attention. "He wanted to shut her up from everybody," and the old woman clasped her meagre hands with a sudden gesture. "I suppose there are still some convents about the world."

"You and the *patronne* are mad together," declared Peyrol. "All this only shows what an ass the curé is. I don't know much about these things, though I have seen some nuns in my time, and some very queer ones, too, but it seems to me that they don't take crazy people into convents. Don't you be afraid. I tell you that." He stopped because the inner door of the kitchen came open and Lieutenant Réal stepped in. His sword hung on his forearm by the belt, his hat was on his head. He dropped his little valise on the floor and sat down in the nearest chair to put on his shoes which he had brought down in his other hand. Then he came up to the table. Peyrol, who had kept his eyes on him, thought: "Here is one who looks like a moth scorched in the fire." Réal's eyes were sunk, his cheeks seemed hollowed, and the whole face had an arid and dry aspect.

"Well, you are in a fine state for the work of deceiving the enemy," Peyrol observed. "Why, to look at you, nobody would believe a word you said. You are not going to be ill, I hope. You are on service. You haven't got the right to be ill. I say, Mademoiselle Catherine, produce the bottle—you know, my private bottle. . . ." He snatched it from Catherine's hand, poured some brandy into the lieutenant's coffee, pushed the bowl towards him, and waited. *"Nom de nom!"* he said forcibly, "don't you know what this is for? It's for you to drink." Réal obeyed with a strange, automatic docility. "And now," said Peyrol, getting up, "I will go to my room and shave. This is a great day—the day we are going to see the lieutenant off."

Till then Réal had not uttered a word, but directly the door closed behind Peyrol he raised his head.

"Catherine!" His voice was like a rustle in his throat. She was looking at him steadily and he continued: "Listen, when she finds I am gone you tell her I will return soon. To-morrow. Always to-morrow."

"Yes, my good Monsieur," said Catherine in an unmoved voice but clasping her hands convulsively. "There is nothing else I would dare tell her!"

"She will believe you," whispered Réal wildly.

"Yes! She will believe me," repeated Catherine in a mournful tone.

Réal got up, put the sword-belt over his head, picked up the valise. There was a little flush on his cheeks.

"Adieu," he said to the silent old woman. She made no answer, but as he turned away she raised her hand a little, hesitated, and let it fall again. It seemed to her that the women of Escampobar had been sin- gled out for divine wrath. Her niece appeared to her like the scape-

goat charged with all the murders and blasphemies of the Revolution. She herself too had been cast out from the grace of God. But that had been a long time ago. She had made her peace with Heaven since. Again she raised her hand and, this time, made in the air the sign of the cross at the back of Lieutenant Réal.

Meanwhile upstairs Peyrol, scraping his big flat cheek with an English razor-blade at the window, saw Lieutenant Réal on the path to the shore; and high above there, commanding a vast view of sea and land, he shrugged his shoulders impatiently with no visible provocation. One could not trust those epaulette-wearers. They would cram a fellow's head with notions either for their own sake or for the sake of the service. Still, he was too old a bird to be caught with chaff; and besides, that long-legged stiff beggar going down the path with all his officer airs, was honest enough. At any rate he knew a seaman when he saw one, though he was as cold-blooded as a fish. Peyrol had a smile which was a little awry.

Cleaning the razor-blade (one of a set of twelve in a case) he had a vision of a brilliantly hazy ocean and an English Indiaman with her yards braced all ways, her canvas blowing loose above her blood-stained decks overrun by a lot of privateersmen and with the island of Ceylon swelling like a thin blue cloud on the far horizon. He had always wished to own a set of English blades and there he had got it, fell over it as it were, lying on the floor of a cabin which had been already ransacked. "For good steel—it was good steel," he thought looking at the blade fixedly. And there it was, nearly worn out. The others too. That steel! And here he was holding the case in his hand as though he had just picked it up from the floor. Same case. Same man. And the steel worn out.

He shut the case brusquely, flung it into his sea-chest which was standing open, and slammed the lid down. The feeling which was in his breast and had been known to more articulate men than himself, was that life was a dream less substantial than the vision of Ceylon lying like a cloud on the sea. Dream left astern. Dream straight ahead. This disenchanted philosophy took the shape of fierce swearing. "*Sacré nom de nom de nom. . . . Tonnerre de bon Dieu!*"

While tying his neckcloth he handled it with fury as though he meant to strangle himself with it. He rammed a soft cap on to his venerable locks recklessly, seized his cudgel—but before leaving the room walked up to the window giving on the east. He could not see the

Petite Passe on account of the lookout hill, but to the left a great portion of the Hyères roadstead lay spread out before him, pale grey in
the morning light, with the land about Cape Blanc swelling in the distance with all its details blurred as yet and only one conspicuous
object presenting to his sight something that might have been a lighthouse by its shape, but which Peyrol knew very well was the English
corvette already under way and with all her canvas set.

This sight pleased Peyrol mainly because he had expected it.
The Englishman was doing exactly what he had expected he would
do, and Peyrol looked towards the English cruiser with a smile of
malicious triumph as if he were confronting her captain. For some
reason or other he imagined Captain Vincent as long-faced, with
yellow teeth and a wig, whereas that officer wore his own hair and
had a set of teeth which would have done honour to a London belle
and was really the hidden cause of Captain Vincent appearing so
often wreathed in smiles.

That ship at this great distance and steering in his direction held
Peyrol at the window long enough for the increasing light of the
morning to burst into sunshine, colouring and filling-in the flat outline of the land with tints of wood and rock and field, with clear dots
of buildings enlivening the view. The sun threw a sort of halo around
the ship. Recollecting himself, Peyrol left the room and shut the door
quietly. Quietly, too, he descended the stairs from his garret. On the
landing he underwent a short inward struggle, at the end of which he
approached the door of Catherine's room and, opening it a little, put
his head in. Across the whole width of it he saw Arlette fast asleep.
Her aunt had thrown a light coverlet over her. Her low shoes stood at
the foot of the bed. Her black hair lay loose on the pillow; and Peyrol's
gaze became arrested by the long eyelashes on her pale cheek. Suddenly he fancied she moved, and he withdrew his head sharply,
pulling the door to. He listened for a moment as if tempted to open it
again, but judging it too risky, continued on his way downstairs. At
his reappearance in the kitchen Catherine turned sharply. She was
dressed for the day, with a big white cap on her head, a black bodice,
and a brown skirt with ample folds. She had a pair of varnished sabots
on her feet over her shoes.

"No signs of Scevola," she said, advancing towards Peyrol. "And
Michel too has not been here yet."

Peyrol thought that if she had been only shorter, what with her black eyes and slightly curved nose she would have looked like a witch. But witches can read people's thoughts, and he looked openly at Catherine with the pleasant conviction that she could not read his thoughts. He said:

"I took good care not to make any noise upstairs, Mademoiselle Catherine. When I am gone the house will be empty and quiet enough."

She had a curious expression. She struck Peyrol suddenly as if she were lost in that kitchen in which she had reigned for many years. He continued:

"You will be alone all the morning."

She seemed to be listening to some distant sound, and after Peyrol had added, "Everything is all right now," she nodded and after a moment said in a manner that for her was unexpectedly impulsive:

"Monsieur Peyrol, I am tired of life."

He shrugged his shoulders and with somewhat sinister jocosity remarked:

"I will tell you what it is; you ought to have been married."

She turned her back on him abruptly.

"No offence," Peyrol excused himself in a tone of gloom rather than of apology. "It is no use to attach any importance to things. What is this life? Phew! Nobody can remember one-tenth of it. Here I am; and, you know, I would bet that if one of my old-time chums came along and saw me like this, here with you—I mean one of those chums that stand up for a fellow in a scrimmage and look after him should he be hurt—well, I bet," he repeated, "he wouldn't know me. He would say to himself perhaps, 'Hullo! here's a comfortable married couple.' "

He paused. Catherine, with her back to him and calling him, not "Monsieur," but "Peyrol," *tout court*, remarked, not exactly with displeasure, but rather with an ominous accent that this was no time for idle talk. Peyrol, however, continued, though his tone was very far from being that of idle talk:

"But you see, Mademoiselle Catherine, you were not like the others. You allowed yourself to be struck all of a heap, and at the same time you were too hard on yourself."

Her long thin frame bent low to work the bellows under the enormous overmantel, she assented: "Perhaps! We Escampobar women were always hard on ourselves."

"That's what I say. If you had had things happen to you which happened to me. . . ."

"But you men, you are different. It doesn't matter what you do. You have got your own strength. You need not be hard on yourselves. You go from one thing to another thoughtlessly."

He remained looking at her searchingly with something like a hint of a smile on his shaven lips, but she turned away to the sink where one of the women working about the farm had deposited a great pile of vegetables. She started on them with a broken-bladed knife, preserving her sibylline air even in that homely occupation.

"It will be a good soup, I see, at noon to-day," said the rover suddenly. He turned on his heels and went out through the *salle*. The whole world lay open to him, or at any rate the whole of the Mediterranean, viewed down the ravine between the two hills. The bell of the farm's milch-cow, which had a talent for keeping herself invisible, reached him from the right, but he could not see as much as the tips of her horns, though he looked for them. He stepped out sturdily. He had not gone twenty yards down the ravine when another sound made him stand still as if changed into stone. It was a faint noise resembling very much the hollow rumble an empty farm-cart would make on a stony road, but Peyrol looked up at the sky, and though it was perfectly clear, he did not seem pleased with its aspect. He had a hill on each side of him and the placid cove below his feet. He muttered, "H'm! Thunder at sunrise. It must be in the west. It only wanted that!" He feared it would first kill the little breeze there was and then knock the weather up altogether. For a moment all his faculties seemed paralyzed by that faint sound. On that sea, ruled by the gods of Olympus he might have been a pagan mariner subject to Jupiter's caprices; but like a defiant pagan he shook his fist vaguely at space which answered him by a short and threatening mutter. Then he swung on his way till he caught sight of the two mastheads of the tartane, when he stopped to listen. No sound of any sort reached him from there, and he went on his way thinking, "Go from one thing to another thoughtlessly! Indeed . . . ! That's all old Catherine knows about it." He had so many things to think of that he did not know which to lay hold of first. He just let them lie jumbled up in his head. His feelings too were in a state of confusion, and vaguely he felt that his conduct was at the mercy of an internal conflict. The consciousness of that fact accounted perhaps for his sardonic attitude towards himself and outwardly towards those whom he perceived on board the tartane; and especially towards the lieutenant whom he saw sitting on the deck leaning against the head of the rudder, characteristically aloof from the two other persons on board. Michel, also characteristically, was standing on the top of the little cabin scuttle, obviously looking out for his "*maître*." Citizen Scevola, sitting on deck, seemed at first sight to be at liberty, but as a matter of fact he was not. He was loosely tied up to a stanchion by three turns of the mainsheet with the knot in such a position that he could not get at it without attracting attention; and that situation seemed also somewhat characteristic of Citizen Scevola with its air of half liberty, half suspicion and, as it were, contemptuous restraint. The sans-culotte, whose late experiences had nearly unsettled his reason, first by their utter incomprehensibility and afterwards by the enigmatical attitude of Peyrol, had dropped his head and folded his arms on his breast. And that attitude was dubious too. It might have been resignation or it might have been profound sleep. The rover addressed himself first to the lieutenant.

"*Le moment approche*," said Peyrol with a queer twitch at a corner of his lip, while under his soft woollen cap his venerable locks stirred in the breath of a suddenly warm air. "The great moment—eh?"

He leaned over the big tiller, and seemed to be hovering above the lieutenant's shoulder.

"What's this infernal company?" murmured the latter without even looking at Peyrol.

"All old friends—*quoi?*" said Peyrol in a homely tone. "We will keep that little affair amongst ourselves. The fewer the men the greater the glory. Catherine is getting the vegetables ready for the noonday soup and the Englishman is coming down towards the Passe where he will arrive about noon, too, ready to have his eye put out. You know, Lieutenant, that will be your job. You may depend on me for sending you off when the moment comes. For what is it to you? You have no friends, you have not even a *petite amie*. As to expecting an old rover like me—oh no, Lieutenant! Of course liberty is sweet, but what do you know of it, you epaulette-wearers? Moreover, I am no good for quarter-deck talks and all that politeness."

"I wish, Peyrol, you would not talk so much," said Lieutenant Réal, turning his head slightly. He was struck by the strange expression on the old rover's face. "And I don't see what the actual moment matters. I am going to look for the fleet. All you have to do is to hoist the sails for me and then scramble ashore."

"Very simple," observed Peyrol through his teeth, and then began to sing:

> "*Quoique leurs chapeaux sont bien laids*
> *God-dam! Moi, j'aime les Anglais*
> *Ils ont un si bon caractère!*"

but interrupted himself suddenly to hail Scevola:

"*Hé! Citoyen!*" and then remarked confidentially to Réal: "He isn't asleep, you know, but he isn't like the English, he has a *sacré mauvais caractère*. He got into his head," continued Peyrol, in a loud and innocent tone, "that you locked him up in this cabin last night. Did you notice the venomous glance he gave you just now?"

Both Lieutenant Réal and the innocent Michel appeared surprised at his boisterousness; but all the time Peyrol was thinking: "I wish to goodness I knew how that thunderstorm is getting on and what course it is shaping. I can't find that out unless I go up to the farm and get a view to the westward. It may be as far as the Rhône Valley; no doubt it is and it will come out of it too, curses on it. One won't be able to reckon on half an hour of steady wind from any quarter." He directed a look of ironic gaiety at all the faces in turn. Michel met it with a faithful-dog gaze and innocently open mouth. Scevola kept his chin buried on his chest. Lieutenant Réal was insensible to outward impressions and his absent stare made nothing of Peyrol. The rover himself presently fell into thought. The last stir of air died out in the little basin, and the sun clearing Porquerolles inundated it with a sudden light in which Michel blinked like an owl.

"It's hot early," he announced aloud but only because he had formed the habit of talking to himself. He would not have presumed to offer an opinion unless asked by Peyrol.

His voice having recalled Peyrol to himself, he proposed to masthead the yards and even asked Lieutenant Réal to help in that operation which was accomplished in silence except for the faint squeaking of the blocks. The sails, however, were kept hauled up in the gear.

"Like this," said Peyrol, "you have only to let go the ropes and you will be under canvas at once."

Without answering Réal returned to his position by the rudder-head. He was saying to himself: "I am sneaking off. No, there is honour, duty. And of course I will return. But when? They will forget all about me and I shall never be exchanged. This war may last for years—" and illogically he wished he could have had a God to whom he could pray for relief in his anguish. "She will be in despair," he thought, writhing inwardly at the mental picture of a distracted Arlette. Life, however, had embittered his spirit early, and he said to himself: "But in a month's time will she even give me a thought?" Instantly he felt remorseful with a remorse strong enough to lift him to his feet as if he were morally obliged to go up again and confess to Arlette this sacrilegious cynicism of thought. "I am mad," he muttered, perching himself on the low rail. His lapse from faith plunged him into such a depth of unhappiness that he felt all his strength of will go out of him. He sat there apathetic and suffering. He meditated dully: "Young men have been known to die suddenly; why should not I? I am, as a matter of fact, at the end of my endurance. I am half dead already. Yes! but what is left of that life does not belong to me now."

"Peyrol," he said in such a piercing tone that even Scevola jerked his head up; but he made an effort to reduce his shrillness and went on speaking very carefully: "I have left a letter for the secretary general at the Majorité to pay twenty-five hundred francs to Jean—you are Jean, are you not?—Peyrol, price of the tartane in which I sail. Is that right?"

"What did you do that for?" asked Peyrol with an extremely stony face. "To get me into trouble?"

"Don't be a fool, gunner, nobody remembers your name. It is buried under a stack of blackened paper. I must ask you to go there and tell them that you have seen with your own eyes Lieutenant Réal sail away on his mission."

The stoniness of Peyrol persisted but his eyes were full of fury. "Oh, yes, I see myself going there. Twenty-five hundred francs! Twenty-five hundred fiddlesticks." His tone changed suddenly. "I heard someone say that you were an honest man, and I suppose this is a proof of it. Well, to the devil with your honesty." He glared at the lieutenant and then thought: "He doesn't even pretend to listen to what I say"—and another sort of anger, partly contemptuous and with something of dim sympathy in it, replaced his downright

fury. "Pah!" he said, spat over the side, and walking up to Réal with
great deliberation, slapped him on the shoulder. The only effect of this
proceeding was to make Réal look up at him without any expression
whatever.

Peyrol then picked up the lieutenant's valise and carried it down
into the cuddy. As he passed by, Citizen Scevola uttered the word
"*Citoyen*" but it was only when he came back again that Peyrol condescended to say, "Well?"

"What are you going to do with me?" asked Scevola.

"You would not give me an account of how you came on board
this tartane," said Peyrol in a tone that sounded almost friendly,
"therefore I need not tell you what I will do with you."

A low muttering of thunder followed so close upon his words that
it might have come out of Peyrol's own lips. The rover gazed uneasily
at the sky. It was still clear overhead, and at the bottom of that little
basin surrounded by rocks there was no view in any other direction;
but even as he gazed there was a sort of flicker in the sunshine suc-
ceeded by a mighty but distant clap of thunder. For the next half hour
Peyrol and Michel were busy ashore taking a long line from the tartane to the entrance of the little basin where they fastened the end of it
to a bush. This was for the purpose of hauling the tartane out into the
cove. Then they came aboard again. The bit of sky above their heads
was still clear, but while walking with the hauling line near the cove
Peyrol had got a glimpse of the edge of the cloud. The sun grew
scorching all of a sudden, and in the stagnating air a mysterious
change seemed to come over the quality and the colour of the light.
Peyrol flung his cap on the deck, baring his head to the subtle menace
of the breathless stillness of the air.

"Phew! *Ça chauffe*," he muttered, rolling up the sleeves of his
jacket. He wiped his forehead with his mighty forearm upon which a
mermaid with an immensely long fishtail was tattooed. Perceiving the
lieutenant's belted sword lying on the deck, he picked it up and
without any ceremony threw it down the cabin stairs. As he was
passing again near Scevola, the sans-culotte raised his voice.

"I believe you are one of those wretches corrupted by English
gold," he cried like one inspired. His shining eyes, his red cheeks, tes-
tified to the fire of patriotism burning in his breast, and he used that
conventional phrase of revolutionary time, a time when, intoxicated
with oratory, he used to run about dealing death to traitors of both

sexes and all ages. But his denunciation was received in such profound silence that his own belief in it wavered. His words had sunk into an abysmal stillness and the next sound was Peyrol speaking to Réal.

"I am afraid you will get very wet, Lieutenant, before long," and then, looking at Réal, he thought with great conviction: "Wet! He wouldn't mind getting drowned." Standing stock-still he fretted and fumed inwardly, wondering where precisely the English ship was by this time and where the devil that thunderstorm had got to: for the sky had become as mute as the oppressed earth. Réal asked:

"Is it not time to haul out, gunner?" And Peyrol said:

"There is not a breath of wind anywhere for miles." He was gratified by the fairly loud mutter rolling apparently along the inland hills. Over the pool a little ragged cloud torn from the purple robe of the storm floated, arrested and thin like a bit of dark gauze.

Above at the farm Catherine had heard, too, the ominous mutter and came to the door of the *salle*. From there she could see the purple cloud itself, convoluted and solid, and its sinister shadow lying over the hills. The oncoming of the storm added to her sense of uneasiness at finding herself all alone in the house. Michel had not come up. She would have welcomed Michel, to whom she hardly ever spoke, simply as a person belonging to the usual order of things. She was not talkative, but somehow she would have liked somebody to speak to just for a moment. This cessation of all sound, voices or footsteps, around the buildings was not welcome; but looking at the cloud, she thought that there would be noise enough presently. However, stepping back into the kitchen, she was met by a sound that made her regret the oppressive silence, by its piercing and terrifying character; it was a shriek in the upper part of the house where, as far as she knew, there was only Arlette asleep. In her attempt to cross the kitchen to the foot of the stairs, the weight of her accumulated years fell upon the old woman. She felt suddenly very feeble and hardly able to breathe. And all at once the thought, "Scevola! Was he murdering her up there?" paralyzed the last remnant of her physical powers. What else could it be? She fell, as if shot, into a chair under the first shock and found herself unable to move. Only her brain remained active, and she raised her hands to her eyes as if to shut out the image of the horrors upstairs. She heard nothing more from above. Arlette was dead. She thought that now it was her turn. While her body quailed before the brutal violence, her weary spirit longed ardently for the end. Let him come! Let all this be over at last, with a blow on the head or a stab in the breast. She had not the courage to uncover her eyes. She waited. But after about a minute—it seemed to her interminable—she heard rapid footsteps overhead. Arlette was running here and there. Catherine uncovered her eyes and was about to rise when she heard at the top of the stairs the name of Peyrol shouted with a desperate accent. Then, again, after the shortest of pauses, the cry of: "Peyrol, Peyrol!" and then the sound of feet running downstairs. There was another shriek, "Peyrol!" just outside the door before it flew open. Who was pursuing her? Catherine managed to stand up. Steadying herself with one hand on the table she presented an undaunted front to her niece who ran into the kitchen with loose hair flying and the appearance of wildest distraction in her eyes.

The staircase door had slammed to behind her. Nobody was pursuing her; and Catherine, putting forth her lean brown arm, arrested Arlette's flight with such a jerk that the two women swung against each other. She seized her niece by the shoulders.

"What is this, in Heaven's name? Where are you rushing to?" she cried, and the other, as if suddenly exhausted, whispered:

"I woke up from an awful dream."

The kitchen grew dark under the cloud that hung over the house now. There was a feeble flicker of lightning and a faint crash, far away. The old woman gave her niece a little shake. "Dreams are nothing," she said. "You are awake now. . . ." And indeed Catherine thought that no dream could be so bad as the realities which kept hold of one through the long waking hours.

"They were killing him," moaned Arlette, beginning to tremble and struggle in her aunt's arms. "I tell you they were killing him."

"Be quiet. Were you dreaming of Peyrol?"

She became still in a moment and then whispered: "No. Eugène."

She had seen Réal set upon by a mob of men and women, all dripping with blood, in a livid cold light, in front of a stretch of mere shells of houses with cracked walls and broken windows, and going down in the midst of a forest of raised arms brandishing sabres, clubs, knives, axes. There was also a man flourishing a red rag on a stick, while another was beating a drum which boomed above the sickening sound of broken glass falling like rain on the pavement. And away round the corner of an empty street came Peyrol whom she recognized by his white head, walking without haste, swinging his cudgel regularly. The terrible thing was that Peyrol looked straight at her, not noticing anything, composed, without a frown or a smile, unseeing and deaf, while she waved her arms and shrieked desperately to him for help. She woke up with the piercing sound of his name in her ears and with the impression of the dream so powerful that even now, looking distractedly into her aunt's face, she could see the bare arms of that murderous crowd raised above Réal's sinking head. Yet the name that had sprung to her lips on waking was the name of Peyrol. She pushed her aunt away with such force that the old woman staggered backwards and to save herself had to catch hold of the overmantel above her head. Arlette ran to the door of the salle, looked in, came back to her aunt and shouted: "Where is he?"

Catherine really did not know which path the lieutenant had taken. She understood very well that "he" meant Réal.

She said: "He went away a long time ago"; grasped her niece's arm and added with an effort to steady her voice: "He is coming back, Arlette—for nothing will keep him away from you."

Arlette, as if mechanically, was whispering to herself the magic name, "Peyrol, Peyrol!" then cried: "I want Eugène now. This moment."

Catherine's face wore a look of unflinching patience. "He has departed on service," she said. Her niece looked at her with enormous eyes, coal-black, profound, and immovable, while in a forcible and distracted tone she said: "You and Peyrol have been plotting to rob me of my reason. But I will know how to make that old man give him up. He is mine!" She spun round wildly like a person looking for a way of escape from a deadly peril, and rushed out blindly.

About Escampobar the air was murky but calm, and the silence was so profound that it was possible to hear the first heavy drops of rain striking the ground. In the intimidating shadow of the storm-cloud, Arlette stood irresolute for a moment, but it was to Peyrol, the man of mystery and power, that her thoughts turned. She was ready to embrace his knees, to entreat, and to scold. "Peyrol, Peyrol!" she cried twice, and lent her ear as if expecting an answer. Then she shouted: "I want him back."

Catherine, alone in the kitchen, moving with dignity, sat down in the armchair with the tall back, like a senator in his curule chair awaiting the blow of a barbarous fate.

Arlette flew down the slope. The first sign of her coming was a faint thin scream which really the rover alone heard and understood. He pressed his lips in a particular way, showing his appreciation of the coming difficulty. The next moment he saw, poised on a detached boulder and thinly veiled by the first perpendicular shower, Arlette, who, catching sight of the tartane with the men on board of her, let out a prolonged shriek of mingled triumph and despair: "Peyrol! Help! Pey——rol!"

Réal jumped to his feet with an extremely scared face, but Peyrol extended an arresting arm. "She is calling to me," he said, gazing at the figure poised on the rock. "Well leaped! *Sacré nom!* . . . Well leaped!" And he muttered to himself soberly: "She will break her legs or her neck."

"I see you, Peyrol," screamed Arlette, who seemed to be flying through the air. "Don't you dare."

"Yes, here I am," shouted the rover, striking his breast with his fist.

Lieutenant Réal put both his hands over his face. Michel looked on open-mouthed, very much as if watching a performance in a circus; but Scevola cast his eyes down. Arlette came on board with such an impetus that Peyrol had to step forward and save her from a fall which would have stunned her. She struggled in his arms with extreme violence. The heiress of Escampobar with her loose black hair seemed the incarnation of pale fury. "*Misérable!* Don't you dare!" A roll of thunder covered her voice, but when it had passed away she was heard again in suppliant tones. "Peyrol, my friend, my dear old friend. Give him back to me," and all the time her body writhed in the arms of the old seaman. "You used to love me, Peyrol," she cried without ceasing to struggle, and suddenly struck the rover twice in the face with her clenched fist. Peyrol's head received the two blows as if it had been made of marble, but he felt with fear her body become still, grow rigid in his arms. A heavy squall enveloped the group of people on board the tartane. Peyrol laid Arlette gently on the deck. Her eyes were closed, her hands remained clenched; every sign of life had left her white face. Peyrol stood up and looked at the tall rocks streaming with water. The rain swept over the tartane with an angry swishing roar to which was added the sound of water rushing violently down the folds and seams of the precipitous shore vanishing gradually from his sight, as if this had been the beginning of a destroying and universal deluge—the end of all things.

Lieutenant Réal, kneeling on one knee, contemplated the pale face of Arlette. Distinct, yet mingling with the faint growl of distant thunder, Peyrol's voice was heard saying:

"We can't put her ashore and leave her lying in the rain. She must be taken up to the house." Arlette's soaked clothes clung to her limbs while the lieutenant, his bare head dripping with rain water, looked as if he had just saved her from drowning. Peyrol gazed down inscrutably at the woman stretched on the deck and at the kneeling man. "She has fainted from rage at her old Peyrol," he went on rather dreamily. "Strange things do happen. However, Lieutenant, you had better take her under the arms and step ashore first. I will help you. Ready? Lift."

The movements of the two men had to be careful and their progress was slow on the lower, steep part of the slope. After going up more than two-thirds of the way, they rested their insensible burden on a flat stone. Réal continued to sustain the shoulders but Peyrol lowered the feet gently.

"Ha!" he said. "You will be able to carry her yourself the rest of the way and give her up to old Catherine. Get a firm footing and I will lift her and place her in your arms. You can walk the distance quite easily. There. . . . Hold her a little higher, or her feet will be catching on the stones."

Arlette's hair was hanging far below the lieutenant's arm in an inert and heavy mass. The thunderstorm was passing away, leaving a cloudy sky. And Peyrol thought with a profound sigh: "I am tired."

"She is light," said Réal.

"*Parbleu*, she is light. If she were dead, you would find her heavy enough. *Allons*, Lieutenant. No! I am not coming. What's the good? I'll stay down here. I have no mind to listen to Catherine's scolding."

The lieutenant, looking absorbed into the face resting in the hollow of his arm, never averted his gaze—not even when Peyrol, stooping over Arlette, kissed the white forehead near the roots of the hair, black as a raven's wing.

"What am I to do?" muttered Réal.

"Do? Why, give her up to old Catherine. And you may just as well tell her that I will be coming along directly. That will cheer her up. I used to count for something in that house. *Allez*. For our time is very short."

With these words he turned away and walked slowly down to the tartane. A breeze had sprung up. He felt it on his wet neck and was grateful for the cool touch which recalled him to himself, to his old wandering self which had known no softness and no hesitation in the face of any risk offered by life.

As he stepped on board, the shower passed away. Michel, wet to the skin, was still in the very same attitude gazing up the slope. Citizen Scevola had drawn his knees up and was holding his head in his hands; whether because of rain or cold or for some other reason, his teeth were chattering audibly with a continuous and distressing rattle. Peyrol flung off his jacket, heavy with water, with a strange air as if it was of no more use to his mortal envelope, squared his broad shoulders and directed Michel in a deep, quiet voice to let go the lines holding the tartane to the shore. The faithful henchman was taken aback and required one of Peyrol's authoritative *"Allez"* to put him in motion. Meantime the rover cast off the tiller lines and laid his hand with an air of mastery on the stout piece of wood projecting horizontally from the rudder-head about the level of his hip. The voices and the movements of his companions caused Citizen Scevola to master the desperate trembling of his jaw. He wriggled a little in his bonds and the question that had been on his lips for a good many hours was uttered again.

"What are you going to do with me?"

"What do you think of a little promenade at sea?" Peyrol asked in a tone that was not unkindly.

Citizen Scevola, who had seemed totally and completely cast down and subdued, let out a most unexpected screech.

"Unbind me. Put me ashore."

Michel, busy forward, was moved to smile as though he had possessed a cultivated sense of incongruity. Peyrol remained serious.

"You shall be untied presently," he assured the blood-drinking patriot, who had been for so many years the reputed possessor not only of Escampobar, but of the Escampobar heiress that, living on appearances, he had almost come to believe in that ownership himself. No wonder he screeched at this rude awakening. Peyrol raised his voice: "Haul on the line, Michel."

As, directly the ropes had been let go, the tartane had swung clear of the shore, the movement given her by Michel carried her towards the entrance by which the basin communicated with the cove. Peyrol attended to the helm, and in a moment, gliding through the narrow gap, the tartane carrying her way, shot out almost into the middle of the cove.

A little wind could be felt, running light wrinkles over the water, but outside the overshadowed sea was already speckled with white caps. Peyrol helped Michel to haul aft the sheets and then went back to the tiller. The pretty spick-and-span craft that had been lying idle for so long began to glide into the wide world. Michel gazed at the shore as if lost in admiration. Citizen Scevola's head had fallen on his knees while his nerveless hands clasped his legs loosely. He was the very image of dejection.

"Hé, Michel! Come here and cast loose the citizen. It is only fair that he should be untied for a little excursion at sea."

When his order had been executed, Peyrol addressed himself to the desolate figure on the deck.

"Like this, should the tartane get capsized in a squall, you will have an equal chance with us to swim for your life."

Scevola disdained to answer. He was engaged in biting his knee with rage in a stealthy fashion.

"You came on board for some murderous purpose. Who you were after unless it was myself, God only knows. I feel quite justified in giving you a little outing at sea. I won't conceal from you, citizen, that it may not be without risk to life or limb. But you have only yourself to thank for being here."

As the tartane drew clear of the cove, she felt more the weight of the breeze and darted forward with a lively motion. A vaguely contented smile lighted up Michel's hairy countenance.

"She feels the sea," said Peyrol, who enjoyed the swift movement of his vessel. "This is different from your lagoon, Michel."

"To be sure," said Michel with becoming gravity.

"Doesn't it seem funny to you, as you look back at the shore, to think that you have left nothing and nobody behind?"

Michel assumed the aspect of a man confronted by an intellectual problem. Since he had become Peyrol's henchman he had lost the habit of thinking altogether. Directions and orders were easy things to apprehend; but a conversation with him whom he called *"notre maître"* was a serious matter demanding great and concentrated attention.

"Possibly," he murmured, looking strangely self-conscious.

"Well, you are lucky, take my word for it," said the rover, watching the course of his little vessel along the head of the peninsula. "You have not even a dog to miss you."

"I have only you, Maître Peyrol."

"That's what I was thinking," said Peyrol half to himself, while Michel, who had good sea-legs, kept his balance to the movements of the craft without taking his eyes from the rover's face.

"No," Peyrol exclaimed suddenly, after a moment of meditation, "I could not leave you behind." He extended his open palm towards Michel.

"Put your hand in there," he said.

Michel hesitated for a moment before this extraordinary proposal. At last he did so, and Peyrol, holding the bereaved fisherman's hand in a powerful grip, said:

"If I had gone away by myself, I would have left you marooned on this earth like a man thrown out to die on a desert island." Some dim perception of the solemnity of the occasion seemed to enter Michel's primitive brain. He connected Peyrol's words with the sense of his own insignificant position at the tail of all mankind; and, timidly, he murmured with his clear, innocent glance unclouded, the fundamental axiom of his philosophy:

"Somebody must be last in this world."

"Well, then, you will have to forgive me all that may happen between this and the hour of sunset."

The tartane, obeying the helm, fell off before the wind, with her head to the eastward.

Peyrol murmured: "She has not forgotten how to walk the seas." His unsubdued heart, heavy for so many days, had a moment of buoyancy—the illusion of immense freedom.

At that moment Réal, amazed at finding no tartane in the basin, was running madly towards the cove, where he was sure Peyrol must be waiting to give her up to him. He ran out on to the very rock on which Peyrol's late prisoner had sat after his escape, too tired to care, yet cheered by the hope of liberty. But Réal was in a worse plight. He could see no shadowy form through the thin veil of rain which pitted the sheltered piece of water framed in the rocks. The little craft had been spirited away. Impossible! There must be something wrong with his eyes! Again the barren hillsides echoed the name of "Peyrol," shouted with all the force of Réal's lungs. He shouted it only once, and about five minutes afterwards appeared at the kitchen-door, panting, streaming with water as if he had fought his way up from the bottom of the sea. In the tall-backed armchair Arlette lay, with her limbs relaxed, her head on Catherine's arm, her face white as death. He saw her open her black eyes, enormous and as if not of this world; he saw old Catherine turn her head, heard a cry of surprise, and saw a sort of struggle beginning between the two women. He screamed at them like a madman: "Peyrol has betrayed me!" and in an instant, with a bang of the door, he was gone.

The rain had ceased. Above his head the unbroken mass of clouds moved to the eastward, and he moved in the same direction as if he too were driven by the wind up the hillside, towards the lookout. When he reached the spot and, gasping, flung one arm round the trunk of the leaning tree, the only thing he was aware of during the sombre pause in the unrest of the elements was the distracting turmoil of his thoughts. After a moment he perceived through the rain the English ship with her topsails lowered on the caps, forging ahead slowly across the northern entrance of the Petite Passe. His distress fastened insanely on the notion of there being a connection between that enemy ship and Peyrol's inexplicable conduct. That old man had always meant to go himself! And when a moment after, looking to the southward, he made out the shadow of the tartane coming round the land in the midst of another squall, he muttered to himself a bitter: "Of course!" She had both her sails set. Peyrol was indeed pressing her to the utmost in his shameful haste to traffic with the enemy. The truth was that from the position in which Réal first saw him, Peyrol could not yet see the English ship, and held confidently on his course up the middle of the strait. The man-of-war and the little tartane saw each other quite unexpectedly at a distance that was very little over a mile. Peyrol's heart flew into his mouth at finding himself so close to the enemy. On board the *Amelia* at first no notice was taken. It was simply a tartane making for shelter on the north side of Porquerolles. But when Peyrol suddenly altered his course, the master of the man-of-war, noticing the manœuvre, took up the long glass for a look. Captain Vincent was on deck and agreed with the master's remark that "there was a craft acting suspiciously." Before the *Amelia* could come round

in the heavy squall, Peyrol was already under the battery of Porquerolles and, so far, safe from capture. Captain Vincent had no mind
to bring his ship within reach of the battery and risk damage in his
rigging or hull for the sake of a small coaster. However, the tale
brought on board by Symons of his discovery of a hidden craft, of his
capture, and his wonderful escape, had made every tartane an object
of interest to the whole ship's company. The *Amelia* remained hove to
in the strait while her officers watched the lateen sails gliding to and
fro under the protecting muzzles of the guns. Captain Vincent himself
had been impressed by Peyrol's manœuvre. Coasting craft as a rule
were not afraid of the *Amelia*. After taking a few turns on the quarter-
deck he ordered Symons to be called aft.

The hero of a unique and mysterious adventure, which had been
the only subject of talk on board the corvette for the last twenty-four
hours, came along rolling, hat in hand, and enjoying a secret sense of
his importance.

"Take the glass," said the captain, "and have a look at that vessel
under the land. Is she anything like the tartane that you say you have
been aboard of?"

Symons was very positive. "I think I can swear to those painted
mastheads, your honour. It is the last thing I remember before that
murderous ruffian knocked me senseless. The moon shone on them. I
can make them out now with the glass." As to the fellow boasting to
him that the tartane was a dispatch-boat and had already made some
trips, well, Symons begged his honour to believe that the beggar was
not sober at the time. He did not care what he blurted out. The best
proof of his condition was that he went away to fetch the soldiers
and forgot to come back. The murderous old ruffian! "You see, your
honour," continued Symons, "he thought I was not likely to escape
after getting a blow that would have killed nine out of any ten men. So
he went away to boast of what he had done before the people ashore;
because one of his chums, worse than himself, came down thinking he
would kill me with a dam' big manure fork, saving your honour's
presence. A regular savage he was."

Symons paused, staring, as if astonished at the marvels of his own
tale. The old master, standing at his captain's elbow, observed in a dis-
passionate tone that, anyway, that peninsula was not a bad jumping-
off place for a craft intending to slip through the blockade. Symons,
not being dismissed, waited hat in hand while Captain Vincent

directed the master to fill on the ship and stand a little nearer to the
battery. It was done, and presently there was a flash of a gun low
down on the water's edge and a shot came skipping in the direction of
the *Amelia*. It fell very short, but Captain Vincent judged the ship was
close enough and ordered her to be hove to again. Then Symons was
told to take a look through the glass once more. After a long interval
he lowered it and spoke impressively to his captain:

"I can make out three heads aboard, your honour, and one is
white. I would swear to that white head anywhere."

Captain Vincent made no answer. All this seemed very odd to him;
but after all it was possible. The craft had certainly acted suspiciously.
He spoke to the first lieutenant in a half-vexed tone.

"He has done a rather smart thing. He will dodge here till dark and
then get away. It is perfectly absurd. I don't want to send the boats too
close to the battery. And if I do he may simply sail away from them
and be round the land long before we are ready to give him chase.
Darkness will be his best friend. However, we will keep a watch on
him in case he is tempted to give us the slip late in the afternoon. In
that case we will have a good try to catch him. If he has anything
aboard I should like to get hold of it. It may be of some importance,
after all."

On board the tartane Peyrol put his own interpretation on the
ship's movements. His object had been attained. The corvette had
marked him for her prey. Satisfied as to that, Peyrol watched his
opportunity and taking advantage of a long squall, with rain thick
enough to blur the form of the English ship, he left the shelter of the
battery to lead the Englishman a dance and keep up his character of a
man anxious to avoid capture.

Réal, from his position on the lookout, saw in the thinning down-
pour the pointed lateen sails glide round the north end of Porquerolles and vanish behind the land. Some time afterwards the
Amelia made sail in a manner that put it beyond doubt that she meant
to chase. Her lofty canvas was shut off too presently by the land of
Porquerolles. When she had disappeared Réal turned to Arlette.

"Let us go," he said.

Arlette, stimulated by the short glimpse of Réal at the kitchen door,
whom she had taken for a vision of a lost man calling her to follow
him to the end of the world, had torn herself out of the old woman's
thin, bony arms which could not cope with the struggles of her body

and the fierceness of her spirit. She had run straight to the lookout, though there was nothing to guide her there except a blind impulse to seek Réal wherever he might be. He was not aware of her having found him until she seized hold of his arm with a suddenness, energy, and determination of which no one with a clouded mind could have been capable. He felt himself being taken possession of in a way that tore all his scruples out of his breast. Holding on to the trunk of the tree, he threw his other arm round her waist, and when she confessed to him that she did not know why she had run up there, but that if she had not found him she would have thrown herself over the cliff, he tightened his clasp with sudden exultation, as though she had been a gift prayed for instead of a stumbling block for his pedantic conscience. Together they walked back. In the failing light the buildings awaited them, lifeless, the walls darkened by rain and the big slopes of the roofs glistening and sinister under the flying desolation of the clouds. In the kitchen Catherine heard their mingled footsteps, and rigid in the tall armchair awaited their coming. Arlette threw her arms round the old woman's neck while Réal stood on one side, looking on. Thought after thought flew through his mind and vanished in the strong feeling of the irrevocable nature of the event handing him to the woman whom, in the revulsion of his feelings, he was inclined to think more sane than himself. Arlette, with one arm over the old woman's shoulders, kissed the wrinkled forehead under the white band of linen that, on the erect head, had the effect of a rustic diadem.

"To-morrow you and I will have to walk down to the church."

The austere dignity of Catherine's pose seemed to be shaken by this proposal to lead before the God, with whom she had made her peace long ago, that unhappy girl chosen to share in the guilt of impious and unspeakable horrors which had darkened her mind.

Arlette, still stooping over her aunt's face, extended a hand towards Réal, who, making a step forward, took it silently into his grasp.

"Oh, yes, you will, Aunt," insisted Arlette. "You will have to come with me to pray for Peyrol, whom you and I shall never see any more."

Catherine's head dropped, whether in assent or grief; and Réal felt an unexpected and profound emotion, for he, too, was convinced that none of the three persons in the farm would ever see Peyrol again. It was as though the rover of the wide seas had left them to themselves on a sudden impulse of scorn, of magnanimity, of a passion weary of itself. However come by, Réal was ready to clasp for ever to his breast that woman touched by the red hand of the Revolution; for she, whose little feet had run ankle-deep through the terrors of death, had brought to him the sense of triumphant life.

CHAPTER XVI

ASTERN OF THE tartane, the sun, about to set, kindled a
streak of dull crimson glow between the darkening sea and
the overcast sky. The peninsula of Giens and the islands of
Hyères formed one mass of land detaching itself very black against
the fiery girdle of the horizon; but to the north the long stretch of
the Alpine coast continued beyond sight its endless sinuosities under
the stooping clouds.

The tartane seemed to be rushing together with the run of the
waves into the arms of the oncoming night. A little more than a mile
away on her lee quarter, the *Amelia*, under all plain sail, pressed to the
end of the chase. It had lasted now for a good many hours, for Peyrol,
when slipping away, had managed to get the advantage of the *Amelia*
from the very start. While still within the large sheet of smooth water
which is called the Hyères roadstead, the tartane, which was really a
craft of extraordinary speed, managed to gain positively on the sloop.
Afterwards, by suddenly darting down the eastern passage between
the two last islands of the group, Peyrol actually got out of sight of the
chasing ship, being hidden by the Ile du Levant for a time. The *Amelia*
having to tack twice in order to follow, lost ground once more.
Emerging into the open sea, she had to tack again, and then the position became that of a stern chase, which proverbially is known as
a long chase. Peyrol's skilful seamanship had twice extracted from
Captain Vincent a low murmur accompanied by a significant com-

pression of lips. At one time the *Amelia* had been near enough the tartane to send a shot ahead of her. That one was followed by another which whizzed extraordinarily close to the mastheads, but then Captain Vincent ordered the gun to be secured again. He said to his first lieutenant, who, his speaking trumpet in hand, kept at his elbow: "We must not sink that craft on any account. If we could get only an hour's calm, we would carry her with the boats."

The lieutenant remarked that there was no hope of a calm for the next twenty-four hours at least.

"No," said Captain Vincent, "and in about an hour it will be dark, and then he may very well give us the slip. The coast is not very far off and there are batteries on both sides of Fréjus, under any of which he will be as safe from capture as though he were hove up on the beach. And look," he exclaimed after a moment's pause, "this is what the fellow means to do."

"Yes, sir," said the lieutenant, keeping his eyes on the white speck ahead, dancing lightly on the short Mediterranean waves, "he is keeping off the wind."

"We will have him in less than an hour," said Captain Vincent, and made as if he meant to rub his hands, but suddenly leaned his elbow on the rail. "After all," he went on, "properly speaking, it is a race between the *Amelia* and the night."

"And it will be dark early to-day," said the first lieutenant, swinging the speaking trumpet by its lanyard. "Shall we take the yards off the back-stays, sir?"

"No," said Captain Vincent. "There is a clever seaman aboard that tartane. He is running off now, but at any time he may haul up again. We must not follow him too closely, or we shall lose the advantage which we have now. That man is determined on making his escape."

If those words by some miracle could have been carried to the ears of Peyrol, they would have brought to his lips a smile of malicious and triumphant exultation. Ever since he had laid his hand on the tiller of the tartane every faculty of his resourcefulness and seamanship had been bent on deceiving the English captain, that enemy whom he had never seen, the man whose mind he had constructed for himself from the evolutions of his ship. Leaning against the heavy tiller he addressed Michel, breaking the silence of the strenuous afternoon.

"This is the moment," his deep voice uttered quietly. "Ease off the mainsheet, Michel. A little now, only."

When Michel returned to the place where he had been sitting to windward, the rover noticed his eyes fixed on his face wonderingly. Some vague thoughts had been forming themselves slowly, incompletely, in Michel's brain. Peyrol met the utter innocence of the unspoken inquiry with a smile that, beginning sardonically on his manly and sensitive mouth, ended in something resembling tenderness.

"That's so, *camarade*," he said with particular stress and intonation, as if those words contained a full and sufficient answer. Most unexpectedly Michel's round and generally staring eyes blinked as if dazzled. He, too, produced from somewhere in the depths of his being a queer, misty smile from which Peyrol averted his gaze.

"Where is the citizen?" he asked, bearing hard against the tiller and staring straight ahead. "He isn't gone overboard, is he? I don't seem to have seen him since we rounded the land near Porquerolles Castle."

Michel, after craning his head forward to look over the edge of the deck, announced that Scevola was sitting on the keelson.

"Go forward," said Peyrol, "and ease off the foresheet now a little. This tartane has wings," he added to himself.

Alone on the after-deck Peyrol turned his head to look at the *Amelia*. That ship, in consequence of holding her wind, was now crossing obliquely the wake of the tartane. At the same time she had diminished the distance. Nevertheless, Peyrol considered that had he really meant to escape, his chances were as eight to ten—practically an assured success. For a long time he had been contemplating the lofty pyramid of canvas towering against the fading red belt on the sky, when a lamentable groan made him look round. It was Scevola. The citizen had adopted the mode of progression on all fours, and while Peyrol looked at him he rolled to leeward, saved himself rather cleverly from going overboard, and holding on desperately to a cleat, shouted in a hollow voice, pointing with the other hand as if he had made a tremendous discovery: "*La terre! La terre!*"

"Certainly," said Peyrol, steering with extreme nicety. "What of that?"

"I don't want to be drowned!" cried the citizen in his new hollow voice. Peyrol reflected a bit before he spoke in a serious tone:

"If you stay where you are, I assure you that you will . . ." he glanced rapidly over his shoulder at the *Amelia* . . . "not die by drowning." He jerked his head sideways. "I know that man's mind."

"What man? Whose mind?" yelled Scevola with intense eagerness and bewilderment. "We are only three on board."

But Peyrol's mind was contemplating maliciously the figure of a man with long teeth, in a wig, and with large buckles to his shoes. Such was his ideal conception of what the captain of the *Amelia* ought to look like. That officer, whose naturally good-humoured face wore then a look of severe resolution, had beckoned his first lieutenant to his side again.

"We are gaining," he said quietly. "I intend to close with him to windward. We won't risk any of his tricks. It is very difficult to outmanœuvre a Frenchman, as you know. Send a few armed marines on the forecastle-head. I am afraid the only way to get hold of this tartane is to disable the men on board of her. I wish to goodness I could think of some other. When we close with her, let the marines fire a well-aimed volley. You must get some marines to stand by aft as well. I hope we may shoot away his halliards; once his sails are down on his deck he is ours for the trouble of putting a boat over the side."

For more than half an hour Captain Vincent stood silent, elbow on rail, keeping his eye on the tartane, while on board the latter Peyrol steered silent and watchful but intensely conscious of the enemy ship holding on in her relentless pursuit. The narrow red band was dying out of the sky. The French coast, black against the fading light, merged into the shadows gathering in the eastern board. Citizen Scevola, somewhat soothed by the assurance that he would not die by drowning, had elected to remain quiet where he had fallen, not daring to trust himself to move on the lively deck. Michel, squatting to windward, gazed intently at Peyrol in expectation of some order at any minute. But Peyrol uttered no word and made no sign. From time to time a burst of foam flew over the tartane, or a splash of water would come aboard with a scurrying noise.

It was not till the corvette had got within a long gunshot from the tartane that Peyrol opened his mouth.

"No!" he burst out, loud in the wind, as if giving vent to long anxious thinking, "No! I could not have left you behind with not even a dog for company. Devil take me if I don't think you would not have thanked me for it either. What do you say to that, Michel?"

A half-puzzled smile dwelt persistently on the guileless countenance of the ex-fisherman. He stated what he had always thought in respect of Peyrol's every remark: "I think you are right, *maître*."

"Listen then, Michel. That ship will be alongside of us in less than half an hour. As she comes up they will open on us with musketry."

"They will open on us . . . ," repeated Michel, looking quite interested. "But how do you know they will do that, *maître*?"

"Because her captain has got to obey what is in my mind," said Peyrol, in a tone of positive and solemn conviction. "He will do it as sure as if I were at his ear telling him what to do. He will do it because he is a first-rate seaman, but I, Michel, I am just a little bit cleverer than he." He glanced over his shoulder at the *Amelia* rushing after the tartane with swelling sails, and raised his voice suddenly. "He will do it because no more than half a mile ahead of us is the spot where Peyrol will die!"

Michel did not start. He only shut his eyes for a time, and the rover continued in a lower tone:

"I may be shot through the heart at once," he said: "and in that case you have my permission to let go the halliards if you are alive yourself. But if I live I mean to put the helm down. When I do that you will let go the foresheet to help the tartane to fly into the wind's eye. This is my last order to you. Now go forward and fear nothing. *Adieu*." Michel obeyed without a word.

Half a dozen of the *Amelia*'s marines stood ranged on the forecastle-head ready with their muskets. Captain Vincent walked into the lee waist to watch his chase. When he thought that the jib-boom of the *Amelia* had drawn level with the stern of the tartane he waved his hat and the marines discharged their muskets. Apparently no gear was cut. Captain Vincent observed the white-headed man, who was steering, clap his hand to his left side, while he hove the tiller to leeward and brought the tartane sharply into the wind. The marines on the poop fired in their turn, all the reports merging into one. Voices were heard on the decks crying that they "had hit the white-haired chap." Captain Vincent shouted to the master.

"Get the ship round on the other tack."

The elderly seaman who was the master of the *Amelia* took a critical look before he gave the necessary orders; and the *Amelia* closed on her chase with her decks resounding to the piping of boatswain's mates and the hoarse shout: "Hands shorten sail. About ship."

Peyrol, lying on his back under the swinging tiller, heard the calls shrilling and dying away; he heard the ominous rush of *Amelia*'s bow wave as the sloop foamed within ten yards of the tartane's stern; he even saw her upper yards coming down, and then everything vanished out of the clouded sky. There was nothing in his ears but the sound of the wind, the wash of the waves buffeting the little craft left without guidance, and the continuous thrashing of its foresail the sheet of which Michel had let go according to orders. The tartane began to roll heavily, but Peyrol's right arm was sound and he managed to put it round a bollard to prevent himself from being flung about. A feeling of peace sank into him, not unmingled with pride. Everything he had planned had come to pass. He had meant to play that man a trick, and now the trick had been played. Played by him better than by any other old man on whom age had stolen, unnoticed, till the veil of peace was torn down by the touch of a sentiment unexpected like an intruder and cruel like an enemy.

Peyrol rolled his head to the left. All he could see were the legs of Citizen Scevola sliding nervelessly to and fro to the rolling of the vessel as if his body had been jammed somewhere. Dead, or only scared to death? And Michel? Was he dead or dying, that man without friends whom his pity had refused to leave behind marooned on the earth without even a dog for company? As to that, Peyrol felt no compunction; but he thought he would have liked to see Michel once more. He tried to utter his name, but his throat refused him even a whisper. He felt himself removed far away from that world of human sounds, in which Arlette had screamed at him: "Peyrol, don't you dare!" He would never hear anybody's voice again! Under that grey sky there was nothing for him but the swish of breaking seas and the ceaseless furious beating of the tartane's foresail. His plaything was knocking about terribly under him, with her tiller flying madly to and fro just clear of his head, and solid lumps of water coming on board over his prostrate body. Suddenly, in a desperate lurch which brought the whole Mediterranean with a ferocious snarl level with the slope of the little deck, Peyrol saw the *Amelia* bearing right down upon the tartane. The fear, not of death but of failure, gripped his slowing-down heart. Was this blind Englishman going to run him down and sink the dispatches together with the craft? With a mighty effort of his ebbing strength Peyrol sat up and flung his arm round the shroud of the mainmast.

The *Amelia*, whose way had carried her past the tartane for a quarter of a mile, before sail could be shortened and her yards swung on the other tack, was coming back to take possession of her chase. In the deepening dusk and amongst the foaming seas it was a matter of difficulty to make out the little craft. At the very moment when the master of the man-of-war, looking out anxiously from the forecastle-head, thought that she might perhaps have filled and gone down, he caught sight of her rolling in the trough of the sea, and so close that she seemed to be at the end of the *Amelia*'s jib-boom. His heart flew in his mouth. "Hard a starboard!" he yelled, his order being passed along the decks.

Peyrol, sinking back on the deck in another heavy lurch of his craft, saw for an instant the whole of the English corvette swing up into the clouds as if she meant to fling herself upon his very breast. A blown sea-top flicked his face noisily, followed by a smooth interval, a silence of the waters. He beheld in a flash the days of his manhood, of strength and adventure. Suddenly an enormous voice like the roar of an angry sea-lion seemed to fill the whole of the empty sky in a mighty and commanding shout: "Steady!" . . . And with the sound of that familiar English word ringing in his ears Peyrol smiled to his visions and died.

The *Amelia*, stripped down to her topsails and hove to, rose and fell easily while on her quarter about a cable's length away Peyrol's tartane tumbled like a lifeless corpse amongst the seas. Captain Vincent, in his favourite attitude of leaning over the rail, kept his eyes fastened on his prize. Mr. Bolt, who had been sent for, waited patiently till his commander turned round.

"Oh, here you are, Mr. Bolt. I have sent for you to go and take possession. You speak French, and there may still be somebody alive in her. If so, of course you will send him on board at once. I am sure there can be nobody unwounded there. It will anyhow be too dark to see much, but just have a good look round and secure everything in the way of papers you can lay your hands on. Haul aft the foresheet and sail her up to receive a tow-line. I intend to take her along and ransack her thoroughly in the morning; tear down the cuddy linings and so on, should you not find at once what I expect. . . ." Captain Vincent, his white teeth gleaming in the dusk, gave some further orders in a lower tone, and Mr. Bolt departed in a hurry. Half an hour afterwards he was back on board, and the *Amelia*, with the tartane in tow, made sail to the eastward in search of the blockading fleet.

Mr. Bolt, introduced into a cabin strongly lighted by a swinging lamp, tendered to his captain across the table a sail-cloth package corded and sealed, and a piece of paper folded in four, which, he explained, seemed to be a certificate of registry, strangely enough mentioning no name. Captain Vincent seized the grey canvas package eagerly.

"This looks like the very thing, Bolt," he said, turning it over in his hands. "What else did you find on board?"

Bolt said that he had found three dead men, two on the after-deck and one lying at the bottom of the open hold with the bare end of the foresheet in his hand—"shot down, I suppose, just as he had let it go," he commented. He described the appearance of the bodies and reported that he had disposed of them according to orders. In the tartane's cabin there was half a demijohn of wine and a loaf of bread in a locker; also, on the floor, a leather valise containing an officer's uniform coat and a change of clothing. He had lighted the lamp and saw that the linen was marked "E. Réal." An officer's sword on a broad shoulder-belt was also lying on the floor. These things could not have belonged to the old chap with the white hair, who was a big man. "Looks as if somebody had tumbled overboard," commented Bolt. Two of the bodies looked nondescript, but there was no doubt about that fine old fellow being a seaman.

"By Heavens!" said Captain Vincent, "he was that! Do you know, Bolt, that he nearly managed to escape us? Another twenty minutes would have done it. How many wounds had he?"

"Three I think, sir. I did not look closely," said Bolt.

"I hated the necessity of shooting brave men like dogs," said Captain Vincent. "Still, it was the only way; and there may be something here," he went on, slapping the package with his open palm, "that will justify me in my own eyes. You may go now."

Captain Vincent did not turn in but only lay down fully dressed on the couch till the officer of the watch, appearing at the door, told him that a ship of the fleet was in sight away to windward. Captain Vincent ordered the private night signal to be made. When he came on deck the towering shadow of a line-of-battle ship that seemed to reach to the very clouds was well within hail and a voice bellowed from her through a speaking trumpet:

"What ship is that?"

"His Majesty's sloop *Amelia*," hailed back Captain Vincent. "What ship is that, pray?"

Instead of the usual answer there was a short pause and another voice spoke boisterously through the trumpet:

"Is that you, Vincent? Don't you know the *Superb* when you see her?"

"Not in the dark, Keats. How are you? I am in a hurry to speak to the admiral."

"The fleet is lying by," came the voice now with painstaking distinctness across the murmurs, whispers, and splashes of the black lane of water dividing the two ships. "The admiral bears S. S. E. If you stretch on till daylight as you are, you will fetch him on the other tack in time for breakfast on board the *Victory*. Is anything up?"

At every slight roll the sails of the *Amelia*, becalmed by the bulk of the seventy-four, flapped gently against the masts.

"Not much," hailed Captain Vincent. "I made a prize."

"Have you been in action?" came the swift inquiry.

"No, no. Piece of luck."

"Where's your prize?" roared the speaking trumpet with interest.

"In my desk," roared Captain Vincent in reply. . . . "Enemy dispatches. . . . I say, Keats, fill on your ship. Fill on her, I say, or you will be falling on board of me." He stamped his foot impatiently. "Clap some hands at once on the tow-line and run that tartane close under our stern," he called to the officer of the watch, "or else the old *Superb* will walk over her without ever knowing anything about it."

When Captain Vincent presented himself on board the *Victory* it was too late for him to be invited to share the admiral's breakfast. He was told that Lord Nelson had not been seen on deck yet, that morning; and presently word came that he wished to see Captain Vincent at once in his cabin. Being introduced, the captain of the *Amelia*, in undress uniform, with a sword by his side and his hat under his arm, was received kindly, made his bow, and with a few words of explanation laid the packet on the big round table at which sat a silent secretary in black clothes, who had been obviously writing a letter from his lordship's dictation. The admiral had been walking up and down, and after he had greeted Captain Vincent he resumed his pacing of a nervous man. His empty sleeve had not yet been pinned on his breast and swung slightly every time he turned in his walk. His thin locks fell lank against the pale cheeks, and the whole face in repose had an expression of suffering with which the fire of his one eye presented a startling contrast. He stopped short and exclaimed while Captain Vincent towered over him in a respectful attitude:

"A tartane! Captured on aboard a tartane! How on earth did you pitch upon that one out of the hundreds you must see every month?"

"I must confess that I got hold accidentally of some curious information," said Captain Vincent. "It was all a piece of luck."

While the secretary was ripping open with a penknife the cover of
the dispatches Lord Nelson took Captain Vincent out into the stern
gallery. The quiet and sunshiny morning had the added charm of a
cool, light breeze; and the *Victory*, under her three topsails and lower
staysails, was moving slowly to the southward in the midst of the
scattered fleet carrying for the most part the same sail as the admiral.
Only far away two or three ships could be seen covered with canvas
trying to close with the flag. Captain Vincent noted with satisfaction
that the first lieutenant of the *Amelia* had been obliged to brace by his
afteryards in order not to overrun the admiral's quarter.

"Why!" exclaimed Lord Nelson suddenly, after looking at the
sloop for a moment, "you have that tartane in tow!"

"I thought that your lordship would perhaps like to see a forty-ton
lateen craft which has led such a chase to, I daresay, the fastest sloop in
His Majesty's service."

"How did it all begin?" asked the admiral, continuing to look at
the *Amelia*.

"As I have already hinted to your lordship, certain information
came in my way," began Captain Vincent, who did not think it necessary to enlarge upon that part of the story. "This tartane, which is not
very different to look at from the other tartanes along the coast
between Cette and Genoa, had started from a cove on the Giens Peninsula. An old man with a white head of hair was entrusted with the service and really they could have found nobody better. He came round
Cape Esterel intending to pass through the Hyères roadstead. Apparently he did not expect to find the *Amelia* in his way. And it was there
that he made his only mistake. If he had kept on his course I would
probably have taken no more notice of him than of two other craft that
were in sight then. But he acted suspiciously by hauling up for the battery on Porquerolles. This manœuvre in connection with the information of which I spoke decided me to overhaul him and see what he
had on board." Captain Vincent then related concisely the episodes of
the chase. "I assure your lordship that I never gave an order with
greater reluctance than to open musketry fire on that craft; but the old
man had given such proofs of his seamanship and determination that
there was nothing else for it. Why! at the very moment he had the
Amelia alongside of him he still made a most clever attempt to prolong
the chase. There were only a few minutes of daylight left, and in the

darkness we might very well have lost him. Considering that they all could have saved their lives simply by striking their sails on deck, I can not refuse them my admiration and especially to the white-haired man."

The admiral, who had been all the time looking absently at the *Amelia* keeping her station with the tartane in tow, said:

"You have a very smart little ship, Vincent. Very fit for the work I have given you to do. French built, isn't she?"

"Yes, my lord. They are great shipbuilders."

"You don't seem to hate the French, Vincent," said the admiral, smiling faintly.

"Not that kind, my lord," said Captain Vincent with a bow. "I detest their political principles and the characters of their public men, but your lordship will admit that for courage and determination we could not have found worthier adversaries anywhere on this globe."

"I never said that they were to be despised," said Lord Nelson. "Resource, courage, yes. . . . If that Toulon fleet gives me the slip, all our squadrons from Gibraltar to Brest will be in jeopardy. Why don't they come out and be done with it? Don't I keep far enough out of their way?" he cried.

Vincent remarked the nervous agitation of the frail figure with a concern augmented by a fit of coughing which came on the admiral. He was quite alarmed by its violence. He watched the commander-in-chief in the Mediterranean choking and gasping so helplessly that he felt compelled to turn his eyes away from the painful spectacle; but he noticed also how quickly Lord Nelson recovered from the subsequent exhaustion.

"This is anxious work, Vincent," he said. "It is killing me. I aspire to repose somewhere in the country, in the midst of fields, out of reach of the sea and the admiralty and dispatches and orders, and responsibility, too. I have been just finishing a letter to tell them at home I have hardly enough breath in my body to carry me on from day to day. . . . But I am like that white-headed man you admire so much, Vincent," he pursued, with a weary smile, "I will stick to my task till perhaps some shot from the enemy puts an end to everything. . . . Let us see what there may be in those papers you have brought on board."

The secretary in the cabin had arranged them in separate piles.

"What is it all about?" asked the admiral, beginning again to pace restlessly up and down the cabin.

"At the first glance the most important, my lord, are the orders for marine authorities in Corsica and Naples to make certain dispositions in view of an expedition to Egypt."

"I always thought so," said the admiral, his eye gleaming at the attentive countenance of Captain Vincent. "This is a smart piece of work on your part, Vincent. I can do no better than send you back to your station. Yes ... Egypt ... the East.... Everything points that way," he soliloquized under Vincent's eyes while the secretary, picking up the papers with care, rose quietly and went out to have them translated and to make an abstract for the admiral.

"And yet who knows!" exclaimed Lord Nelson, standing still for a moment. "But the blame or the glory must be mine alone. I will seek counsel from no man." Captain Vincent felt himself forgotten, invisible, less than a shadow in the presence of a nature capable of such vehement feelings. "How long can he last?" he asked himself with sincere concern.

The admiral, however, soon remembered his presence, and at the end of another ten minutes Captain Vincent left the *Victory*, feeling, like all officers who approached Lord Nelson, that he had been speaking with a personal friend; and with a renewed devotion for the great sea-officer's soul dwelling in the frail body of the commander-in-chief of his Majesty's ships in the Mediterranean. While he was being pulled back to his ship a general signal went up in the *Victory* for the fleet to form line, as convenient, ahead and astern of the admiral; followed by another to the *Amelia* to part company. Vincent accordingly gave his orders to make sail, and, directing the master to shape a course for Cape Cicié, went down into his cabin. He had been up nearly the whole of the last three nights and he wanted to get a little sleep. His slumbers, however, were short and disturbed. Early in the afternoon he found himself broad awake and reviewing in his mind the events of the day before. The order to shoot three brave men in cold blood, terribly distasteful at the time, was lying heavily on him. Perhaps he had been impressed by Peyrol's white head, his obstinacy to escape him, the determination shown to the very last minute, by something in the whole episode that suggested a more than common devotion to duty and a spirit of daring defiance. With his robust health, simple good nature, and sanguine temperament touched with a little irony, Captain Vincent was a man of generous feelings and of easily moved sympathies.

"Yet," he reflected, "they have been asking for it. There could be only one end to that affair. But the fact remains that they were defenceless and unarmed and particularly harmless-looking, and at the same time as brave as any. That old chap now. . . ." He wondered how much of exact truth there was in Symons' tale of adventure. He concluded that the facts must have been true but that Symons' interpretation of them made it extraordinarily difficult to discover what really there was under all that. That craft certainly was fit for blockade running. Lord Nelson had been pleased. Captain Vincent went on deck with the kindliest feelings towards all men, alive and dead.

The afternoon had turned out very fine. The British Fleet was just out of sight with the exception of one or two stragglers, under a press of canvas. A light breeze in which only the *Amelia* could travel at five knots, hardly ruffled the profundity of the blue waters basking in the warm tenderness of the cloudless sky. To south and west the horizon was empty except for two specks very far apart, of which one shone white like a bit of silver and the other appeared black like a drop of ink. Captain Vincent, with his purpose firm in his mind, felt at peace with himself. As he was easily accessible to his officers his first lieutenant ventured a question to which Captain Vincent replied:

"He looks very thin and worn out, but I don't think he is as ill as he thinks he is. I am sure you all would like to know that his lordship is pleased with our yesterday's work—those papers were of some importance you know—and generally with the *Amelia*. It was a queer chase, wasn't it?" he went on. "That tartane was clearly and unmistakably running away from us. But she never had a chance against the *Amelia*."

During the latter part of that speech the first lieutenant glanced astern as if asking himself how long Captain Vincent proposed to drag that tartane behind the *Amelia*. The two keepers in her wondered also as to when they would be permitted to get back on board their ship. Symons, who was one of them, declared that he was sick and tired of steering the blamed thing. Moreover, the company on board made him uncomfortable; for Symons was aware that in pursuance of Captain Vincent's orders, Mr. Bolt had had the three dead Frenchmen carried into the cuddy which he afterwards secured with an enormous padlock that, apparently, belonged to it, and had taken the key on board the *Amelia*. As to one of them, Symons' unforgiving verdict was that it would have served him right to be thrown ashore for crows to peck his eyes out. And anyhow, he could not understand why he should have been turned into the coxswain of a floating hearse, and be damned to it. . . . He grumbled interminably.

Just about sunset, which is the time of burials at sea, the *Amelia* was hove to and, the rope being manned, the tartane was brought alongside and her two keepers ordered on board their ship. Captain Vincent, leaning over with his elbows on the rail, seemed lost in thought. At last the first lieutenant spoke.

"What are we going to do with that tartane, sir? Our men are on board."

"We are going to sink her by gunfire," declared Captain Vincent suddenly. "His ship makes a very good coffin for a seaman, and those men deserve better than to be thrown overboard to roll on the waves. Let them rest quietly at the bottom of the sea in the craft to which they had stuck so well."

The lieutenant, making no reply, waited for some more positive order. Every eye on the ship was turned on the captain. But Captain Vincent said nothing and seemed unable or unwilling to give it yet. He was feeling vaguely, that in all his good intentions there was something wanting.

"Ah! Mr. Bolt," he said, catching sight of the master's mate in the waist. "Did they have a flag on board that craft?"

"I think she had a tiny bit of ensign when the chase began, sir, but it must have blown away. It is not at the end of her mainyard now." He looked over the side. "The halliards are rove, though," he added.

"We must have a French ensign somewhere on board," said Captain Vincent.

"Certainly, sir," struck in the master, who was listening.

"Well, Mr. Bolt," said Captain Vincent, "you have had most to do with all this. Take a few men with you, bend the French ensign on the halliards, and sway his mainyard to the masthead." He smiled at all the faces turned towards him. "After all they never surrendered and, by heavens, gentlemen, we will let them go down with their colours flying."

A profound but not disapproving silence reigned over the decks of the ship while Mr. Bolt with three or four hands was busy executing the order. Then suddenly above the topgallant rail of the *Amelia* appeared the upper curve of a lateen yard with the tricolour drooping from the point. A subdued murmur from all hands greeted this apparition. At the same time Captain Vincent ordered the line holding the tartane alongside to be cast off and the mainyard of the *Amelia* to be swung round. The sloop shooting ahead of her prize left her stationary on the sea, then putting the helm up, ran back abreast of her on the other side. The port bow-gun was ordered to fire a round, aiming well forward. That shot, however, went just over, taking the foremast out of the tartane. The next was more successful, striking the little hull between wind and water, and going out well under water on the other side. A third was fired, as the men said, just for luck, and that, too, took effect, a splintered hole appearing at the bow. After that the guns were secured and the *Amelia*, with no brace being touched, was brought to her course towards Cape Cicié. All hands on board of her with their backs to the sunset sky, clear like a pale topaz above the hard blue gem of the sea, watched the tartane give a sudden dip, followed by a slow, unchecked dive. At last the tricolour flag alone remained visible for a tense and interminable moment, pathetic and lonely, in the centre of a brimful horizon. All at once it vanished, like a flame blown upon, bringing to the beholders the sense of having been left face to face with an immense, suddenly created solitude. On the decks of the *Amelia* a low murmur died out.

WHEN LIEUTENANT RÉAL sailed away with the Toulon fleet on the great strategical cruise which was to end in the battle of Trafalgar, Madame Réal returned with her aunt to her hereditary house at Escampobar. She had only spent a few weeks in town where she was not much seen in public. The lieutenant and his wife lived in a little house near the western gate, and the lieutenant's official position, though he was employed on the staff to the last, was not sufficiently prominent to make her absence from official ceremonies at all remarkable. But this marriage was an object of mild interest in naval circles. Those—mostly men—who had seen Madame Réal at home, told stories of her dazzling complexion, of her magnificent black eyes, of her personal and attractive strangeness, and of the Arlesian costume she insisted on wearing, even after her marriage to an officer of the navy, being herself sprung from farmer stock. It was also said that her father and mother had fallen victims in the massacres of Toulon after the evacuation of the town; but all those stories varied in detail and were on the whole very vague. Whenever she went abroad Madam Réal was attended by her aunt who aroused almost as much curiosity as herself: a magnificent old woman with upright carriage and an austere, brown, wrinkled face showing signs of past beauty. Catherine was also seen alone in the streets where, as a matter of fact, people turned round to look after the thin and dignified figure, remarkable amongst the passers-by, whom she, herself, did not seem to see. About her escape from the massacres most wonderful tales were told, and she acquired the reputation of a heroine. Arlette's aunt was known to frequent the churches, which were all open to the faithful now, carrying even into the house of God her sibylline aspect of a prophetess and her austere manner. It was not at the services that she was seen most. People would see her oftener in an empty nave, standing slim and as straight as an arrow in the shadow of a mighty pillar as if making a call on the Creator of all things with whom she had made her peace generously, and now would petition only for pardon and reconciliation with her niece Arlette. For Catherine for a long time remained uncertain of the future. She did not get rid of her involuntary awe of her niece as a selected object of God's wrath, until towards the end of her life. There was also another soul for which she was concerned. The pursuit of the tartane by the *Amelia* had been observed from various points of the islands that close the roadstead of Hyères, and the English ship had been seen from the Fort de la Vigie opening fire on her chase. The result, though the two vessels soon ran out of sight, could not be a matter of doubt. There was also the story told by a coaster that got into Fréjus, of a tartane being fired on by a square-rigged man-of-war; but that apparently was the next day. All these rumours pointed one way and were the foundation of the report made by Lieutenant Réal to the Toulon Admiralty. That Peyrol went out to sea in his tartane and was never seen again, was of course an incontrovertible fact.

The day before the two women were to go back to Escampobar, Catherine approached a priest in the church of Ste. Marie Majeure, a little unshaven fat man with a watery eye, in order to arrange for some masses to be said for the dead.

"But for whose soul are we to pray?" mumbled the priest in a wheezy low tone.

"Pray for the soul of Jean," said Catherine. "Yes, Jean. There is no other name."

Lieutenant Réal, wounded at Trafalgar, but escaping capture, retired with the rank of Capitaine de Frégate and vanished from the eyes of the naval world in Toulon and indeed from the world altogether. Whatever sign brought him back to Escampobar on that momentous night, was not meant to call him to his death but to a quiet and retired life, obscure in a sense but not devoid of dignity. In the course of years he became the Mayor of the Commune in that very same little village which had looked on Escampobar as the abode of iniquity, the sojourn of blood-drinkers and of wicked women.

One of the earliest excitements breaking the monotony of the Escampobar life was the discovery at the bottom of the well, one dry year when the water got very low, of some considerable obstruction. After a lot of trouble in getting it up, this obstruction turned out to be a garment made of sail-cloth, which had armholes and three horn buttons in front, and looked like a waistcoat; but it was lined, positively quilted, with a surprising quantity of gold pieces of various ages, coinages, and nationalities. Nobody but Peyrol could have put it there. Catherine was able to give the exact date; because she remembered seeing him doing something at the well on the very morning before he went out to sea with Michel, carrying off Scevola. Captain Réal could guess easily the origin of that treasure, and he decided with his wife's approval to give it up to the Government as the hoard of a man who had died intestate with no discoverable relations, and whose very name had been a matter of uncertainty, even to himself. After that event the uncertain name of Peyrol found itself oftener and oftener on Monsieur and Madame Réal's lips, on which before it was but seldom heard; through the recollection of his white-headed, quiet, irresistible personality haunted every corner of the Escampobar fields. From that time they talked of him openly, as though he had come back to live again amongst them.

Many years afterwards, one fine evening, Monsieur and Madame Réal, sitting on the bench outside the *salle* (the house had not been altered at all outside except that it was now kept whitewashed), began to talk of that episode and of the man who, coming from the seas, had crossed their lives to disappear at sea again.

"How did he get all that lot of gold?" wondered Madame Réal innocently. "He could not possibly want it; and, Eugène, why should he have put it down there?"

"That, *ma chère amie,*" said Réal, "is not an easy question to answer. Men and women are not so simple as they seem. Even you, *fermière* (he used to give his wife that name jocularly, sometimes), are not so simple as some people would take you to be. I think that if Peyrol were here he could not perhaps answer your question himself."

And they went on, reminding each other in short phrases separated by long silences, of his peculiarities of person and behaviour, when above the slope leading down to Madrague, there appeared first, the pointed ears, and then the whole body of a very diminutive donkey of a light grey colour with dark points. Two pieces of wood, strangely shaped, projected on each side of his body as far as his head, like very long shafts of a cart. But the donkey dragged no cart after him. He was carrying on his back on a small pack saddle the torso of a man who did not seem to have any legs. The little animal, beautifully groomed and with an intelligent and even impudent physiognomy, stopped in front of Monsieur and Madame Réal. The man, balancing himself cleverly on the pack saddle with his withered legs crossed in front of him, slipped off, disengaged his crutches from each side of the donkey smartly, propped himself on them, and with his open palm gave the animal a resounding thwack which sent it trotting into the yard. The cripple of the Madrague in his quality of Peyrol's friend (for the rover had often talked of him both to the women and to Lieutenant Réal with great appreciation—"C'est un homme, ça") had become a member of the Escampobar community. His employment was to run about the country on errands, most unfit, one would think, for a man without legs. But the donkey did all the walking while the cripple supplied the sharp wits and an unfailing memory. The poor fellow, snatching off his hat and holding it with one hand alongside his right crutch, approached to render his account of the day in the simple words: "Everything has been done as you ordered, madame"; then lingered, a privileged servant, familiar but respectful, attractive with his soft eyes, long face, and his pained smile.

"We were just talking of Peyrol," remarked Captain Réal.

"Ah, one could talk a long time of him," said the cripple. "He told me once that if I had been complete—with legs like everybody else, I suppose he meant—I would have made a good comrade away there in the distant seas. He had a great heart."

"Yes," murmured Madame Réal thoughtfully, then turning to her husband, she asked: "What sort of man was he really, Eugène?" Captain Réal remained silent. "Did you ever ask yourself that question?" she insisted.

"Yes," said Réal. "But the only certain thing we can say of him is that he was not a bad Frenchman."

"Everything's in that," murmured the cripple, with fervent conviction in the silence that fell upon Réal's words and Arlette's faint sigh of memory.

The blue level of the Mediterranean, the charmer and the deceiver of audacious men, kept the secret of its fascination—hugged to its calm breast the victims of all the wars, calamities, and tempests of its history, under the marvellous purity of the sunset sky. A few rosy clouds floated high up over the Esterel range. The breath of the evening breeze came to cool the heated rocks of Escampobar; and the mulberry tree, the only big tree on the head of the peninsula, standing like a sentinel at the gate of the yard, sighed faintly in a shudder of all its leaves, as if regretting the Brother of the Coast, the man of dark deeds, but of large heart, who often at noonday would lie down to sleep under its shade.

ABOUT THE EDITORS

The Heart of Oak Sea Classics book series is edited by DEAN KING, author of *A Sea of Words: A Lexicon and Companion for Patrick O'Brian's Seafaring Tales* (Henry Holt, 1995; second edition, 1997) and *Harbors and High Seas: An Atlas and Geographical Guide to the Aubrey-Maturin Novels of Patrick O'Brian* (Holt, 1996; second edition, 1999), and editor, with John B. Hattendorf, of *Every Man Will Do His Duty: An Anthology of Firsthand Accounts from the Age of Nelson, 1793–1815* (Holt, 1997). In the past, King has sailed on board the replica of the 1757 frigate HMS *Rose*, a sail-training ship which operates out of Bridgeport, Connecticut. He is the author of a forthcoming biography of Patrick O'Brian.

Comments on or suggestions for the Heart of Oak Sea Classics series can be sent to Dean King, c/o Henry Holt and Company, 115 West 18th Street, New York, New York 10011 or E-mailed to him at DeanHKing@aol.com. For more information on the series, visit www.HeartOfOak.com on the Internet.

The series' scholarly advisors are JOHN B. HATTENDORF, Ernest J. King, Professor of Maritime History at the U.S. Naval War College, and CHRISTOPHER MCKEE, Samuel R. and May-Louise Rosenthal, Professor and Librarian of the College, Grinnell College, author of, most recently, *A Gentlemanly and Honorable Profession: The Creation of the U.S. Naval Officer Corps, 1794–1815* (Naval Institute Press, 1991).